DEATH MARCH
TO THE
PARALLEL WORLD RHAPSODY 5

AT THE
BANQUET
IN THE
DWARF CITY

MIA
A taciturn elf who
loves music.

NANA
An expressionless
homunculus.

LIZA
A scalefolk girl.

POCHI
A dog-eared girl.

SATOU

A twenty-nine-year-old programmer who has been transported to a parallel universe.

LULU

Born in the Kuvork Kingdom. She is Arisa's older sister.

TAMA

A cat-eared girl.

ARISA

A former princess of the Kuvork Kingdom. She was Japanese in her previous life.

"Satou... do you think... you can change fate?"

Her faint smile looked about to disappear at any moment, and I...

DEATH MARCH
TO THE PARALLEL WORLD
RHAPSODY

5

★ ★ ★

HIRO AINANA
ILLUSTRATION BY SHRI

YEN
ON

NEW YORK

Death March to the Parallel World Rhapsody, Vol. 5
Hiro Ainana

Translation by Jenny McKeon
Cover art by shri

© Hiro Ainana, shri 2015
First published in Japan in 2015 by KADOKAWA CORPORATION, Tokyo.
English translation rights arranged with KADOKAWA CORPORATION, Tokyo through Tuttle-Mori Agency, Inc., Tokyo.

English translation © 2018 by Yen Press, LLC

Yen On
1290 Avenue of the Americas
New York, NY 10104

Visit us at yenpress.com
facebook.com/yenpress
twitter.com/yenpress
yenpress.tumblr.com
instagram.com/yenpress

First Yen On Edition: May 2018

Yen On is an imprint of Yen Press, LLC.
The Yen On name and logo are trademarks of Yen Press, LLC.

The publisher is not responsible for websites (or their content) that are not owned by the publisher.

Library of Congress Cataloging-in-Publication Data
Names: Ainana, Hiro, author. | Shri, illustrator. | McKeon, Jenny, translator.
Title: Death march to the parallel world rhapsody / Hiro Ainana ; illustrations by shri ; translation by Jenny McKeon.
Other titles: Desu machi kara hajimaru isekai kyosokyoku. English
Description: First Yen On edition. | New York, NY : Yen ON, 2017–
Identifiers: LCCN 2016050512 | ISBN 9780316504638 (v. 1 : pbk.) |
ISBN 9780316507974 (v. 2 : pbk.) | ISBN 9780316556088 (v. 3 : pbk.) |
ISBN 9780316556095 (v. 4 : pbk.) | ISBN 9780316556101 (v. 5 : pbk.)
Subjects: | GSAFD: Fantasy fiction.
Classification: LCC PL867.5.I56 D413 2017 | DDC 895.6/36d—dc23
LC record available at https://lccn.loc.gov/2016050512

ISBNs: 978-0-316-55610-1 (paperback)
978-0-316-55617-0 (ebook)

1 3 5 7 9 10 8 6 4 2

LSC-C

Printed in the United States of America

CONTENTS

Sara of the Tenion Temple

Satou here. Destiny is a mysterious thing. An unexpected reunion with someone you've met on a journey is more than just a dramatic interlude. The second meeting might be a coincidence, but when they keep piling up...could you call that fate?

"It is a great pleasure to meet you. I am Sara, the oracle priestess of the Tenion Temple."

A mysterious voice like an angelic melody rang through the audience room of Muno Castle.

She gazed directly at me, her eyes the bright green of newly sprouted leaves.

In the sunlight that trickled into the audience room, her pale hair shone with a curious luster somewhere between gold and silver.

Was this what they call "platinum blond" hair? It was especially lovely next to her pale white skin.

Her nose, situated somewhat lower on her face than the average person in the Shiga Kingdom, drew a splendid line in profile and led the gaze toward her soft lips, neither too thick nor too thin. They were stunningly glossy despite the presumable lack of lipstick, contributing to her charming appearance as a healthy young lady.

The girl was wearing Western-style priestess garb with a simple embroidered pattern in blue and gold thread—similar in design to what Miss Ohna, the priestess from Parion Temple, had worn when we met her in Seiryuu City.

Though the garment was designed to be modest, an impressive amount of her bust was asserting its presence nonetheless.

It wasn't nearly on the level of Nana or Miss Karina, but they were undoubtedly large for the girl's age.

Of course, I had no interest in hitting on a girl barely old enough for middle or high school, but in another five years or so, she'd definitely be one to watch.

Miss Nina, the magistrate, nudged me pointedly, and I realized everyone was waiting on me to introduce myself. All the others had finished their introductions while I was daydreaming about this girl's future prospects.

Every eye in the audience room of Muno Castle was resting on me.

This included Baron Muno, Miss Nina, Miss Sara and her escort knights, and a handsome civil official.

"It's a pleasure to meet you, Lady Sara. I am Satou Pendragon, a hereditary knight and vassal of the Muno Barony. I have only recently received the honor of this title, so I hope you'll look kindly upon me."

I offered her the standard greeting I had learned from my etiquette coach, Yuyurina.

Miss Sara smiled back at me, but the stern glowers of the two male knights standing behind her were unchanged.

According to the AR display, Miss Sara was level 30, with the skills "Holy Magic: Tenion Faith," "Oracle," "Meditation," and "Perceive Malice."

The knights escorting her were fairly high-level as well: Temple Knight Keon Bobino, the one with short blond hair, was level 31, and Imperial Knight Ipasa Lloyd, the one with a shock of red hair, was level 33.

The handsome official of the Ougoch Duchy behind them was a much more average level 12.

As I understood it, Miss Sara and company had come to assist with the restoration of order and revitalization efforts in the Muno Barony after the recent demon attack.

In the plaza outside the castle, a large force of eight knights, four priests, three hundred soldiers, and forty wagons was waiting on standby. With all that power, they could probably bring down Muno Castle if they wanted to.

Softhearted baron or no, however, if a shrewd tactician like Miss Nina had let them onto castle grounds, in all likelihood they were perfectly friendly.

"I'm surprised that the duke permitted his lovely young grand-daughter to leave the territory," Miss Nina commented.

"Having left my house, I no longer have any connection to the duke, I'm afraid."

Miss Sara maintained a sweet smile as she answered. Her family name hadn't appeared in the AR display, but when I checked the more detailed information, it turned out that she was indeed the grandchild of Duke Ougoch.

"What of the temple, then, sending their precious oracle into such danger?"

"The head priestess was kind enough to support me."

...Hmm?

Something about Miss Sara's words struck me as odd, but before I could figure out what it was, my attention was drawn elsewhere.

"I see. So the holy woman of Tenion Temple is as graceful yet bold as ever, then."

Though Miss Nina and Miss Sara referred to her by different names, the "head priestess" and the "holy woman" of the temple were one and the same. I had assumed that Miss Sara herself was the "holy woman" I'd heard about, but it seemed I was mistaken.

So this holy woman is even more saintly than Miss Sara? My pitiful imagination couldn't even begin to picture it.

When we visited the old capital, I'd have to find a way to see her, even if just from a distance.

"Besides, I must also exorcise the traces of the Undead King's curse, which the head priestess was unable to do."

"Is she unwell, then?"

"I'm afraid so. Recently, she has been unable to even leave the sanctuary of the temple grounds."

I wasn't sure what the "sanctuary" was—maybe like a hospital's IC unit or something?

I had always imagined that high-ranking Holy Magic would be able to heal anything, but apparently, there were some things even magic couldn't do.

"...And so...in the end, the masked hero and the forest giants did away with the demon army, but the castle would have fallen before reinforcements arrived were it not for Sir Pendragon and his comrades."

After relocating to the parlor, Miss Nina was relaying the story of the recent demon attack to Miss Sara and company.

There were a total of seven people in the room: Baron Muno, the magistrate Miss Nina, Miss Sara, her two knights (courtesy of the duke), the handsome civil official, and me.

"What a splendid feat of gallantry for one so young to not only survive an encounter with a demon unharmed but to defeat him. We could use someone like yourself in our ranks," the imperial knight commended.

I appreciated the compliment, but I could've done without the rather hungry smile.

"Personally, I don't believe it. This young lad defeated a demon?"

"Sir Keon, hold your tongue."

The imperial knight scolded the temple knight, whose scowl only deepened.

"It takes a full squadron to stand a chance at defeating even a lesser hell demon, and you still risk losing half. And we are to believe that a group of women and children defeated one? Impossible!"

"Am I to understand that you do not take me at my word, then, Sir Temple Knight...?"

The knight's words must have struck a nerve; Miss Nina's tone changed harshly. The more polite her words, the more likely she was about to go on the attack.

"S-Sir Keon!"

The handsome official had turned pale and quickly stood to mediate the situation.

"Lady Nina, I am terribly sorry. He means you no ill, I assure you. P-please find it in your heart to hold back your rage."

At the moment, I just looked like a slender fifteen-year-old boy. It was no wonder the temple knight didn't believe I'd defeated a demon.

Still, this tense mood was less than desirable.

"I can appreciate your skepticism, Sir Knight. However, it was not my power alone that defeated the demon. I owe that to the help of trustworthy friends, as well as a special artifact that temporarily weakens the power of a demon."

"An artifact! I see!"

At my explanation, the civil official chimed in with a rather melodramatic show of appreciation.

He's got a tough job. To keep the ball rolling, I went into more detail about the demon-sealing bell I'd received from the chief of the forest giants, which helped appease the temple knight.

In a tag-team effort between the official and me, we made it through the crisis unscathed, and the topic shifted to the battle between the demon and the masked hero.

"H-he assimilated with a hydra?! A lesser demon shouldn't be able to take over a demi-dragon!"

"He must have been an intermediate one, then..."

The imperial knight and Miss Sara mused aloud.

My map search had labeled him a lesser demon, but I kept that to myself.

"So what was the demon's goal in attacking this territory?" the temple knight cut in, blatantly trying to turn this into an interrogation. Evidently, this man was a dependent of a high-ranking aristocrat called Count Bobino from the old capital, so he tended toward the haughty.

Miss Nina gave him a sharp look for his insolent tone, and Baron Muno answered in her stead:

"Ahem... The letter from the masked hero suggested that the demon's goal was the resurrection of the demon lord."

That letter had been my effort to convey the demon's plan after the incident was over.

"Wh-what did you say?!"

"This is a serious matter!"

The two knights leaped to their feet at the shocking revelation from Baron Muno.

The civil official blanched even paler, unable to speak.

It seemed like the phrase *demon lord* carried considerable weight here.

"Please remain calm, both of you," Miss Sara chided them gently.

Despite her outward composure, there was no hiding the way the blood had drained from her previously rosy complexion.

"B-but my lady...!"

"This is not the time to be calm!"

"And yet you call yourselves knights defending the Ougoch Duchy and Tenion Temple? Baron Muno here is perfectly at peace. This can only mean that the resurrection attempt has already been thwarted, does it not?"

After Miss Sara admonished them in a dignified voice, she looked to Baron Muno for confirmation.

"Yes, indeed. The masked hero prevented the demon's plan from succeeding."

"What was he attempting, then?"

The imperial knight composed himself and returned to his seat, but the temple knight seemed unconvinced and pressed with more questions.

"The demon was oppressing people in the barony and gathering their negative feelings into a cursed vessel called a chaos jar. The hero destroyed the vessel along with the demon."

"A chaos jar, eh? I see. So it was destroyed."

The temple knight heaved an apparent sigh of relief.

To me, it felt more like the disappointed lament of the demon lord whose resurrection I'd prevented.

Once the discussion in the parlor was over, Miss Nina and the handsome official headed toward the office to take care of clerical work or something.

In the meantime, Miss Sara requested a tour of the castle and the city.

The two knights left Miss Sara's side to complete duties of their own, leaving two new temple knights to guard her in their place. This pair, a man and a woman, were each only level 13.

The man's name was Heath, and the woman's name was Ina. Since it didn't seem like we'd be spending time together for very long, I decided to just remember them as "Guy Knight" and "Lady Knight." Both were from the lower aristocracy of the old capital.

"Now then, where would you like to go?"

"Could I ask you to guide me to the Tenion Temple of Muno City first? After that, I should very much like to pay a visit to the city's orphanage, if it's all right with you."

I understood the first request well enough, but it was unusual for a high-ranking aristocratic young lady to want to visit an orphanage.

Unlike modern Japan, orphanages in the Shiga Kingdom were hardly sanitary places, due to their low budget and generally poor grasp of hygiene. Besides, there was no orphanage in Muno City.

"My apologies. I can certainly take you to the Tenion Temple, but I'm afraid it won't be possible to visit the orphanage."

"Whyever not? I shan't be repulsed or offended, no matter what the conditions might be."

"No, that isn't the issue. You see..."

I explained to Miss Sara that the former magistrate, who was actually the demon in disguise, had shut down the city's orphanage two years ago.

"Then the children..."

Oops, I guess I should have given her the good news first. Miss Sara's face was clouded with concern.

"Please, do not worry. The children are being cared for in the castle."

The castle had taken in the children only recently after the demon attack, but there was probably no need to dive into the details.

The two thousand people who had lost their homes along the wall of the city in the process of rezoning had been living in the spare barracks of the castle, but they'd recently been moved into the newly completed temporary housing. The only people remaining in the barracks were mostly children and the elderly.

Those in temporary housing had been given jobs creating gabo-fruit fields to combat the famine on the land that was now dedicated to agriculture.

If possible, I would've liked to suggest a better-tasting crop, but the difference in productivity between gabo fruits and other crops was simply too large to justify that until the overall food situation improved.

"In...the castle?"

"That's right. I can show you, if you'd like. Or would you prefer to start with the Tenion Temple, as originally planned?"

"No, I will visit them first. Please show me the way." Miss Sara responded with remarkable warmth.

I would have expected her to be tired from such a long journey, but she seemed energetic, if anything—even impatient.

She acted almost like she'd been told she had only a little time left to live and was desperate not to waste a single minute.

It wasn't far enough for a carriage, and we walked toward where the children were staying, chatting along the way.

As we passed through the inner wall to the area around the barracks, we heard soldiers' voices rumbling and lively music in the air.

"Oh? What an unusual sound..."

"It certainly is a merry tune, though I cannot say I've heard it before."

Miss Sara tilted her head curiously with refined grace, and Guy Knight agreed.

As we listened to the music and followed it toward its source, we soon found the small maestro responsible in a corner of the training field.

"Satou."

Mia the elf looked up at us from her lute. Her full name was Misanaria Bolenan.

Though her actual age was more than a hundred and thirty years, she was still a child in elf years and had the appearance of an elementary school student to match.

Her slightly pointed ears, characteristic of her race, peeped out through the shadows of her neat, light-turquoise pigtails. She must have been a little chilly, because she had a pale-yellow cardigan over her periwinkle-blue dress.

"A-an elf? What is Cyriltoa the Songstress doing here?"

"No, if it was her, she'd only be moving one hand."

"Quiet down, please, you two. I cannot hear her song."

Miss Sara scolded the murmuring pair of knights.

In the old capital, there was an elf known as Cyriltoa the Songstress who had the use of only one arm, it seemed.

"Hi, Mia."

"...Mrrrr?"

Mia answered my greeting with a short nod, then squinted rather unpleasantly at Miss Sara behind me.

Must be in a bad mood.

"It's nice to meet you. I am Sara of Tenion Temple."

"Mm. Mia."

Mia barely acknowledged Miss Sara's polite greeting and brusquely offered nothing but her name, without pausing her playing.

"Is that a traditional song of the village of Bolenan?"

"Wagner."

Mia shook her head at Miss Sara's question and answered with a word.

The song Mia strummed on her lute was Wagner's "Ride of the Valkyries."

After I had played my ringtone for her once, she had copied it perfectly by ear. The instrumentation was different, of course, but Mia had made up an arrangement of her own.

"Are you entertaining the soldiers while they train?"

"Requested."

Mia looked past us toward Sir Zotol, a knight who had been appointed to reorganize the barony's armed forces. He appeared to be refereeing for the soldiers' bouts and hadn't noticed us.

"Next! Miss Nana and Miss Karina versus Miss Liza!" he shouted, and three girls appeared from among the soldiers.

The first to enter the field was Liza of the orange Scalefolk tribe, shaking out her long scarlet locks. She would have looked like an ordinary human were it not for her lizard-like tail and patches of orange scales on her arms and neck.

At level 14, she was the highest level of my companions.

The black armor she was wearing was handmade by yours truly.

It was made from hydra leather and ironshell fruit, with defense stronger than steel. It was only slightly heavier than normal leather armor, too, so it wouldn't slow down her agility.

I was very proud of my work. The only problem was that the black color of hydra leather and ironshells made the wearer look very intimidating.

"Hey, get a load of that demi-human's spear."

"A weapon made from monster parts…? That's a rare sight."

"She must be a former labyrinth explorer or monster hunter."

The temple knights murmured among themselves as they eyed Liza's spear.

I'd heard of labyrinth explorers already, but "monster hunter" sounded like a cool title, too. I'd have to get them to tell me about it over dinner or something.

"Master!"

Nana came onto the field after Liza, then noticed us and called out to me with a big wave. The exaggerated movement shook her golden hair as well as her ample breasts.

Nana was wearing the same armor as Liza. Unlike the slender Liza, Nana had a rather large bust, so making her chest piece from the ironshells took some time.

"Liza, master is watching us from over there, I report."

On hearing this, Liza looked to us with a dignified expression and bowed in our direction.

Nana looked like an ordinary human girl of around high school age, but she was actually a homunculus who had been artificially created less than a year ago. It was no surprise that her face was generally a mask and she spoke in a strangely stilted way.

Fortunately, she was wearing a hidden item called an Amulet of Humanity, so there was no danger of her true nature being discovered even if someone analyzed her.

As our shield maiden since we'd entered the Muno Barony, she was up to level 10 now.

The last contender in the ring was Baron Muno's second daughter, Karina.

She made a big entrance, leaping over the soldiers and somersaulting in midair.

The reason she could pull off such superhuman moves was her Intelligent Item, a necklace called Raka that granted her Body Strengthening.

Her blond curls fell perfectly into place as she lined up next to Nana.

Miss Karina was only level 8, but that was a huge improvement from when we first found her collapsed in the forest.

"Whoa…"

"Oh, grow up."

Guy Knight's whistle of admiration met a resentful grumble from Lady Knight.

The reaction was probably to Miss Karina's incredibly bountiful bosom. Even Nana's E cups looked small in comparison.

"Begin!"

On Sir Zotol's signal, Liza readied her spear and charged toward Nana, whose shield was already raised.

Before the weapons could meet, though, a transparent magic shield blocked their path.

"Hmm, so that shield girl's a Practical Magic user? If she's not equipped with a staff, she must have a ring or something as the catalyst."

Guy Knight evaluated Nana.

Sorry, but Nana's not actually using Practical Magic—it's a special ability homunculi have called Foundation.

Unlike Practical Magic, it didn't require an incantation to cast, but the disadvantage was that she could use only preset techniques. Installing new spells would require a special facility.

Plus, a magic rune appeared on her forehead when she used it, so it'd draw attention if she wasn't wearing a helmet.

"That girl with the curly hair... Was that a blue light?!"

"Is she wearing some kind of Holy Armor?!"

The knights exclaimed with surprise at Miss Karina, who was hiding behind Nana.

"Lady Karina!!"

"Yes, Mr. Raka!"

At the urging of her necklace's low, masculine voice, Miss Karina jumped out from behind Nana for a surprise attack on Liza.

The blue light from Raka's core left a faint afterimage, making her movements clearer.

"So fast! How can she do that?!"

To intercept Miss Karina's inhumanly swift surprise attack, Liza swung up her spear with one hand and fended her off.

Then Nana fired off a Magic Arrow.

Hey, I told her not to use attack magic in a practice match. I'll have to scold Nana later.

"Whoa, that must've been one fast chant!"

"No way, how's she gonna dodge?"

Liza avoided the Magic Arrow by quickly dropping to the ground.

With Liza's stance compromised, Nana swept in to strike with her large shield.

But the shield was a bit too high. Plus...

With a heavy *thud*, the shield sent someone rolling across the practice field.

"Oh dear, some friendly fire there..."

Miss Karina had jumped into the fray without thinking, and Nana's shield clocked her instead.

Raka's scalelike white shields flashed in and out around her, easing the impact.

"Is she all right?"

"Don't worry; she's fine. See? She's already standing up." I smiled back at Miss Sara to assuage her concern for Miss Karina.

Raka's defense power was pretty high, so even an attack from a level-20 lesser demon wouldn't leave a scratch on her equipment. So

far, I was the only person who'd managed to break through Raka's defense.

The three-person battle continued in Liza's favor. This was not due to the difference in their levels but poor communication between Nana and Miss Karina.

Between Nana's Foundation techniques and Miss Karina's Strength Enhancement from Raka, the level gap would have been a poor excuse.

Eventually, Nana was deemed unable to battle, and it became a showdown between Liza and Miss Karina.

Liza's magic spear cut a red streak through the air as she barreled toward Karina with all her might.

"...'Spellblade'?"

"No, it's incomplete..."

The knights' words caught my attention, so I turned toward them inquisitively.

"Incomplete, you say?"

"Yeah, that girl hasn't mastered 'Spellblade' yet. About half a year before one of my superiors learned 'Spellblade,' her weapon left magic traces like that while she was fighting."

I see. That's good to know.

Most likely, Liza didn't have enough skill points to acquire the "Spellblade" skill.

Once we set out on the next leg of our journey, I'd have to pit Liza against some more monsters.

As I was thinking about these things, the trio's fight ended, and Sir Zotol began reviewing key points from the match.

I waved to them and left the area, resuming Miss Sara's tour.

"So that young lady with the curls was Baron Muno's daughter?!"

"That's right. She was even on the front lines in the defense of Muno City a few days ago."

When I told the temple knights and Miss Sara about Miss Karina's identity, the latter was especially shocked.

"Mistress, she sounds just like your elder sister, Lady Linegrande."

"Please refrain from calling me 'mistress.' You are not wrong, though... My sister, though the daughter of a duke, always did enjoy training for battle."

"And magic, too! Why, she revived the lost magic of two family lines at the royal academy, defeated a floormaster in the labyrinth of Celivera, and a hero even personally requested her to become an attendant!"

Lady Knight's eyes sparkled as she gushed about the accomplishments of Miss Sara's sister.

If these stories were true, then this Lady Linegrande must be an exceptionally talented person.

Miss Sara appeared to have some reservations about her sister, though, as she gave no response to the praise.

In fact, upon closer inspection, I saw that her hands were clenched so tightly that her fingers were turning white.

She seemed to be suppressing some powerful emotions. Perhaps a well of passion lurked beneath that perpetually calm exterior.

As I speculated about her inner conflict, an excited voice rang out from the second floor of the barracks in front of us.

"Ah! It's master, sir!"

Tail whipping back and forth, the dog-eared Pochi leaned out the window and waved.

She was in charge of cleaning the barracks with the children in the castle's custody, so she was wearing loose, comfortable clothes: a white shirt and yellow shorts. The ribbon tied in a bow beneath her collar was a charming touch.

The maids had kindly cut her tawny-brown hair into a neat bob, and now she was more adorable than ever.

"It's truuue?"

Tama, with her feline ears and tail, popped up eagerly behind Pochi. Her pure-white hair was short and fluffy as usual. Despite her sporty appearance, Tama had a penchant for cute, girlie clothing and was wearing a pink culotte skirt. Her top was the same white shirt as Pochi's.

Her shirt had a similar ribbon, too, but this one had a lace border.

"...Animal-eared folk?!"

I heard an exclamation of surprise from Miss Sara.

Guess the likes of cat-eared folk and dog-eared folk are rare even in the Ougoch Duchy.

Tama and Pochi disappeared from the window and before long came dashing out the entrance of the barracks.

They seemed to be carrying something in their arms.

"Did you finish cleaning up?"

"Aaaye!"

"We were all exploring the attic together, sir."

The two of them were puffed up with pride and hoping for some praise.

"Great job," I told them, petting their heads; both of them scrunched up their faces and giggled. "By the way, what are you two carrying?"

In response, they both held their objects out toward me.

"Preeey!"

"Look at this, master!"

Next to me, Miss Sara couldn't seem to resist taking a peek herself.

"Waah!"

She let out a cute little scream and grabbed my right arm against her chest.

Just as I thought, she was probably a C cup. Might even be coming up on a D cup.

Evidently, the dead rats in the girls' hands had startled her.

"How dare you expose Lady Sara to such things!" Lady Knight gave an angry shout behind me, and I heard her starting to draw her sword.

"Just a moment, please."

I turned around to protect the kids, reaching out my free hand to stop her.

It was a total coincidence that I ended up almost hugging Miss Sara, who was still attached to my arm.

Maybe it was a divine gift from the lucky lecher god.

"You insolent cur! Get away from Lady Sara!"

The indignant Lady Knight swung her sword at my head.

Her intention seemed to be only to strike me with the flat, but a hit from a steel object at that speed would probably still be a serious injury for most people.

I bent down in the nick of time to avoid the sword.

"Oh my!"

I swear on my life that I was not planning to face-plant into Miss Sara's chest on my way down.

Shaking off the momentary happiness that swathed my face, I quickly pulled away from Miss Sara and apologized sincerely.

"I'm terribly sorry, Lady Sara."

"N-not to worry... I know it wasn't intentional."

Miss Sara forgave me with only a slight flush of embarrassment on her cheeks, but her attendants didn't seem so generous.

"Stand behind me, Lady Sara."

Lady Knight stepped in front of Sara, pointing her sword at me.

"Please put the sword away, Ina."

"But…"

"Ina. Put it down."

"…Very well."

After Miss Sara and Guy Knight insisted, Lady Knight reluctantly returned the sword to its sheath.

"Master, did me and Tama do something wrong, sir?"

"Well, some people don't like rats, so it's best not to show them to others without warning, okay?" I gently explained to the teary-eyed children.

"I understand, sir. I'm sorry for scaring you, ma'am."

"We're sorry."

The girls bowed regretfully, and Miss Sara accepted their apologies with a kind smile.

At the entrance of the barracks, the children who had been cleaning with Pochi and Tama were peeking this way.

"That was quite a surprise. But everything is fine now."

Miss Sara noticed them and called out gently, and one by one the children ventured toward us.

"Mister Viscount, we cleaned it all up."

"It's good an' clean now."

"We worked real hard."

One after another, the elementary school–aged children joined the crowd around me.

"Great job, everyone," I told them. I reached into Storage by way of my pocket and handed each one a sweet pastry as a reward for their hard work.

We walked along with the children toward the barracks where they were currently living and that they had just cleaned. This was where the soldiers from the Ougoch Duchy would be staying.

"Is it fun living here?"

"Yup! We get to have breakfast and supper every day!"

"There's even dried meat once in a while!"

The older children enthusiastically answered Miss Sara's question.

I wanted to give them better food to eat, but I kept that impulse down to avoid raising their expectations too much for their lives once we left Muno Barony.

Yeah, I know I just gave them treats for finishing their work, but cut me some slack.

As we approached the children's barracks, the scents of steamed fish and fresh herbs wafted through the air.

"Smells gooood?"

"Smells like *sasakama*, sir!"

"And what might *sasakama* be?" Unable to follow, Miss Sara looked to me to help.

"It's thinly diced fish steamed with herbs and grilled in the shape of a small board."

Unlike the fish we'd eaten upstream, our catches in the river in front of Muno City were rather dirty, so we steamed them with herbs before shaping them into an oval and cooking them. Their only similarity to the Japanese dish *sasa kamaboko* was the oval shape, but Arisa had mentioned the name. It stuck, hence *sasakama*.

With the creation of *sasakama*, we were aiming to improve the food in Muno City while also creating a new local specialty.

As I explained all this to Miss Sara, we arrived at the area next to the barracks where a group of young women was preparing the aforementioned dish.

At the center of the group was a young girl in a maid outfit teaching the others.

"Master!"

The cheerful call came from Lulu, with her black hair, dark eyes, and Japanese features. If there were, say, three of her, I'd be willing to bet that her simple beauty could conquer a castle, maybe even the whole solar system.

She pattered up to me, the indigo skirt of her maid outfit fluttering in the breeze. I'd designed this prototype with Arisa to look like something you'd see in Akihabara.

She was smiling so widely that if she had a tail like Pochi's, I was sure it would be wagging away.

"Yikes, she's a homely one."

"Cut it out. It's unseemly for a temple knight to poke fun at someone's appearance."

"Yeah, but…"

Behind me, the temple knights muttered about Lulu as she rushed toward us.

I'd come to learn that beauty standards in the Shiga Kingdom were very different from Japan; to them, Lulu's incredible loveliness was repulsive.

It really was a terrible thing that no one else appreciated her looks. If they had spoken loudly enough for Lulu to hear, I would've demanded an apology.

"Master, we've finished a test dish with burdock and carrots. Could I ask you to taste it for us, please?"

"Yeah, of course. Lulu, this is Lady Sara of the Tenion Temple."

"I-it's nice to meet you!" Flustered, Lulu bowed hurriedly to Miss Sara.

Seeing these two together was like a heavenly combination of Western- and Eastern-style beauty. *If the pair formed an idol unit, I swear they could take over the world.*

"Taaaste?"

"Pochi would be premist not to taste it, sir."

You mean "remiss," Pochi.

Tama and Pochi grabbed Lulu's hands and dragged her back toward the spot where the *sasakama* was cooking.

I beckoned to Miss Sara and followed toward the other women.

"Sir Knight." As we approached, one of the *sasakama* cooks came to meet us.

"How's it going?"

"Thanks to you, sir, everyone is healthy, without a hungry or freezing soul in sight."

This person was the former director of the orphanage, an old woman with surprisingly good manners for someone from the poorer parts of town.

"How might I be of service today?"

Somewhat perplexed, the former director eyed Miss Sara and the temple knights behind me.

"No need to be alarmed. These kind people came from the Tenion Temple to visit."

I gave a simple explanation, then left the rest to Miss Sara.

"A sympathy call, is it? We are certainly most grateful to have you."

"Please, no need to be so formal. I've only come in the hopes of healing anyone who might be sick or injured. Could I ask you to show me around?" Miss Sara smiled warmly at the former director.

"Well, you see…" Faltering, the former director looked back toward me.

"What's wrong?" Sara watched us a bit doubtfully.

"You see, there are no sick or injured here."

"Whyever not…? Have they been quarantined elsewhere?"

Misunderstanding, Sara drew closer to the former director with a grave expression.

"No, it's not that. It's just that Sir Pendragon has…"

"He what?"

Sara's intensity was clearly overwhelming the director.

"He used magic potions to cure 'em all!"

"Miss Mia used magic to heal 'em, too!"

A group of children hiding in my shadow chimed in in the former director's place.

"Magic potions?!"

"He gave out something that expensive?!"

The two temple knights exclaimed behind me.

"Is this true?"

"It is indeed. From the mortally wounded to those rendered immobile by broken bones, dozens of people were healed thanks to the hereditary knight Pendragon's generous gift of his potions."

To hear the former director tell it, I sounded like a real saint.

I had wanted to heal them, of course, but I also wanted to test out the effectiveness of my various magic concoctions.

The treatment for such diverse ailments varied depending on the symptoms, so the information I'd gleaned was promising for the future. In particular, I found that just about any venereal disease (which were quite common) could be cured as long as it wasn't in the very late stages.

"On top of that, he is even training apprentices so that we might be self-sufficient in the future."

"Goodness, how very wonderful!"

The admiring gazes from the former director and Miss Sara made me a little uncomfortable.

I hadn't really been thinking so far ahead. I just wanted some help making special potions.

Fortunately, a loud voice resounding off the walls of the barracks rescued me from this awkward situation.

"There you aaare! Masterrr!"

Arisa came barreling toward me, her lilac hair loose and disheveled.

She was wearing a pink dress and a wine-red cardigan, and she had something white clasped in her hands.

The sparkle in her violet eyes was even more brilliant than usual.

"Violet hair?"

"I hope she doesn't curse us…"

Again, the temple knights muttered behind me upon seeing her.

While Arisa normally wore a blond wig while traveling, she could go out and about with her natural color in Muno Castle, where fewer people held such prejudices.

"You mustn't look down on others based on superstition." Sara reprimanded the knights again.

"Look, look! It's *onigiri*! Here, I'll give you one, master!"

Arisa gleefully handed me a ball of white rice.

"Where did you get white rice?"

I raised my eyebrows at Arisa as I accepted the food.

"In the relief supplies from the duke's army! So obviously I had the head chef Miss Gert cook some up, and I ran off to find you so you could have one!"

Arisa was wheezing, her face flushed from excitement.

She must have sprinted here from the castle, despite being terrible at exercising. I was surprised she could track me down like that.

"Thank you, Arisa."

"Hee-hee! They do say that happiness is meant to be shared!"

My thanks brought a satisfied grin to Arisa's face, and without further ado, she bit into the other rice ball in her hand.

"Yummyyy?"

"Pochi wants a bite, too, sir!"

Tama and Pochi gazed at Arisa pitifully.

"I'm sorry. I only brought two. There are more in the kitchen, so we'll go get them later, all right?"

"Aye!"

"Yes, sir!"

As I listened to the trio's exchange, I discreetly slipped the rice ball into my fluttering sleeve and deposited it in Storage.

I was excited about having *onigiri* for the first time in so long, but not so much that I would forget myself and chow down in the middle of Miss Sara's tour.

Still, I wasn't a jerk who would tell Arisa and rain on her parade. There wouldn't be time tonight, but maybe the next morning I could make some Japanese food to complement the rice and give it to her.

After that, we paid a visit to the Tenion Temple in the city, then toured around to inspect the in-progress gabo fields in the slum quarters and the tenement construction sites.

That evening, dinner was served in the nobles' dining room in Muno Castle.

The participants from Muno Barony were the baron; his daughters, Lady Soluna and Lady Karina; Magistrate Nina; and myself, which made five. The Ougoch Duchy participants were Miss Sara, a priest, the handsome civil official, and eight temple knights: eleven in total.

I was sitting at the far end of the Muno Barony side, next to Miss Karina.

Because there were more people from the Ougoch Duchy than would fit on one side, the young temple knights were seated near me.

"Now then, let us toast to the peace and prosperity of the Ougoch Duchy and the Tenion Temple."

Baron Muno raised his glass, and a rare feast for the barony began.

In the Shiga Kingdom, this generally took the form of courses that were presented one at a time, as in French dining.

The difference, though, was that the Shiga Kingdom's traditional order of courses was soup, appetizers, salad, seafood, bread, a meat dish, and dessert.

I had helped out with the recipes and preparation, but I left the rest to the skillful hands of Gert and her chefs.

No doubt they had prepared an exquisite feast for us.

First, deep soup bowls arrived in front of each person.

"Hey, Heath. Is it just me, or is salt soup for a lord's supper rather...?"

"Quiet, Ina. It's inevitable in a barony with a food shortage."

"I suppose. And I do smell something good back there, so I'm sure the later dishes will be more impressive."

My "Keen Hearing" skill picked up on Lady Knight whispering with Guy Knight next to me.

Rather reluctantly, the two of them dipped their spoons into the transparent broth.

The moment they put the spoons to their mouths, they froze completely.

"...Delicious! What *is* this?"

"Don't talk to me. Let me enjoy my soup."

In contrast with Lady Knight's surprised cry, Guy Knight maintained a stoic expression as he reverently brought the next spoonful to his mouth.

Similar reactions were occurring elsewhere.

The maids were hiding smiles at the feedback from the dinner guests, and I stealthily gave them a thumbs-up.

"Never in my life have I tasted such a soup. Whatever is this dish called, pray tell?"

"Go ahead and tell her, Sir Pendragon."

Surprised, Miss Sara asked a question that Miss Nina deflected toward me.

"This is called a consommé soup. It may look simple, but it's actually a remarkable blend of flavors from different ingredients."

My answer sounded like I was parroting some gourmet critic.

Chef Gert of Muno Castle had helped me reproduce this soup based on my vague memories. It was supposed to be more of an amber color, but it came out clear. I must have missed a step somewhere.

Maybe that was because we used Mia's magic to reduce the cooking time, or maybe I shouldn't have used "Transmutation" to extract the flavors. But it didn't cause any problems other than disguising it as salt soup, so I wasn't terribly concerned about making it look right.

"Hey, do you think we can get seconds?"

"I'm sure we *could*, but as for whether we *should*..."

I overheard the young knights talking again.

Lady Knight especially seemed to have taken a liking to the soup, as she flagged down one of the waitresses standing against the wall and requested another helping.

As far as I could tell, this encouraged the other guests: Several more people asked for seconds, and this continued until the soup ran out.

Next came hors d'oeuvres consisting of *sasakama* and cheese, with fried potatoes and potato chips on the side. The unique texture of the chips was very well received. The combination of *sasakama* and cheese was especially popular with beer drinkers.

After the appetizer came the salad, which consisted of decorative, thin slices of celery over leafy greens with strips of daikon radish arranged to look like a feather on top.

I heard someone asking a waitress about the dressings that came with the salad.

We had mayonnaise and tartar sauce, which were very popular at Muno Castle, and a sweet-and-sour orange sauce that was commonly used in the Shiga Kingdom.

The more reserved adults chose the orange sauce, but most people requested that the servants pour a little of each kind over their salads.

"This white stuff is great. I've never found vegetables so tasty before."

"What is this vegetable anyway? The transparent white one. I've never had a texture like this."

"Mmm, it has a little kick that goes well with the white sauce."

The knights continued chatting as they ate the salad.

"Radish, you say?!" exclaimed Sir Keon, a temple knight, after a short exchange with a maid.

When I'd first suggested the daikon salad, Chef Gert did warn me that some people in the old capital despised radishes.

"That was daikon radish? But I ate all of it…!"

"The rumor that eating radishes summons orcs is only a superstition, y'know."

"But…daikon, though!"

"I mean, I've never eaten it before, but it was delicious. Didn't you like it, Ina?"

"Well… It *was* good, but…"

Judging by the knights' conversation, superstitious people had an intense dislike for daikon.

Nobody made any complaints, but the reaction was stronger than I'd expected, so perhaps it'd be best to shelve the radishes for any future dinner guests from the old capital.

We hadn't caught any really good fish this time, so instead we tried making tempura for the seafood portion of the meal. Shrimp was the main focus of this course, with three kinds of vegetable tempura as well.

Normal tempura sauce accompanied it. Salt is a fine topping and all, but this time I wanted to try making a particular variety.

"What is this lumpy yellow stuff?"

"I don't know, but I bet it's delicious."

Clearly, we'd won the trust of the knights. I was a little proud.

I watched the other guests' reactions as I brought a piece of shrimp to my mouth.

For my first bite, I used the tempura sauce sparingly.

The sweetness tickled my tongue lightly along with the crunchy coating.

As my teeth came down on it, they reached the slightly chewy body of the shrimp for a tantalizing sensation.

I bit through the shrimp and began chewing.

The different textures mixed in my mouth, with the sauce adding to the flavors blending on my tongue.

Absolute bliss.

I doused the second piece thoroughly in the tempura sauce, enjoying the thick coating.

Some people might have frowned upon that, but I thought this deep, thick flavor was one of the true charms of tempura.

I was relieved that the tempura made with the local analogue to beefsteak leaves went over well. Deep down, I'd been worried that someone might be enraged that we would dare to make them eat such a thing.

Next, the main dish: fried cutlets from long-haired cows.

Instead of large slabs of meat, these were bite-size pieces that we'd tried flavoring in various ways.

There were three normal pieces, one coated in red pepper powder, and one fried with cheese.

I had made sure to color each coating so that the guests could tell them apart. A thick *tonkatsu* sauce accompanied them. This was an exquisite condiment that we'd only recently perfected.

"These are crispy and delicious, too!"

"Mmf, spicy!"

"Spicy? This reddish one, you mean?"

"It's spicy, but it's good. And cheese comes out of the yellowish one! That was a surprise."

"C'mon, don't spoil it for me. I could really get addicted to this combination of crunchiness and thick cheese."

If the knights' exchange was any indication, they were thoroughly enjoying the meal now.

I thought that having two fried dishes in a row might be too heavy, but just as Miss Gert and the other chefs had assured me, it was fine.

Unfortunately for them, there were no seconds for the fried foods. Long-haired cow beef was pretty rare.

"Oh my! So the final dish is pancakes?!"

"Ho-ho, these are all the rage in the royal capital, I hear!"

Miss Sara couldn't withhold a little exclamation of joy when she saw the pancakes decorated with fresh cream. The handsome official next to her looked pleased as well.

"Is this the same white stuff as earlier?"

"I dunno if that sauce would go very well with pancakes..."

"I mean, I've never had pancakes before, have you?"

Even lower-class nobles don't eat pancakes, then? Maybe eggs are expensive or something?

"Delicious... This is incredibly good!"

"No kidding. It's even better than the ones I had in the royal capital. And look, there are two cakes, with sliced fruit in the middle!"

"I wonder how they make the white stuff on top? Wish I could bring some back with me."

"It's so sweet and delicious. I bet they could make some truly incredible desserts if they worked together with the famous confectioners of Gururian City."

Happily, the last dish seemed to be a hit as well.

I'd definitely like to try that dessert Guy Knight mentioned.

I added **eat cake in Gururian City** to my planning memo for the duchy.

Thus, the dinner ended with contented sighs and countless compliments from the guests.

After that, at the invitation of Baron Muno, most of the men moved on to a drinking party in the salon, while the women went with his eldest daughter, Soluna, to have tea in the parlor.

After an hour or so, the get-together in the salon was becoming a little rowdy.

"Sir Pendragon! You should come and serve the Lloyd family!"

"I beg your pardon, Lord Ipasa. I wouldn't go poaching the third noble of the Muno Barony if I were you, unless you want to learn why they call me Iron-Blooded Nina…"

They nicknamed me the "third noble" because there were only three people in the whole territory with a noble title.

This was the fourth time that the gourmand Lord Ipasa had attempted to recruit me as a vassal and the third time that Miss Nina had interfered.

As I smiled blandly at the pair's conversation, I felt a tug on my shoulder from the seat behind me.

"Are you listening, Sir Pendragon?"

"Yes, of course."

"Most people will go their whole lives without meeting a demon, ya know. The only difference between you and me is that you were lucky enough to fight one. You got that?"

You call that "lucky"? Wish I could give you the rest of my luck, then.

I didn't actually say that, of course. *We Japanese people are especially good at this sort of thing, if I do say so myself.*

"Yes, you're quite right."

"No, I don't think you do—"

"You've had too much to drink, Sir Keon."

"Right this way, Sir Pendragon."

Two other temple knights stepped in to rescue me from the drunken Sir Keon.

Another young temple knight, Sir So-and-So, led me to the corner of the room, where the handsome official and Baron Muno were engaged in a rousing discussion about heroes.

"…and have you heard this theory? According to that same book, the ancestral king Yamato continued traveling around for the betterment of the world even after abdicating, and then he unearthed corruption in several territories as the duke of Mitsukuni!"

"Yes, so I have heard."

"Ooh! You are one of the leading hero researchers, after all! Still, it's impressive that you would know a story only passed around among commoners!"

"You flatter me greatly. Truly, the 'Depths of Celivera' story has become so famous that most people believe that the ancestral king Yamato exorcised the Corpse King and the Origin Vampire before falling in battle against the Ogre King. It is a great shame that only commoners know the tale of the travels that took place after."

"Indeed. Nobles and knights prefer stories of pulse-pounding battles, alas."

...I didn't know how much of this was true, but it sounded to me like the ancestral king Yamato lived a pretty exciting and dramatic life.

As the two of them fell silent for a moment, I took this opportunity to interject.

"Would you mind terribly if I listen in?"

"Oh heavens, what an honor to share tales of legend with the hero of Muno City!"

The handsome official was pretty drunk. His manner of speaking was getting stranger by the minute.

Wait, who are you calling a "hero"?

"I pride myself on my knowledge of the ancestral king Yamato, rivaled only by his lordship the baron here. Please, ask me anything."

I didn't actually have any questions; I just wanted to hear cool stories about a hero.

But I couldn't bring myself to say that to the handsome civil official as he puffed his chest out with childish pride, so I picked a question at random.

"What sort of demon lord did the ancestral king Yamato fight?"

"Ah yes, the Golden Boar Lord."

...Golden?

Was that the same as the "Golden Lord" or whatever that the lesser demon had mentioned before?

He was talking about resurrection, too, so considering that this ancient demon lord might be making a reappearance at some point, I should probably listen carefully.

"His body shone with gold that repelled even a Holy Sword, and his twin sabers slew two heroes... Yes, he was truly a lord of demon lords, said to be the strongest ever known. Even the ancestral king Yamato fell to him twice before finally defeating him with the help of the flying dragons."

Clearly in his element, the handsome official expounded at great length.

I wasn't sure how much his drunken testimony could be trusted, but if it was true, that meant there had been at least three heroes.

If this demon lord could repel even Holy Swords, did that mean he was basically invincible?

"Hmm, I must make a small objection to that view. Wouldn't the strongest demon lord be the Dogheaded Demon Lord, who traveled the world destroying gods in ancient mythology, or perhaps the Goblin Demon Lord, who forced Parion to implore the dragon god to summon the first hero?"

"Hmm-hmm. I'll grant you that the Goblin Demon Lord was perhaps stronger, as he sank even the light boats of the elves and could not be eliminated even by the gods. That much is true. However! I take issue with your suggestion of the Dogheaded Demon Lord."

"Even though the scriptures of many temples report his strength to have rivaled a god's?"

"True, I certainly do not deny his power. However, this 'Doghead' was not in fact a demon lord but an offspring of the Demon God. In fact, it is now believed by yours truly that this creature would be more accurately named the 'Dogheaded Evil God.'"

The civil official got even more worked up, reeling as he spoke.

Yeah, I didn't really need information about some unreasonably strong enemy.

What if it jinxed me and ended up with their being revived one after another?

I especially don't want to meet this Mr. Doghead guy, okay? Let's change the subject...

"Are there any records of what level the ancestral king Yamato was?"

"There are varying opinions, but some texts, like the 'Depths of Celivera' that I mentioned before, suggest a superhuman level of eighty-nine."

"Indeed. However, successive generations of heroes have rarely exceeded level seventy..."

"I beg your pardon, Baron Muno...! The Saga Kingdom's first hero was level eighty-eight. Are you suggesting that a later Shigan king falsified this information to compete with him?!"

Guess nations get competitive in fantasy worlds, too.

Their conversation was becoming heated, so I took the first opportunity I saw to change the subject again.

"Could you tell me about King Yamato's Holy Sword?"

"Do you mean the Holy Sword Gjallarhorn he created?"

The ancestral king made that sword, too...? These legends were starting to sound made-up.

I wondered if this meant that the Holy Sword recipe I found also came from him.

"Or did you perhaps mean the Heavenly Holy Sword gifted to the king by the goddess Parion?"

"The latter, if you please."

"Truth be told, there are several differing anecdotes about the ancestral king Yamato's summoning to the Saga Kingdom, but it is theorized that the sword the king wielded at the time was either Durandal or Claíomh Solais..."

The Holy Sword Durandal was actually tucked away in my Storage.

"Well, which was the sword that the ancestral king wielded against the demon lord?"

"That would be Claíomh Solais! There is a famous verse that goes thusly: 'Dance, Claíomh Solais, become thirteen blades whirling through the skies...'"

After sharing an absurd description of the ludicrous sword—which apparently boasted a homing function, the ability to break into smaller blades, and elasticity—the handsome official went on to explain other anecdotes about the ancestral king, and we had great fun until he finally drank himself unconscious.

With all the information I got, I felt like I could put together a whole book about the adventures of Yamato the Hero myself.

◆

Four days after the night of the feast, when Miss Sara and her party were departing, we decided to leave the Muno Barony as well.

Miss Sara had already left, and now our wagon was the last to depart.

We weren't the only ones hitting the road along with her; Miss Karina and her attendants were leaving as well.

The baron's daughter was going to the royal capital by way of the old capital, in order to deliver a letter to the king summarizing the events of the demon attack in the Muno Barony. As I understood it, the only people in this territory with titles befitting a messenger to the king were Miss Nina and the baron himself, neither of whom could leave at present.

For that reason, it was decided that sending a member of the baron's family would be the next best option, and ultimately the duty fell to Miss Karina.

It seemed that a report to the king had already been made using the City Core, but it was considered courteous for the lord to send a messenger to explain in person nonetheless.

As I mulled over this information, Lulu called out to me from the coachman's seat.

"Master, I believe we'll be departing soon."

Indeed, the number of wagons departing from Muno Castle's parking area had greatly decreased, and it would soon be our turn next.

"Satou, please take care of my dear Karina."

"Of course. We'll be parting ways at Bolehart City, but until then, you can certainly count on me."

I smiled reassuringly at the worried Baron Muno.

Bolehart City was the dominion of the dwarves in the Ougoch Duchy. I had yet to meet a dwarf, one of the most famous denizens of any fantasy world, so I was very much looking forward to the visit.

"You know you can come back here once you've seen Lady Karina to her destination, don't you?"

"I'm afraid that won't be possible. We need to bring Mia back home to the Bolenan Forest."

Miss Nina's comment was offhand yet serious, so I responded sincerely.

She had also given me a letter of introduction to several influential aristocrats, as well as a few personal letters that she'd asked me to deliver.

"I wish you'd at least leave Miss Arisa with me. Without her, my workload's about to double."

"Oh, I couldn't! I just can't bear to live unless I'm by my darling's side." Arisa appeared out of nowhere to respond to Miss Nina's complaint.

I would've liked to object to the whole "darling" bit, but this was standard practice for Arisa. I just pretended not to hear it.

Arisa was peeking at me hopefully, clearly expecting me to jab back at her, but she'd just have to wait.

More importantly, I was a bit concerned about the maids who were slowly but surely drawing closer.

They were all clutching their hands to their chests and gazing at me rather tearfully.

...Ummm?

I hadn't so much as touched a single one of them, yet they were looking at me like a litter of abandoned puppies.

"Please don't go, Lord Hereditary Knight."

One of the maids, a slender redhead, rushed forward with a cry and clung to me.

Sadly, she was a little lacking in volume.

She had opened the floodgates, as a wave of maids cascaded toward me to embrace me and try to stop me from leaving.

Some of them even tried to kiss my cheek or my forehead. If I were a lolicon, this would probably be a moment to remember.

Instead, thanks to the enthusiasm of the younger maids, I missed my chance at a little intimacy with the shapely adults.

Arisa and Mia kicked me from behind in protest ("Enough with the swooning!"), but I ignored them.

"Sir Knight, please stay here forever!"

"Yes! Who will make crepes if you are gone, my lord?"

"Forget crepes! Can't we get one more taste of that fried chicken?"

"No, marry me and cook for me forever!"

"At least leave little Tama with us!"

"What are you saying? Pochi is much cuter!"

"I want to hear Lady Mia's music forever…!"

…So at least half their reasons for wanting me to stay were food-related. I never knew I'd captured their stomachs so thoroughly.

…Oh?

I felt a familiar tugging on my legs, so I looked down to see Pochi and Tama.

Why were they hanging off me like that?

They were looking up at me keenly, their eyes sparkling. Did they think all this shoving was some new game?

The head maid clapped her hands briskly, drawing her subordinates' attention away from me.

"Everyone! I understand we're all sad to see Sir Knight go, but you mustn't trouble him so."

"That's right. Besides, he baked a pound cake for us that's sitting in the dining room right now. Once you finish your work, you can come and have a piece each."

With this announcement from Chef Gert, the maids all flooded away from me like the ebbing tide.

…I'll admit it hurt my feelings a little.

"You haven't had breakfast yet, right? It may not measure up to your cooking, Sir Knight, but please take this if you'd like."

"Thank you very much. I'm sure it will be delicious."

I accepted the boxed lunch that the head chef Gert handed to me and passed it to Lulu in the coachman stand.

"Are you heading out? If you get bored of traveling, please come back anytime."

"Once we've trained in Labyrinth City for a year or two, I promise we'll return awhile."

Nodding to Miss Nina, I boarded the carriage.

"Please take care of little Tama and Pochi."

Baron Muno spoke in the same tone he'd used when entrusting his own daughter to me. No, if anything, it was even more emotional.

During our stay, he'd doted on the two like they were his grand-children, so it wasn't surprising that he was sad to see them go.

"Don't worry—I will."

The baron still looked worried.

"It's okaaay!"

"Pochi is fine anywhere, sir!"

Tama and Pochi, who were busy receiving little pouches of sweets from Miss Soluna, turned to the baron and grinned cheerfully.

I helped the pair board the carriage, then joined them in waving out the window to our Muno Barony friends.

Behind the baron and company, the rest of the castle staff, as well as the children and elderly in the care of the castle, had all gathered to see us off.

Of course, this also included Miss Soluna and the former fake hero, Hauto; Sir Zotol; and the other soldiers.

With Liza and Nana leading the way on horseback, our carriage departed from Muno Castle.

We said our farewells to our unexpectedly cozy visit in Muno City and set off for the Ougoch Duchy.

The Home of the Dwarves

Satou here. Sometime in junior high, I learned that there were different kinds of dwarves than the ones I saw in picture books as a kid. I remember being surprised to read that female dwarves had beards.

Five days after we left Muno City, we finally reached the fork in the road that branched off toward Bolehart City.

Not only was our party large, but the mountainous region at the border of the territory was quite difficult to traverse, so it took longer than I'd expected.

Monsters attacked us a few times over the course of our journey, but the soldiers and knights traveling in front of us took care of them each time, so we never had to battle for ourselves.

"Well, here we are. I hope we meet again in the old capital."

"Indeed. If you go to the old capital, please do visit the Tenion Temple."

At the crossroads, we bade farewell to Miss Sara and company—or rather, we exchanged a promise to meet again.

"S-Sa… Sir Pendragon. Are you certain there's no way you might accompany me to the old capital?" Lady Karina gazed at me like an abandoned kitten.

As usual, she seemed to be too embarrassed to call me by my first name.

"I'm sorry, Lady Karina. I am duty bound to deliver Miss Nina's letter to Bolehart City."

I depended on my "Poker Face" skill to keep my expression from faltering as I apologized.

I couldn't tell her that I was too excited to see dwarves to go with her.

"Hee-hee. You seem to be quite close to Sir Pendragon, Lady Karina."

Miss Sara might be a priestess, but she was still a girl, too. Evidently this meant she had a fondness for romance, as she was watching us with an amused smile.

It was a misunderstanding, of course, but I didn't have the heart to...

"I—I have no such r-relationship with this person, I'll have you know!"

"Oh? Denying it so fervently is rather insulting, is it not?"

Miss Sara's smile only deepened at Miss Karina's desperate denial.

...All right, I guess I should help her out.

"Lady Sara... Lady Karina is quite innocent at heart, so please don't tease her any further."

"Hee-hee, I suppose you're right." Miss Sara accepted my suggestion easily enough and returned to the original subject. "We will be waiting in the riverbed city of Gururian for a few days, so if your business is brief enough, Sir Pendragon, perhaps we will meet again there."

"Then I shall have to put our cart horses to work and bring that to fruition."

I didn't think it would actually be possible, given our itinerary, but I responded diplomatically just in case.

To be honest, though, I didn't really want to work our horses too hard.

We shouldn't keep blocking the road, so we parted ways with Sara and her party and journeyed toward Bolehart.

We'd acquired a new four-horse carriage for the journey.

Since this doubled our horses while lightening the weight of the carriage itself, we were able to travel an extra 30 percent or so per day with our newfound speed and endurance.

Thanks to the shock absorber I'd made with earth and stones on the journey to Muno Barony, as well as the new cushions, the journey had become considerably more comfortable.

In addition, I'd installed a mechanism to quickly transform the seats into beds.

And two additional horses accompanied us at all times, usually ridden by the armored Liza and Nana.

This was intended to fend off thieves. I had spotted more than a few bandits when I was surveying the Ougoch Duchy with a handmade hang glider before we departed, so we needed to make the proper precautions.

It would be easy enough to defeat them, but taking care of what came next was much more involved than just beating monsters, so I wanted to avoid that if at all possible.

I opened the door that connected the carriage to the coachman's stand and spoke to Lulu.

"Lulu, let me take over for you."

"That won't do, master. You're a noble now, so you must leave the coach driving to your servants."

True enough. I could still see the soldiers from Miss Sara's group behind us.

I didn't think it would be that big of a deal if they saw me driving, but Lulu seemed to be enjoying herself. I gave up for the time being.

"All right. But may I sit beside you, at least?"

"Yes, of course!"

Lulu shifted to one side, then patted the seat next to her in an exceptionally cute gesture.

I thanked her as I sat down and looked around.

Fresh green leaves were beginning to bud all around, bringing the first signs of spring to the Ougoch Duchy.

In this world, Ritual Magic could affect the change of the seasons using City Cores, so I wasn't sure how much the conventional wisdom of Japan applied here.

Still, though, any weather that let you steer a carriage without freezing half to death was welcome in my book.

"There you are, you big flirt."

Arisa popped out to join us, latching onto me and making a deadpan joke. Naturally, she chose to squeeze herself between Lulu and me.

"Arisa, you're such a green-eyed monster sometimes." Lulu smiled and patted the other girl's hair.

Then, Tama and Pochi shoved their way in, crushing Arisa.

"Geh!"

"Flirtiiiing?"

"That's forbidden, sir."

The two of them seemed happy that it was just our little group again.

"Forbidden."

Mia, who had started riding on Nana's horse with her a while back, puffed out her cheeks and prodded me lightly with her staff.

"Master, please look ahead, I suggest."

Nana pointed forward, drawing my attention to the path before us.

When I followed her gaze, I saw that Liza had dismounted a short ways down the road and was crouching next to a brown lump on the shoulder.

According to the AR display, it was a **large wild boar**.

Most likely, it had tried to attack Liza and was soundly defeated for its troubles.

"I guess we'll have boar hot pot tonight."

"Yaaay, hot pooot!"

"We'll help break it down, sir!"

I opened my map to see if there were any sources of water nearby.

"Liza, there's a village a little ways away, so perhaps you can find out if we can use some water there."

"Yes, master!"

I took a long stick and a rope from the Garage Bag and handed it to Liza to transport the wild boar.

The Garage Bag was a Magic Item that could hold much more than its appearance suggested.

I'd recently acquired a lesser one, which was currently the saddlebag of Liza's horse. It was primarily used to store Liza's magic spear.

That evening, we butchered the wild boar and shared some of the meat with the villagers, then parked the horse-drawn carriage in the village square to spend the night.

As soon as he found out I was a noble, the village chief offered to let us stay in his home; I didn't want to trouble him with so many guests, so I politely declined.

◆

Two days after our stay at the village, seven total after leaving the Muno capital, we arrived at Bolehart City.

The self-governed area was a blank spot on the Ougoch Duchy map, so I used my "Search Entire Map" skill for the first time in a long while to gain information about it.

A dwarf city might call to mind an underground society, but according to my newfound information, at least half of them lived aboveground normally in a fortress city. The other half, more in line with my imagination, lived in the mines connected to the city.

At only twelve miles in diameter, including several mountains, the dwarf territory wasn't very large.

There was one city and several villages within the Bolehart dominion. The city's population was about 60 percent dwarves, 20 percent ratfolk, 10 percent rabbitfolk, and the last 10 percent were mostly humans and miscellaneous demi-humans.

Unlike the other cities I'd seen so far, there were hardly any slaves or serfs.

The only slaves who showed up in my map search were owned by merchants visiting from outside the city. The traders were all human-folk or weaselfolk, mostly the former.

The only fairyfolk besides the dwarves were a handful of gnomes and spriggans; there were no elves at all. Maybe the old fantasy trope of enmity between elves and dwarves was true?

Absentmindedly, I filtered my map search.

When I searched by level, there were a little more than ten people who had reached at least level 40. They were all dwarves. The highest level was an elderly dwarf called Dohal, who was level 51.

Dwarves overall averaged at level 7 or so, so these people were probably exceptions.

I also checked to be sure that there were no demons, reincarnations, or anything of the sort. Like in the Ougoch Duchy, I found none.

As a bonus, there were no members of the demon lord–worshipping Wings of Freedom, either. We should be able to sightsee normally here for once.

As I was checking the map, the landscape around us changed. The number of tall trees decreased, while there were more bushes and reddish-brown thickets.

"Mine pollution, perhaps?" Arisa murmured as she looked out the window.

"You think so? I've never been close to a mine before, so I have no idea."

I had been sightseeing in an abandoned mine before, but I'd never visited one that was still in use.

Instead, Mia answered Arisa's question.

"Mrrrr? Spirits." She made an X over her mouth with her fingers.

"It's because of spirits, you mean?"

"No. No spirits."

"They're withering because there are no spirits, then?"

"Mm." Mia nodded, satisfied.

Well, that's fantasy logic if I've ever heard it.

"Mana shortage," the elf added, and Arisa nodded rapidly.

With her sage expression still on her face, she turned toward me. "…Master, explain?"

I gave a light chop to Arisa's forehead before obliging.

"As I understand, spirits convey mana to everything in the natural world. I don't know what effect it has on plants, but I think there's an adverse effect if they don't get enough."

I'd obtained this information from Trazayuya's journals in the Cradle incident.

According to the documents, mana affected not only living and non-living things but also phenomena. This probably included natural phenomena like wind currents and temperature changes.

"Huh. Have you ever seen a spirit, master?"

Arisa's question drew to mind the youthful image of a dryad.

"Well, we've seen a dryad, remember? She was a tree sprite, so that makes her a spirit, right?"

"No." Mia shook her head.

"So…not a spirit?"

"Mm." She nodded.

I didn't really understand the difference, but Mia was a kind of fairyfolk and all. She would know better than I would.

I'd probably have to get an adult elf to explain it to me when we brought Mia to Bolenan Forest.

Shelving that line of thought for now, I answered Arisa's original question. "Well, if dryads aren't spirits, then I guess I've never seen one. You probably need a skill like Mia's 'Spirit Vision' to see them."

Arisa nodded, then twisted around toward Mia.

"Mia, what do spirits look like?"

"Pretty."

"Well, that's not much to go on."

"Mrrrr." Mia scrunched up her eyebrows and thought a moment. "Glowy pearls. Fluffy. Nice."

Her usual one- or two-word statements didn't suffice this time, so she strung together a longer explanation for once.

"Hmm! I'd like to see one for myself, then."

"Me too."

Arisa murmured enviously, and I nodded in agreement.

I'd certainly like to meet a graceful undine or a free-spirited sylph sometime. Preferably of the sexy mature-woman variety.

"Mrrrr."

"You're drooling, master!"

Without thinking, I automatically pressed a hand to my face at Arisa's words, causing her to exclaim, "I knew it!" and cling to me to prevent me from "cheating." Mia began doing the same.

"Cheeeater?"

"Cheetah, sir!"

Tama and Pochi had been dozing off until the fuss woke them up, and they started imitating Arisa and Mia, first hugging and then climbing all over me.

I patted the young girls' heads in a vague attempt at reassurance. All the noise made Lulu poke her head in through the door to the coachman's box. "Looks like you're all getting along swimmingly," she remarked with a giggle.

"Master, there's a great deal of smoke up ahead."

Just then, Liza, who'd brought her horse close to the carriage, reported to me with some anxiety.

The map didn't show me anything out of the ordinary going on in Bolehart City.

"Don't worry. It's just fumes from smelting iron."

"I-is that so? I apologize for disturbing you."

I assured Liza not to worry about it, put the children back in their seats, and headed up to the coachman's stand.

After a while, the trees thinned out, and we entered into a wasteland of stones and bare soil.

Beyond this wasteland, I could see a fortress city that appeared to be carved into a gray mountain, belching white smoke from an array of chimneys.

Similar hazy streams billowed out from several openings in the side of the mountain.

Though we arrived in the afternoon, there was a long line waiting for entry at the gates of Bolehart City.

We stopped our carriage at the back and waited for our turn.

"Looks like there are maybe twenty carts in front of us? We might be waiting quite a while."

"Seems that way."

Arisa clambered over me in the coachman's stand to size up the line.

Looking closely, I noticed that many of the carts had the same canopy design. We must have arrived right after some merchant party.

Sensing someone behind me, I turned to see Pochi and Tama enviously staring at Arisa. With little else to do, I let them ride piggyback on my shoulders, one at a time.

Before long, I felt a tug on my sleeve. Mia was waiting for her turn, too.

"Next."

Unlike Tama and Pochi, Mia was wearing a skirt, so I lifted her by the waist instead.

"Not fair."

She must have wanted to ride on my shoulders, too.

"It's only because of your skirt. If you were wearing shorts, I'd put you on my shoulders, too."

"Mrrrr."

Mia puffed out her cheeks and went inside the carriage just to change clothes, so I held true to my word and gave her a piggyback ride.

"Tama, Pochi, stand at the back of the carriage and keep watch for thieves."

Bringing her horse up alongside the carriage, Liza gave instructions to Tama and Pochi, who were staring around wide-eyed from the coachman's seat.

"Aye-aye, siiir!"

"Roger, sir!"

With a sharp salute, Tama and Pochi hopped down from the coachman's stand and rushed to the back of the carriage.

Once her instructions were fulfilled, Liza turned toward me.

"Master, it appears that weasels visit this town. They are a cunning tribe, so please be careful."

"All right, got it. Thanks, Liza."

If I remember correctly, the weaselfolk are the race that destroyed Liza's village.

"Nana."

After climbing down from my shoulders, Mia beckoned to Nana.

"Ride."

"Master, I will transfer horse operation duties to Mia, I report. Permission to do so?"

"Sure. Don't go too far, though, all right?"

"Mm."

Mia hopped in front of Nana and took the reins, turning the horse toward the front gate. She probably wanted to check the situation at the front of the line.

As Mia and Nana left, they passed a group of approaching peddlers.

"Mister, won't ya buy some potatoes? They're right tasty."

A woman with an unusual dialect selling boiled potatoes was the first to arrive. One potato cost one copper. This was three times the price that my "Estimation" skill suggested.

"Mister, ferget them potatoes. I got chicken skewers here. They use lots o' rock salt from Bole'art! Only three coppers apiece."

"Master, don'tcha want some real meat? These whole-roasted toads'll fill ya right up. Nice an' chewy."

Maybe I was just being prejudiced, but the weaselfolk sounded shady to me.

The smell wasn't bad, but the appearance of the toad put off my appetite, so I declined.

Seeing this from the back of the carriage, Tama and Pochi looked a little disappointed, but we'd just eaten lunch a little while earlier. *Eating too much is bad for your health, you know.*

As we waited our turn, more peddlers, including more weaselfolk, ratfolk, and rabbitfolk children, accosted us, selling things like sandals and rope. However, we didn't need any of it, so I just checked their prices with "Estimation" and didn't buy anything.

After a while, Nana and Mia came back with a purchase they'd made near the front.

Both of them were wearing flower crowns atop their heads. As a bonus, Mia had something sticking out of her mouth.

"Satou."

Mia took out the long, stemlike object from her mouth and offered the end to me, so I gave it a taste.

…It was sweet. Sweet and somehow nostalgic.

It brought back childhood memories of picking azaleas from the side of the road and sucking up the nectar.

Unlike the sugarcane-y taste of the thorn licorice pulp that I often gave the kids as a snack, this stem had a gentle sweetness like the nectar of a flower.

"Ah!"

"That was an indirect kiss, wasn't it?! That's it, I'm going next!"

Lulu gave a small exclamation of reproach from my side and Arisa a much louder one from behind me.

Indirect kisses? Come on, we're not in junior high— Wait, I guess Lulu is around that age.

Arisa extended her arm, but Mia snatched the stem before the lilac-haired girl could reach it. Sticking it back in her mouth, Mia held up two fingers in a victory sign.

Arisa muttered darkly behind me. I wished Mia would stop provoking her. Even Lulu was looking a little teary-eyed.

Luckily, a weaselfolk child came by just then to sell stems like the one Mia was chewing on, so I bought enough for everyone and distributed them.

They wanted me to put the stems in my mouth first for whatever reason, but I decided to just go along with the strange request.

"Ach, coachman! Does this carriage belong to a noble or what?"

"Or is it a merchant? Hey, coachman!"

I heard gruff voices shouting, but I didn't see anyone.

"Right here, coachman."

"That's right. Down here, y'see."

I lowered my gaze and found two short and stout dwarves, only a little more than four feet tall.

They were wearing gleaming black iron helmets and chain mail, carrying not axes but short spears.

Underneath their triangular helmets, I saw beady eyes, hooked noses, and long beards down to their stomachs. This was indeed the kind of dwarf I often saw in games.

I used "Poker Face" to mask my welling excitement and got down from the carriage to answer their questions.

"Nice to meet you, Sir Dwarves. I am Satou Pendragon, a hereditary knight of Muno Barony."

When I used my "Etiquette" skill to politely introduce myself, the dwarves hurriedly struck their fists against their chests and straightened up.

"S-so terribly sorry. We di'n' realize ye were a noble, ach…"

"Mighty strange noble at that, to be sittin' on the coachman's stand, y'see."

I found their manner of speaking to be rather strange, but I remained polite as I asked, "So, what business did you have with me?"

"We came to say that if ye be a noble, ye needn't wait in line, ach."

"Yes, nobles don't need to wait in line, y'see."

With that, the dwarves led us past the line and into the city.

As it happened, nobles could get preferential treatment in any city, not just Bolehart. This even included the lowest title of hereditary knight, like me.

Even inside, they only checked my identity, making no effort to examine my companions. They took a quick glance inside the carriage—no searches or entrance tax.

Seemed to me that a sneaky noble would have no trouble smuggling.

◆

"It's a pleasure to meet you, Sir Pendragon. I've received the letter from Viscount Lottel. Is the brave lady doing well?"

"Yes, she's ruling with great enthusiasm. And please feel free to call me Satou, if you'd like."

I was visiting the city hall to chat with the mayor, Mr. Dorial.

The other children were relaxing in a separate room, except for Arisa, who was beside me. Miss Nina had asked her to take care of something.

She almost sounded like a different person as she addressed Mr. Dorial.

"If it pleases you, Master Dorial, we would like to formally request your gracious acceptance of exchange students from the Muno territory to study abroad here, as is written in that letter."

"Hmm. Viscount Lottel did look out for me when I was studying abroad in the old capital, so I'm sure we can accept a few exchange students each year."

Mr. Dorial opened the letter as he answered. I'd learned the lord of this dominion was his father, Mr. Dohal, not Mr. Dorial himself, so I had to wonder if he could really make promises like that.

Perhaps sensing my trepidation, Mr. Dorial went on.

"Worry not. My father entrusts me with all but the most important matters."

Oh, good. There was nothing to worry about, then. Personally, the possibility of leaked information seemed pretty important to me, but maybe their stance was along the lines of "If you want to steal our technology, go ahead and try"?

"The letter states that you might be interested in blacksmithing and such, Mr. Satou. Would you like to visit the public workshops and refining facilities?"

"Yes, please!"

Wow, what a godsend.

Deep in my heart, I showered Miss Nina with gratitude. I would have to write her a thank-you letter later.

"This is the biggest blast furnace in the city."

Before me was a building with a ceiling height of about sixty feet.

The only people here were Mr. Dorial, a female dwarf who was acting as his secretary, and me. The female dwarf, named Jojorie, was Mr. Dorial's daughter.

Instead of the cutesy little girls who often represent female dwarves in recent games, she was basically just a beardless version of a male dwarf.

Meanwhile, Arisa had gone off to the commercial district of the city. She declared that she was going to look for a merchant to deliver the response to Muno City.

Jojorie opened the heavy-looking door, releasing a blast of hot air.

The inside of the building was a single large room, like a mill or a factory, with a great number of men hard at work. They seemed to be shoveling black lumps into the hole at the center.

"That there is the top of the furnace."

...The top?

I was doubtful at first, but checking the map resolved my confusion.

The main body of the blast furnace was in the basement of this building, and the black lumps the men were tossing in appeared to be fuel and iron ore.

"Does it use coal?"

"The fuel is transmuted from monster cores and coal to create something called 'refined monster coal.' It's got more heating power than ordinary coal, and using monster cores for the fuel is more cost-efficient than running a magic furnace."

As I listened to Jojorie's explanation, I searched through Trazayuya's documents and found the recipe for this special fuel. It might be more prevalent than I expected.

"It's too hot in here. Let's do our explanations elsewhere."

Mr. Dorial urged us over to an observation area, where the heat was a little milder. According to Mr. Dorial, an insulation spell protected it.

From here, I could fully visualize the blast furnace.

The room was cut in half down the middle, and the far side served as a sort of well that went about two hundred feet underground.

On the lower floor, a large group of shirtless dwarves and beastfolk was hard at work.

Occasionally, red-hot metal would flow out of the furnace, illuminating the dark underground section.

"This is quite a facility you have here."

"Yes, thirty percent of the iron used in the duchy is refined here."

I wasn't just acting impressed to be polite. The technology was different, of course, but this facility was on the same level as the ironworks I'd seen in my old world.

"The smoke is purified when it passes through that pipe there. The inside of the pipe is lined with a catalyst transmuted from water stones and wind stones, which cleans away the soot from the smoke without needing any additional magic power supply."

I see. It probably keeps the overhead lower than using Magic Items or magic to purify it.

Moving on, I also got to tour a rotary kiln and a roller. The latter used a huge magical furnace that was some kind of magic tool, as far as I could tell. This furnace required magic to run, as evidenced by the men stumbling around in robes like sorcerers on the verge of exhausting their magic.

"That seems to be quite a difficult endeavor."

"Indeed. We would normally have more hands on the job, but gnomes are currently visiting home, so we're short on people."

As I nodded along to Jojorie's explanation, my heart went out to the men working overtime due to the staff shortage.

Hearing heavy footsteps, I turned to find a group of little giants around ten feet tall carrying finished bars of iron and steel. According to the information from the AR display, they were a different clan from the little giants we'd met in the Mountain-Tree Village.

I was able to get a fairly thorough tour, but they hadn't yet shown me the mithril-related facilities in the underground caverns. It was probably a highly classified part of Bolehart City.

Unable to resist my curiosity, I decided to ask Mr. Dorial about it, just for kicks.

"Are the mithril facilities underground, then?"

"I-I'm surprised you knew about that. Did Viscount Lottel tell you, perhaps?"

"No, it was just a hunch. Besides, I heard that this city's mithril goods are the finest in the world, so I very much wanted to visit for myself if at all possible."

"Is that so…? I should like to allow it, then, but I would need my father's permission for that."

Mr. Dorial crossed his short arms and furrowed his brow. Unable to watch her father fret any longer, Jojorie spoke up.

"Father, why not simply talk to Grandfather? Surely even he would never command a total stranger to forge a sword or anything like that."

Jojorie, please don't set up flags like that.

◆

"Hmph. Let's see ye forge a sword. Then we'll talk."

…Jojorie…

I glanced over at her, but she quickly avoided my eyes.

After squeezing through a narrow underground tunnel only a few feet high, we reached Elder Dohal's workplace. In the back of the room, high-level dwarves were forging swords.

They were all highly skilled. Each sword was higher in attack power, sharpness, durability, and other parameters than any you'd find on the street by more than half.

And after I was introduced to him, he made the very request Jojorie had joked about.

I sensed his eyes on the Silent Bell of Bolenan attached to my belt, but he said nothing about it. I presumed this Elvish treasure had no effect on him.

"Father, Sir Satou is an acquaintance of Viscount Lottel..."

"Hmm. Certainly we owe Nina a debt of gratitude, but that has nothing to do with this. Seeing someone forge a sword speaks volumes of their character. Zajuul, bring out a heated mithril ingot."

"Of course, master."

Mr. Dorial tried to intervene on my behalf, but Elder Dohal was hearing none of it.

The brawny gray-bearded dwarf Zajuul prepared an ingot and the necessary tools for me.

Well, I'd gotten to see someone working on a sword at a blacksmith in Muno City, so maybe I understood the process well enough to give it a shot. My "Smithing" skill was maxed out anyway, so it would probably be fine.

I grasped the red-hot ingot with smithing tongs and placed it on the anvil. Then, steadying myself, I struck it with the mallet.

A small spark flew through the air, and a shrill metallic *clank* echoed through the room.

...Huh? Something felt wrong just now.

Possibly sensing my hesitation, Elder Dohal took the tool from me and struck the ingot in the same way.

After a single blow, he called Zajuul over and rapped him on the head with his knuckles.

"How many decades have ye been working with mithril now, ye fool? I've said time and again that melting metal into an ingot is the foundation of smithing!"

"Of course, master."

I didn't quite understand what happened, but there must have been some problem with the ingot Zajuul prepared for me.

Was that why I'd felt like something was a little off before?

"All right, we're going to the mithril furnace. Come with me, youngster."

"Certainly."

Guess Elder Dohal was going to take me there himself. I didn't actually end up forging a sword, but I must have passed.

Mr. Dorial and Jojorie followed behind me. Zajuul had already gone ahead, presumably to make some kind of preparations.

I didn't know what to expect from the furnace, but I was looking forward to it.

Compared to the iron blast furnace I'd seen outside, the one for mithril was much smaller. It was probably only about a third of the size.

Unlike the first one, it seemed to operate solely on magical power, so all that went into the hole in the top was mithril ore.

The furnace, which wasn't currently in use, was made of a red metal—according to the AR, the exceptionally heat-resistant **scarlet ore**.

If I remembered correctly, the Japanese name for it was "*hihiiro-kane*," a fantasy metal that appeared in Japanese mythology.

This reminded me of the time I saw Shinto shrine–style archways in Seiryuu County or certain stories about heroes of the past. Why was there so much Japanese aesthetic mixed in with this fantasy world? Maybe it was just the effects of my translation skills, but it made me a little nervous.

In front of the control panel for the furnace, Zajuul was shouting at several other dwarves.

"Brother Zajuul… We only have poor-quality monster cores left, so we can't produce enough heat."

"We need better quality cores or the magic furnace just won't work, no matter how much we plug away at it, y'see."

"Och, if the gnomes were here, they could refill it from the emergency magic supply terminal there…"

Exhausted, the dwarves were slumping to the ground as they explained the situation to Zajuul. It seemed to be a fuel quality issue.

They looked miserable now, but everyone present was a fierce warrior of more than level 30. They all had the "Smithing" skill and some kind of magic skill.

"You morons! The youth of Bolehart shouldn't whine like this!"

Zajuul was obviously a stick person, not a carrot person.

"Lemme see your guts! We're gonna work together to power up the supply terminal!"

"Brother Zajuul?! A-all right, let's do it, then!"

"Och, will it really work with just us?"

"We'll round up all the bastards who are on break, too, o' course!"

They were going to make it work with sheer manpower.

One of the engineers threw a pink core into the magic furnace and started it up.

Then, with Zajuul leading the way, the group of ten men grabbed the "magic supply terminal" thing and started pushing magic into it.

The crimson ore furnace took on a faint golden glow.

However, they didn't seem to be able to produce the magic fast enough, and the glow began flickering on and off.

"Looks like you're a bit short. Let me help out."

"If you're helping, Father, then I will, too."

Even Elder Dohal and Mr. Dorial came to pitch in.

Mr. Dorial was grinning and rolling up his sleeves, excited to get a piece of the action.

I have enough MP to spare anyway, so I ought to help, too.

"Sir Dohal, would you mind if I help as well?"

"Just use a free terminal!"

"M-master!"

Elder Dohal easily granted me permission to help.

Judging by the way Zajuul and the other dwarves gaped at him in disbelief, it was probably unusual for an outsider to be permitted to touch the equipment.

I bowed to Elder Dohal and touched the crystal ball on the metal terminal.

"All right, you lot! Breathe in time!"

""""RIGHT!"""""

Elder Dohal and Zajuul alternately shouted "HEIGH!" and "HO!" to get a rhythm going.

I almost lost it when I heard that signature phrase being shouted over and over, but I managed to keep a straight face.

Trying to focus, I poured more magic power into the terminal. When I felt slight changes, I adjusted accordingly.

At first, I put in only one point at a time out of fear of breaking the furnace, but it seemed to be able to handle a bit more.

After a while, I felt a very slight sense that the flow of magic was being blocked. It was probably an effect of my "Magic-Tool Tuning" skill. Changing my title to Tuner while I was at it, I focused on cleaning the magical path for them.

"HEIGH!"

I added five points of magic to give an extra push to the current from the dwarves.

That seemed to be enough to clear out the blockage in the magic flow.

The flashing glow of the scarlet ore began to stabilize.

"HO!"

This time, I pushed in ten points of magic power.

Along with it, I corrected a slight distortion in the route of the magic.

Yeah, that's better.

The golden glow of the furnace grew.

"It's stabilizing! You can do it!"

Jojorie's cheer put the spark back in the dwarves' eyes.

Looks like men are weak to the cheers of beautiful women in any world.

The furnace began to let off a shrill sound as the repeated shots of magic started to cross the threshold.

"Now! Throw in the mithril ore!"

"Right!"

At Elder Dohal's command, the dwarf who was waiting on standby near the furnace tossed in the ore.

"Mithril blast furnace preparations complete!"

"All hands, equip light protection gear!"

Zajuul followed up Elder Dohal's words with instructions to everyone else.

Immediately, the dwarves all pulled out dark goggles from who-knows-where and put them on.

Um, what? I don't have anything like that, though?!

"Here, Mr. Satou."

Jojorie came up behind me and affixed something like sunglasses to my face.

"It's a light shield. The glow of the furnace can hurt your eyes even when you're wearing these, though, so please avoid looking directly at it."

"Thank you very much."

I nodded gratefully to Jojorie just as Elder Dohal made another declaration.

"Mithril blast furnace, commence operation!"

"Right!"

One dwarf moved away from the magic supply terminal and gave the control panel a hearty smack.

The reddish-gold glow around the furnace gathered at the bottom, creating dazzling rings of light that floated upward rhythmically.

It was a beautiful sight.

The next moment, my eyes were overwhelmed.

I must have been unconsciously using the "Night Vision" skill, rendering the protection of the light shield fairly useless, and the excessive brightness fried my retinas.

Manipulating the menu that floated over my completely dark field of vision, I discovered that my status now read **Blind**.

Luckily, my eyesight returned before I could start panicking about what to do.

My "Self-Healing" must have automatically repaired my retinas. *That's a relief.*

> Skill Acquired: "Light Intensity Adjustment"
> Skill Acquired: "Light Resistance"

I got some weird robot-sounding skills in the process, so I maxed them out with skill points and activated them before my eyes could get burned out again.

Then, as I gazed at the now moderate light of the mithril blast furnace, I heard Elder Dohal yelling at his crew.

"Come on, you lot! The work's not over yet! Keep the magical pressure going!"

""""RIGHT!""""

Apparently, I chose a poor time for the glow to distract me.

I joined the dwarves in supplying more magic power.

By the end, I'd poured in about three hundred points, but my MP recovery was fast enough that I could've kept going indefinitely.

The dwarves, on the other hand, seemed to be pushing themselves too hard and dropped one after another from overwork.

Eventually, the only two left standing aside from me were Elder Dohal and Zajuul.

"Look at you, human! Seems I misjudged ya!"

Zajuul chuckled heartily and smacked my shoulder with a thick palm.

With my high VIT stat, I was fine, but it probably would've knocked a normal human flat on the ground.

"Thanks for your help, Mr. Satou. Are you thirsty? You too, Mr. Zajuul."

I took a gulp of the liquid Jojorie offered me.

Immediately, I felt alcohol burning my throat and caught the refreshing scent of rice wine in my nostrils.

I nearly choked with surprise, but somehow I kept it together.

"...Is this alcohol?"

"Distilled rice wine from the city, yes. It won't get you drunk like strong spirits would, but it's good for you to drink after working up a sweat."

Using highly alcoholic distilled liquor as a substitute for a sports drink...? I guess that's typical for dwarves.

"Zajuul!"

"Yes! Master!"

Zajuul pressed a button on the lower part of the furnace, and the door at the bottom opened, producing the freshly tempered mithril.

Instead of a melted metal like iron, it produced about twenty solid ingots that looked like they weighed around ten pounds each.

They were even in the proper shape already. There must have been a mold inside.

Once they cooled, the completed ingots gleamed silver with a faint green finish.

Hearing thudding sounds, I turned to see that a door on the side of the furnace had opened to discharge some blackish lumps. According to my AR display, it was **mithril slag**.

...Clank.

A metallic sound made me turn back around. There, I saw Elder Dohal hitting one of the ingots with a small hammer to check the sound.

Then he pointed out a few that had met his standards, instructing Zajuul to bring them to the smithing area.

"Come along, youngster. I'll have ye hammer in turn with me."

"Master! A human child can't keep up with your hammering!"

"Silence, you! Don't contradict my decisions!"

I was going to be smithing with Elder Dohal.

"Youngster! Ye'd best assume that ye won't be sleeping till morning. Jojorie, we'll need meat. We still have that smoked basilisk, do we not? Bring the whole thing here. We must fill our stomachs first."

So you can eat basilisk...? I had stowed away the corpse of the one I defeated before because its meat was poisonous, but maybe I should try to figure out how to remove the poison and cook it.

Once we'd moved to the blacksmiths' messroom and Jojorie had served us, I asked her to deliver a message and some food to Arisa and the others.

We had already arranged to spend the night in the mayor's guest-house, so it shouldn't be a problem.

The whole process had taken such a long time that Mr. Dorial had already returned to his mayoral duties, leaving Jojorie behind.

◆

A huge lump of metal shook the floor with a *thud*.

"What's the matter, youngster? Is the giant smithing hammer giving you second thoughts?"

Zajuul smirked and patted the handle of the enormous tool on the floor.

It was basically just a huge unrefined lump of metal with a handle, and it looked like it could easily weigh a ton.

According to the AR display, it was made with an alloy of iron and mithril.

"A dwarf would be able to lift this with one hand, y'know. Put yer back into it!"

The absurd size of it did intimidate me, despite Zajuul's attempt at encouragement.

Dwarves can lift this with one hand? They must be crazy strong.

As if he could hear my admiration, Zajuul did indeed lift it up with one hand to demonstrate.

I pretended not to notice that he was trying to impress Jojorie. I didn't want to make a comment that might earn him another smack from Elder Dohal.

Preparing myself, I put both hands on the handle of the giant hammer.

Thanks to my absurdly high STR stat, I was able to lift it easily. If anything, keeping my balance was the hardest part, because my body was so light.

I did my best to brace my legs and lower my center of gravity until it felt almost unnaturally steady.

It was possible that my "Transport" skill made finding my balance easier despite the heavy load.

While I practiced swinging the giant hammer, Elder Dohal peered into the pot his apprentices had brought.

"It's a little weak. Bring something stronger."

"Och, master, this is all we've got right now."

"Have Ganza formulate some more, then."

"Och, Ganza went back home to take care of some incident in Boleheim."

Guess the chemicals we were supposed to use for smithing didn't meet Elder Dohal's standards.

As the person in charge of formulating them was away right now, it was a bit of a problem.

If I'd known the recipe, I could formulate it instead, but I couldn't imagine they would teach it to outsiders.

"Jojorie! Go up to the surface and get me an alchemist. Anyone will do."

Those instructions were pretty vague…but if anyone would suffice, then maybe I could at least offer.

"Lord Dohal, if you really do mean anyone, perhaps I could formulate it?"

"Hmm? You do alchemy, too, do ye? It's in your hands, then."

Elder Dohal's swift decision seemed to agitate Zajuul and the other apprentices.

However, none of them was able to say that to his face.

One of the apprentices guided me to the alchemy area in the corner of the room.

"I've only helped with formulation before, but…"

According to the dwarf's explanation, the pots were lined up in order of when they should be mixed in, and the assortment of tableware strewn around in front of the pots was used in place of scales to measure the material. It was pretty approximate.

The contents of the jars were supposed to be a secret, but because of my "Analyze" skill and AR display, I could figure it out easily.

The Transmutation Tablet used to finish up the job already had the proper settings in place, so I was able to master the Dwarf Elixir without much trouble.

Checking over my creation, Elder Dohal nodded sagely.

"Well made. Perhaps ye can take over for Ganza."

Elder Dohal didn't sound like he was joking.

He carried the pot containing the elixir into a room next to the smithing workshop.

I figured this was a smithing room for his exclusive use.

The room contained a small furnace made of scarlet ore and an anvil made of mithril alloy.

"■ *Magic Pulse Connection Mamyaku Setsuzoku.*"

Elder Dohal's words caused a golden-red flame to spring up in the melting furnace.

As he spoke the incantation, the gold diadem around his forehead glowed, so he was probably using the power of a City Core granted exclusively to the lord of a territory.

One of his apprentices arranged his smithing tools next to him. In the bucket for cooling was a liquid called Dwarf Water.

Curious, I asked Zajuul about it, since he was standing nearby.

"Is that water in there?"

"It's Dwarf Water, for cooling. Three parts oil and one part spirits. Even the mithril here likes liquor, y'see."

I think that last part was a joke, but other than that, he taught me the recipe easily enough.

I was tempted to comment that it should be called Dwarf Oil not Water, but we were starting soon. I kept my mouth shut.

"Master! Preparations are complete."

"Great. Then let's begin."

The jealous gazes of the dwarves around us bore into me painfully. I supposed smithing along with Elder Dohal was a great honor.

If you've got something to say, say it to Elder Dohal.

I did my best to ignore the envy of those around me and focus on the task at hand. Getting to work with a master sword smith might well be a once in a lifetime chance, so I wanted to enjoy it to the fullest.

◆

By the next morning, the sword was complete.

I'd struck it so many times that I felt like I was in a trance. When I closed my eyes, I could still see the sparks flying on the backs of my eyelids.

The Dwarf Elixir was used to heat the mithril in the melting furnace. With monster core powder as an ingredient, this was probably part of the key to the dwarves' unique weapon-making methods. It seemed to be a different technique from the liquid used for making Magic Swords.

For the final stage, I observed Elder Dohal's precise work on only the finishing touches, but I still learned a lot from it. After this, I felt like I could make a famous sword myself.

"I'm impressed ye finished it without needing someone to take yer place. If ye wish to study in earnest, yer always welcome here. Ye could even surpass me with a little time."

Elder Dohal clapped me on the back mightily.

Oof.

It hurt just as much as that tail attack from the greater hell demon in the Seiryuu City labyrinth.

If he wasn't careful, he might just kill someone with that someday.

"I still have much left to do. Go on and eat without me."

With that, Elder Dohal went off somewhere with the completed sword. Once he had stepped out with Zajuul, the other dwarves promptly gathered around me.

"Yer pretty good for a human!"

"Darn right! Ye sure ye ain't a dwarf wi'out a beard?"

"I didn't think anyone but Master Dohal could swing that giant hammer all night long, och!"

"Yer welcome here anytime, y'hear!"

All I really did was strike with the giant hammer until morning as Elder Dohal instructed, but by all appearances, I'd thoroughly impressed the dwarven blacksmiths.

I was happy about that, although I could've done without the comment on my lack of a beard.

If this body were the same as it was before, it'd be only another five or six years before I started growing one… Probably.

Shaking off the beginnings of an inferiority complex, I headed to the messroom with the dwarves to have breakfast.

As we left, I noticed Jojorie asleep in the corner of the room, so I woke her up and brought her along.

Once I'd replenished my energy with a breakfast of meat and liquor, I was called into the hall in the basement.

This was the atrium of the second level, and the ceiling was about fifteen feet high.

"Give it a swing."

I accepted the mithril sword we'd made together through the night. Elder Dohal appeared to have added some hilt ornamentation that doubled as a grip.

Now that it was completed, the weapon took the form of a double-edged bastard sword. It felt a little light in my hand; I judged that it weighed only about 70 percent of what a standard iron sword might weigh.

The lightness made it easy to handle, but the power of a sword is directly correlated to its weight. I couldn't imagine that being beneficial...

But there's probably a good reason for it, I thought as I tried taking a stance with it.

Its balance was exquisite. It felt just as comfortable as if it were an extension of my hand.

I gave it a light swing. That felt good.

Next, I tried a little faster.

A cheaper sword would feel some kind of air resistance, but this one was on par with a Holy Sword in that department. There was no resistance at all.

Yeah. This was a good sword.

"Now try putting some magic into it and swinging it," Elder Dohal said in a deep voice, watching me test out our creation.

Instead of using the rare skill "Spellblade," I tried just pouring a bit of magic into it in the usual way.

To start with, I put in about ten points.

...Ohh.

It passed through as easily as Liza's spear. So this was the work of a dwarven master sword smith.

Or perhaps it was the power of the mithril itself?

Emerald-green streaks floated on the surface of the sword like ripples. This was a characteristic of high-quality mithril weapons. When I added more power, the ripples started to produce a red glow.

Strangely, the more magic I put into the sword, the heavier it felt. After the first ten points, I thought I was imagining it, but now I could definitely tell a difference. Because it didn't seem to have any kind of magic circuit when we were forging it, this must be a property of the mithril itself.

I didn't want to push it too far and break it, so I stopped adding magic after about fifty points.

In this state, it felt almost twice as heavy as a normal sword of the same size.

If that's how mithril works, couldn't they have made that giant hammer a little smaller?

I asked about this later, but it turned out that making the hammer out of pure mithril and loading it up with magic could have an adverse effect on the mithril being worked on, which was why they used an alloy instead.

"Indeed, fine handling. Let us have a bit of a bout."

With that, Elder Dohal took up a battle-ax and came forward. As soon as the battle-ax entered my line of sight, my "Sense Danger" skill reacted.

According to the AR display, the weapon's status read **Cursed**.

So the elder's favorite weapon was a cursed one for whatever reason.

"Let's begin!"

I avoided Elder Dohal's powerful first swing with a light backstep.

After all, I didn't want to block and end up damaging the sword we'd only just made, but...

"What are ye scurryin' around for, boy? Do ye think so poorly of my smithing that ye expect a few blows to damage that sword?!"

...the act seemed to have injured Elder Dohal's pride.

"My apologies. Here I come, then."

After a shot of magic to my blade, I blocked the next heavy swing from Elder Dohal.

"Yes, that's it! Magic makes the mithril stronger."

Elder Dohal's eyes glittered with enthusiasm.

"Don't stop supplying it, even in the midst of battle!"

Elder Dohal's fighting style was so outrageous that I could barely keep up.

If I focused too much on attacks from the ax's blade, he started aiming for my jaw with the butt of the handle.

And once I started watching both ends of the battle-ax carefully, he came at me with wild attacks like head butts and front kicks, making it difficult to block everything with a single sword.

I did my best to dodge and defend, but there were a few times when his attacks managed to graze me.

I was quick to evade, but not only was he pulling attacks from an endless bag of tricks, he was steadily cutting off my escape options like a chess master. All his firsthand experience in real combat made him an incredible opponent.

Eventually, the match ended in my defeat when he completely backed me into a corner.

Handing off his battle-ax to Zajuul, Elder Dohal walked over to me. In spite of all that zipping around, he wasn't even out of breath.

What an incredibly tough old man. He'd stayed up all night forging a sword, then sparred with me for a good half hour.

"Let me see the sword."

Once I handed it to him, he examined the blade, then swung it a few times to check something.

"There's not a single nick or distortion on the blade. You've a good arm."

At first, I thought he was singing his own praises, but he was complimenting my skill with the sword.

"I do not wish to pry, but ye must be older than ye appear. Ye must have wielded a sword for at least ten or twenty years to have earned that skill."

Well, he was right that I didn't look my age, at least.

I had been doing my best to avoid revealing my high level via my actions, but he had seen through me.

Elder Dohal gazed silently at the sword in his hands for a few moments. Then, coming to some kind of decision, he began chanting.

"Hmm. ■■ *Name Order Meimei!* 'Fairy Sword Trazayuya.'"

...*Trazayuya?*

I was so surprised that it nearly showed on my face. I was lucky that I had the "Poker Face" skill.

"You know of Mr. Trazayuya, Lord Dohal?"

"Indeed. Ye've heard of him as well, have ye? Long, long ago, I used to serve that wise man. This is the best sword I've made in all me life, so I thought to name it for the late sage."

So he used to work for Trazayuya?

Though he didn't shed a tear, Elder Dohal did close his eyes in a moment of deep silence.

Then, opening them again, he wordlessly held out the fairy sword to me. Caught up in the moment as I was, I instinctively accepted it.

"This sword could not have been made without you. I am certain it will accept ye as its owner, too. Use it well."

"...It would be my great honor to do so."

I responded reverently, and Elder Dohal broke into a huge smile.

"Today is a good day! Let us drink to it! Bring a barrel of spirits!"

Slinging an arm over my shoulders, Elder Dohal chuckled heartily and led me to sit on the waiting cushions.

Zajuul carried a large barrel and set it down before us with a *thud*, and the merrymaking began.

A transparent reddish liquid flowed from the barrel into silver bowl-like cups.

"Drink up!"

"...Thank you."

Holding it in my mouth for a moment, I could tell its alcohol content was high. Despite that, it had a good flavor and was easy to drink. If anything, it reminded me of the aged sake I drank in Okinawa long ago.

Unlike the distilled spirits Jojorie had served us yesterday, this drink left a fiery heat in the bottom of my belly.

"Gah-ha-ha-ha, you drink well, youngster!"

"Ye show much promise, to drink raw spirits like that at such an age."

"The last human who drank it was that self-proclaimed master swordsman, and 'e choked half to death on it!"

The other dwarves seated themselves around us and took swigs as well.

Following suit, I drank one cup after another. The drink itself was delicious, but I found myself craving a snack to go with it.

Due to my body having such high stats, I didn't get drunk easily, and it didn't last long. So if you asked me, delicious alcohol should always be paired with a delicious dish.

I was sure they couldn't have heard my inner thoughts, but before long, a group of dwarf women entered the room with plates full of sliced cheese and smoked meat.

Soon there were other snacks, too, like nuts and salted dried fish, all perfect accompaniments for drinking.

Not to be outdone, the other dwarf men aside from the elder left and returned with a great deal of barrels. It seemed that half of them were ale, while the other half were more spirits.

"Oh-ho! Looks good!"

"Don't stuff yourself too much, now! Soon, we'll be back with something from the grill, too!"

The female dwarves scolded the men who jumped at the plates of food.

"Master! There he is, everyone!"

Hearing Arisa's energetic voice, I turned to see my kids entering the banquet hall.

"Masterrr?"

"We missed you, sir!"

"Satou."

It had been a full day now since they'd seen me, and the younger kids immediately pounced. They must have been a little lonely without me.

"Master, the mayor invited us to the banquet, I report."

"Really? I'll have to thank Mayor Dorial later, then."

"Master, it sounds as though you've been through a great deal. Are you all right?"

"I'm fine, thanks. Sorry for worrying you."

"Master, we brought you a change of clothes."

"Thank you. I'll change as soon as the banquet's over."

Nana, Liza, and Lulu each spoke up in turn. *So the older group was worried about me, too.*

At my request, the dwarf women prepared nonalcoholic fruit beverages for the children.

A cry of joy rose from the hallway leading to the kitchen.

"Everyone! They're making some kind of special dish, they said!"

"Meeeat?"

"I don't know this smell, sir!"

Always burning with curiosity, Arisa dashed down the hall with Tama and Pochi.

Liza stayed seated beside me, but she looked rather restless.

She probably wanted to see the meat, too.

"Sorry, Liza, but would you mind keeping an eye on the kids for me?"

"O-of course! I shall return!"

After flashing me a rare smile, Liza hurriedly recovered her stoic expression and just about sprinted away to look after the meat—that is, the children.

"The rest of you can go, too, if you'd like?"

"Perhaps I'll help bring out the food, then."

"Master, for Lulu's protection, I depart."

Both Lulu and Nana took me up on my offer, heading over to check out the unusual cuisine.

"You don't want to go, Mia?"

"Mn."

Mia was leaning against my side, crunching away on a bowlful of nuts like an adorable little woodland creature. I figured nuts alone might be a bit lacking, so I added some dried fruits from Storage. This was a new creation of mine using wild cherries from the Mountain-Tree.

"Oh-ho, aren't ye the child of Bolenan Forest?"

Noticing Mia, Elder Dohal called out to her with surprise.

That said, he didn't take the same tone of sacred reverence toward elves as the fairyfolk and little giants from the Mountain-Tree Village did.

"I'd heard that ye went missing. Ran off with a human, did ye?"

"Mm. Lovers."

That's a bald-faced lie and you know it. Are you trying to ruin my reputation?

"An evil sorcerer kidnapped her, so I rescued her. We're taking her back to the forest now."

"Mrrrr."

Mia puffed out her cheeks sulkily. Guess she was hoping I'd play along.

Of course, the culprit who kidnapped Mia during the Cradle incident was the Undead King Zen, not just some ordinary sorcerer, but I left that part out to avoid a lengthy explanation.

"The Bolenan Senate did issue a notice requesting information on her whereabouts. Would ye mind if we send them a letter?"

"That would be excellent, if it's not too much trouble."

Evidently I was being small-minded when I assumed that elves and dwarves would be on bad terms. They seemed to get along just fine.

At Elder Dohal's request, Mayor Dorial arranged for the letter to be sent.

They should have received a message from the Elvish shop manager of the general store in Seiryuu City, too, but the postal system in this world wasn't as reliable as modern Japan's, so it couldn't hurt to send a backup.

I petted Mia's hair lightly as I chatted with the dwarf blacksmiths and other artisans.

We had some very interesting conversations. However, since the topics mostly revolved around smithing and mining and such, I spent most of the time just listening.

According to them, gnomish magic users were the primary method of combating gas and cave-ins and such, but if no such mage was available to accompany them, the miners used scrolls. Scrolls were expensive, one miner explained, but well worth the price to save lives.

I was also informed that these scrolls were sold in a magic shop in the dwarven mining district, not the one aboveground. Hopefully they would let me buy some!

I did my best to make sure that the children didn't drink, but in the end, I couldn't stop the dwarves from giving the kids alcohol for their own amusement.

"Hee-hee-hee, Satou. Heh-heh... Sa. Tou. Ah-ha-ha, Satou. ♪"

Lulu was at least a happy drunk; she was giggling away as she fawned over me.

The only accurate way to punctuate the singsong way she kept repeating my name was with a little heart or music note.

Though I lifted the cup out of her hands, I dutifully allowed her to keep clinging to me.

"*Hic*... At least I'll get to stay a pure maiden forever. I'm gonna end up all alone in this world, just like last time..."

Meanwhile, Arisa was more of a downer. I made a mental note to be extra careful about keeping alcohol away from her from now on.

"*Hee-hee...this is fun, sooo fun. C'mon, Satou, let's drink more. Hoo-hoo, there're three of you... How nice, sooo nice.*"

The usually reticent Mia wound up blathering on in Elvish.

She was having a ball spinning around like a top, which was fine and all, except that her pigtails were whipping from side to side rather dangerously.

Her skirt looked like it might roll up at this rate, too, so I caught her by the waist and plopped her down at my side opposite Lulu.

"Whee-hee-hee… Ishh mashhter, shirr." Pochi's tongue wasn't cooperating.

"Nyooom."

Tama slid into my lap like liquid, curled up in a ball, and promptly fell asleep. Seeing this, Pochi crawled onto my knee as well.

Argh, please just go to bed already!

"Master, my logic circuits are malfunctioning, I report. This water may contain poison…son…son?"

Shoot, even Nana had gotten some liquor. She was stammering like a broken record, so I gave her a magic potion to treat hangovers and laid her down to rest.

Liza, who'd been drinking serenely by my side, was now sitting upright and fast asleep.

Unlike modern-day Japan, this kingdom didn't have any limitations on underage drinking, but I resolved right then not to let my kids drink again as long as they were minors.

Indifferent to my silent resolution, the merrymaking at the banquet went on late into the night.

> **Title Acquired: Fairy Sword Smith**
> **Title Acquired: Heavy Drinker**
> **Title Acquired: Lush**
> **Title Acquired: Drunkard**
> **Title Acquired: Friend of the Dwarves**

◆

The next morning, four of the younger girls discovered the suffering that is a hangover.

"Ugh… My head… Id hurds so bad…"

"Nyoo…"

"It hurts…sir…"

"Satou. Medicine."

Nana was fine thanks to the potion I'd given her the day before, and Liza and Lulu seemed to be faring well enough.

Lulu busied herself bringing everyone water. When our eyes met, she turned bright red and quickly looked away.

She was probably embarrassed about her behavior at the drinking party. I didn't think it was that big of a deal, but she was being kind of cute, so I didn't say anything.

The children's hangovers would probably be cured if I gave them more of the medicine I'd given Nana, but I decided to leave them be for a little while.

"I'm going out for a bit. I'll pick up the ingredients for a cure, so be good and sit tight, all right?"

"F...fine. Don't be long..."

"We'll be gooood."

"Pochi will be good, too, sir."

"Alcohol...terrible."

I waved a hand at the teary-eyed children and left the room.

Jojorie was taking me to the magic shop that I'd learned about the night before.

At her suggestion, I wore the fairy sword at my waist that I'd just received yesterday. The belt and sheath were new; I'd hastily constructed them myself after the party. They were made from ironshell fruit, the same material as Liza's and Nana's armor, so while they looked plain, they were actually hard enough to block a metal sword.

I figured I would decorate the sheath and reinforce it with metal and such some other time.

Anyway, putting that aside, the magic shop I was looking for was called "Don & Khan," and it was located a little ways past a giant hall with a mithril furnace.

"Hullo, Jojorie, did ye fall for a human? Ye'll break Zajuul's heart, y'know."

"Hey, Jojorie, yer old man'll have yer hide fer bringing a human here, y'know."

Inside the magic shop, a pair of tiny twin elderly men greeted us.

Their accent was similar to the dwarf guards' we'd met at the city gate, but these two were actually gnomes.

I'd heard at the forge that there was a big incident in the gnomes' homeland of Boleheim, though. Why hadn't these two gone back with them?

Out of curiosity, I pulled up the detailed information in the AR display, where I learned that these brothers were from a clan called Braiheim. It was only the gnomes of the Boleheim clan who were having problems.

"Good day, Mr. Don, Mr. Khan. This human has Father's permission to be here, I assure you."

As she spoke, Jojorie pointed to the hilt of my fairy sword. The gnomes demanded to see it up close, so I took it off the sword belt and held it out to them.

"Well, I'll be damned. If it isn't the old man's seal."

"Well, I'll be darned. How drunk did ye have to get him for this?"

As it turned out, the design was Elder Dohal's seal of approval, and it wasn't attached to any ordinary work.

If I showed it to any gnomes or dwarves living in the Bolehart dominion, they explained, I would be treated as warmly as an old friend.

So basically, this was the dwarf version of my Silent Bell of Bolenan.

Elder Dohal...was it really wise to give this to me when we only just met two days ago?

At any rate, thanks to the seal, I could buy whatever I wanted in the store, so I had them show me their magic books and scrolls.

The store turned out to serve as an alchemy shop as well, but they sold only finished products, not tools and ingredients.

"Let me see. We have lesser spell books for all the basic elements—earth, water, fire, wind, ice, flame—and intermediate books for earth, fire, and flame. As for rarer items, we also have books on magic for smithing and workin' in the mountains, y'see."

Mr. Don brought out a stack of spell books.

The tome on smithing was a collection of spells that would be useful for a blacksmith, primarily using the "Fire Magic" skill.

Similarly, mountain magic was for things like excavation and finding ore in the mines, making use of Earth Magic.

I was also warned that a handful of the spells required other elemental magic skills.

With Mr. Don's permission, I skimmed through the lesser spell books.

They were similar to the ones I'd bought in a human town, but certain aspects of the chants were different from the human versions. I ended up buying them all. Both paying for and stowing away the books was a breeze thanks to my Garage Bag.

Next was what I was really here for: buying magic scrolls. Mr. Khan was in charge of scrolls and magic tools.

"Oh-ho? Scrolls, is it? They're just weak spells at a high price, y'know?"

Mr. Khan cautioned me as he took the scrolls down from the shelf.

They had only six kinds.

"Mining engineers bring these with 'em when they're doing a survey unaccompanied just to be safe, y'see. We've got Rock Smasher, which crushes rocks into dust... Freeze Water and Hard Clay, which they use if'n there's a water leak...and the Earth Magic spell Wall, which can reinforce brittle rock. Aside from that, there's just Air Cleaner and Air Curtain, which they use in case of any strange gases."

Of course, I requested one of each, but Mr. Khan had an objection.

"Sorry, boy. Unless ye absolutely must have it, could I ask ye to hold off on Air Cleaner? It's me last one, y'see. I don't want to run out before we restock next month."

"In that case, just one each of the other five is fine."

I was disappointed, but I didn't want it badly enough to inconvenience the dwarves.

So the scrolls I got were as follows:

> **Scroll, Earth Magic: Wall**
> **Scroll, Earth Magic: Rock Smasher**
> **Scroll, Earth Magic: Hard Clay**
> **Scroll, Wind Magic: Air Curtain**
> **Scroll, Ice Magic: Freeze Water**

Testing them out would have to wait until I could do it in a remote place.

◆

I finished my errands within about a half hour and returned to the rest of my group.

"Welcome hooome..."

Arisa greeted me weakly from the floor, where she was sprawled out looking on the verge of death.

Tama, Pochi, and Mia didn't say a word. I must've left them hanging a little too long.

I reached into the Garage Bag, pulled out some hangover medicine, and handed it to the four of them.

"I liiiiive!"

"All betterrr?"

"Master, thank you, sir."

"Thanks."

The magic potion went straight to work, and in a flash they were right as rain. You'd never guess they'd been lying around groaning just moments before.

When they immediately started complaining of hunger, Lulu headed to the kitchen to get some light soup.

Arisa, in particular, seemed even more energetic than usual. She was probably trying to forget the things she'd said in her inebriation the night before, so I decided to steer clear of the subject as much as possible.

I hadn't had the chance yesterday, so I decided to spend the day touring Bolehart City with everyone.

Jojorie even volunteered to show us the sights. We were getting the VIP treatment.

First, at her recommendation, we visited a place called the central square.

"Hold haaands?"

"I wanna hold hands, too, sir."

"Sure."

I held hands with Tama and Pochi as we walked.

"Mrrrr."

"Trade spots with us later!"

"Aaaye!"

"Yes, sir."

So now we were going to be holding hands in shifts.

...Oh?

Shortly after we started walking, I noticed that we were being followed.

According to the map, I discovered that the people trailing us were dwarves, specifically security staff of Bolehart City. When I checked with Jojorie, she confirmed that Mayor Dorial had arranged an escort for us.

Man, we really were getting the VIP treatment, then.

All sorts of people had collected around the fountain in the central square: sword dancers, blade sharpeners, people selling weapons and armor, and many more.

Instead of carts like I'd seen in Seiryuu City, the vendors had their wares spread out on sheets on the ground. Much of it ironware, probably one of the key products of the city.

As I was looking around, I heard an argument between a dwarf and a young man.

"Seriously?! How can a dwarven city not have any mithril swords for sale?!"

"Please be reasonable, Mister Noble. The only smiths who can work with a precious material like mithril are Elder Dohal and his apprentices."

"So I can get one if I talk to this Dohal fellow, then?"

Unlike the indifferent-sounding dwarf, the young man's voice was rapidly rising in desperation.

"Perhaps. But unlike the swords here, a mithril sword would cost you at least a hundred gold coins, eh?"

"Excuse me? This iron sword here was only a single gold coin! How can it be so much more expensive?!"

"A sword that's only worth a single gold coin must be a cheap piece o' work..."

The dwarf responded to the agitated man in an exasperated voice.

It smelled like trouble to me, so I adjusted our sightseeing course toward an area where a lively crowd seemed to be enjoying something.

As it happened, exhibition matches were going on in a corner of the square.

"Do we have any brave challengers?! If anyone can beat me, I'll give you this Mantis Sword, made from one of the bladed arms of a soldier mantis! Isn't there anyone bold enough to bet their own weapon and challenge me in a one-on-one match?!"

A large tigerfolk man was waving around a sword made from a monster part and challenging the people near him.

"The old capital's martial arts tournament is coming up, so there are a lot of warriors gathered here at present."

"A martial arts tournament?"

"That's right. It's held publicly once every three years. Aristocrats often take on participants who do well as vassals, so people travel from far and wide in the hopes of finding success."

Jojorie told me about the competition as we walked around the plaza until I felt a tug on my sleeve.

"Sausaaage?"

I looked where Tama was pointing to see a food cart selling links. They seemed to be served with a sauce made by boiling vegetables and tallow.

"Master, the sauce turns it brown, sir. It's very spicy when it's brown, so you mustn't use the sauce, sir. Pochi knows all about it, sir!"

Pochi's face was very serious as she spoke, and Tama nodded rapidly in assent.

...No way. Trying to keep my rising hopes under control, I walked over to the stall.

"I knew it—it's mustard!"

"The seed spice, you mean? If you prefer yours with an extra kick, the chili pepper–stuffed sausages are three coppers apiece, the regular ones bein' two."

"One regular sausage with the seed spice, please."

"Certainly."

I wasted no time in tasting the mustard-coated sausage.

Right away, vivid heat lit up my taste buds with that familiar sting. Delicious.

Savoring the contrast between the piquant mustard and the hearty sausage, I quickly took another bite.

Yum. It was so good I couldn't stop myself. Before I knew it, I'd wolfed the whole thing down.

"I've never seen you buy and eat something so quickly before, master."

Lulu's eyes were wide as she passed me a handkerchief.

There must have been mustard on my face.

I thanked her and wiped my mouth clean, eliciting a shriek from Arisa, who was jumping up and down next to me.

"Argh! There goes my dream! I wanted to wipe a little boy's cheek with my finger and go, 'Hee-hee, you little glutton...'"

Was it really so upsetting that she needed to pound the ground with her fists?

Ignoring Arisa's eccentric behavior as usual, I recommended the sausages to everyone else.

According to Lulu, though, they'd already bought a bunch of the mustard sausages the day before. When I patted her head and praised their good taste, she turned adorably red.

Pochi, on the other hand, seemed a little forlorn that I hadn't followed her advice.

Next time, I vowed silently, I would eat whatever she recommended.

After exiting the square, we took a street carriage to go through the artisan district.

The clanking of hammers on anvils and the raucous voices of dwarves colored the streets.

"This is quite the hustle and bustle around here."

"Oh yes. There's plenty of demand for forged weapons, of course. But the Bolehart dominion also boasts the finest casting technology in the Shigan Kingdom, so we receive lots of orders every month."

That made sense. Even a relatively violent world like this one had to produce something besides weapons.

"If you're interested, would you like to have a look around?"

"Yes, please!"

I wasted no time in accepting Jojorie's offer, so she took us to a casting workshop run by one of her acquaintances.

"...More or less. To put it simply, we pour heated metal into a mold, remove the hardened cast, shave off any excess with a rasp, and that's that."

The dwarf who owned the workshop was kind enough to explain the casting process. This was another benefit of Elder Dohal's seal.

The area on the other side of the large room was where they poured the liquid metal into the molds. The red glow lit up the shadowy room, and crimson sparks flew as the metal flowed into the molds to create an unexpectedly beautiful sight.

The metallic odor was a bit strong, so I covered my mouth with a handkerchief. Looking to my side, I saw Lulu and Mia do the same.

The workshop owner chortled at our outward daintiness.

"The sparks are prettyyyy?"

"It goes glub glub, sir!"

Tama and Pochi seemed excited about watching the metal river pour into the casts.

The fascinated pair tried to get closer, but as soon as they took a single step forward, Liza swept them up and carried them under her arms like sacks of flour.

The sparks seemed to enchant Nana, too, and she started reeling toward the workers.

"No."

Mia caught the end of Nana's long ponytail and yanked her back mercilessly.

It was so forceful that I half expected to hear Nana's neck crack.

"Mia, that hurts, I protest."

"Mm, sorry."

Nana tearily rubbed the back of her neck, looking toward the sparks. "It is beautiful; thus, it would be best to see it up close, I propose."

"Dangerous," Mia scolded, and Nana looked to me for rescue.

"Master, permission?"

"Sorry, but you'll have to watch it from here. It's too dangerous."

Nana's shoulders slumped in disappointment.

"You'd best stay back, missy. If you venture too close, you could get a burn on that pretty face."

With that, the workshop owner led us to the next room.

As we walked, I asked him a question that had been on my mind. "How are the molds made?"

"First, we make a model out of clay or carved wood. Then we bring it to a magic user, who turns the model to stone. We dunk the stone model in molten metal, then cut the block in half once it hardens. We have the magic user turn the stone to mud to drain it out, and presto! You have a mold."

…I wasn't expecting dwarves to use magic in the casting process.

"Some casters use sand or plaster, but not here. If memory serves, elves make the molds entirely with magic, don't they?"

"Mm."

Mia nodded when the workshop owner looked to her for confirmation.

I imagine it'd be easy enough to make a mold with magic if you had a strong enough spell, maybe something like Shield or Shelter.

After our tour of the workshop, we were served chilled tea in an office decorated with casting samples. We'd just come through some extremely hot rooms, so the cold drink was very refreshing.

Glancing around, I spotted something interesting in the corner of the room.

"Is that a meat grinder for sausages?"

"Yes, that's right. We make all kinds, from small ones for food carts to the big ones used at meat-processing plants."

Aha, so I was right.

"If someone were to place an order, how long would it take to complete?"

"Are you interested in purchasing one?"

"Yes, I am. We had some delicious sausage in the central square, so now I'm rather interested in a machine that would let me make it myself."

It was possible to mince meat with a carving knife, but not only was it a pain, the others probably wouldn't be able to do it without scattering meat everywhere or ruining the texture.

"As far as small cart-size machines go, I believe we do have a completed one. Would you like it delivered to the mayor's estate?"

"Yes, please."

Now I would be able to make a certain something for everyone.

I pictured the kids' happy faces as I paid the workshop owner and filled out the paperwork.

After the caster's, we visited a few other general workshops. Then, at Jojorie's suggestion, we took a little break at a windmill.

In the park in front of the giant blades, I got to taste the city's famous shrimp crackers and watch the younger girls play with some dwarf children.

Once our sightseeing tour was done, I had Jojorie show me the way to one more shop.

"Here we are: Garohal's Magic Shop."

There were no customers to be seen inside, just a single dwarf falling asleep at the counter.

"Honestly, Garohal..." Jojorie marched up to the counter and rapped him on the forehead with her knuckles.

It was easy to tell that she was Elder Dohal's grandchild.

"Ouch..." Mr. Garohal rubbed his head as he looked up.

He was surprisingly thin for a dwarf, and his beard was carefully set with wax. Maybe he was an attractive guy by dwarf standards.

"Are you awake now?"

"Hiya, Jojorie. It's rare to see ye come out to the shop! Did ye finally get fed up with that meathead Zajuul? Wonderful! I couldn't be happier."

"Good morning, Garohal. You mustn't speak so poorly of Mr. Zajuul."

As soon as he saw Jojorie, Garohal started chattering like a machine gun. Jojorie didn't seem overly impressed.

"Oh-ho, are those customers behind ye?"

"That's right. These are Grandfather's honored guests, so be sure to take good care of them."

"Ho-ho, Elder Dohal accepting a human? Is he the son of some important noble?"

"Not quite. Mr. Satou is a blacksmith skilled enough to earn Grandfather's seal."

"Och, really?"

I presented the surprised dwarf the pattern on my fairy sword. Once he was convinced, he finally showed me his wares.

The magic books were mostly the same as the ones in the shop underground, but there was a two-volume set on Everyday Magic by a different author, so I purchased that.

This shop also had various smithing-related materials for alchemy.

Some ore-based materials, like mercury and sulfur, were normally in short supply in other cities, but here they had a large supply at a very low price, so I bought as much as I could without cleaning him out.

I was even able to buy mercury by the barrel, so it would be easy to transmute plating and such in the future.

"Ga-ha-ha, this is the biggest sale I've made since we opened! Jojorie, ye really are my goddess, aren't ye?"

"Enough of that, Garohal! Stop celebrating and take care of your customer, please," Jojorie chided the excited Garohal.

Once his attention was back to me, I requested to see his scrolls.

Now this was what I really came here for.

Their selection of scrolls was different here than the shop underground. According to Mr. Garohal, these were aimed toward nobles and merchants.

"How do ye like that? I went all the way to Yorschka to buy these. Bet ye've never laid eyes on these before, eh?"

"Oh my! I thought that Yorschka was full of monster hunters and weaselfolk merchants. You didn't buy anything too strange, did you?"

Mr. Garohal seemed quite confident, though Jojorie less so.

Yorschka was a town in the southeast of this territory, a major stop on the highway that led to a group of small countries beyond the eastern mountain range.

"Yer such a worrywart, Jojorie." Mr. Garohal set out the scrolls with mild irritation. "Look at this! These are rare Everyday Magic scrolls: Bug Wiper, Anti-Itch, and Deodorant. Perfect for folks who ain't accustomed to long journeys. There's even Pure Water, to prevent any stomachaches from unboiled water."

They were very intriguing scrolls, but the prices seemed a little high. Sure enough, Jojorie's face clouded over as she scanned the collection.

"Say, Garohal. How much is it for one of these scrolls?"

"Well, normally I'd like to sell 'em for one gold coin apiece, but yer a special guest. I'd settle for three silvers."

"You haven't sold a single one of these scrolls, have you?"

Mr. Garohal's proud expression froze.

Then Arisa dealt the finishing blow.

"For these prices, I'd imagine it'd be easier and more cost-efficient to just hire a servant who can use Everyday Magic instead of carrying around all these pricey scrolls."

It seemed many merchants and nobles had had the same thought as Arisa; half a year had passed since Garohal bought these, but they weren't selling at all.

"W-well, we also have Sonar for finding wolves and Fence to prevent thieves from escaping!"

"Wouldn't a beastfolk's sharp senses be far superior?"

Mr. Garohal tried to recover his sales pitch, but Arisa was having none of it.

"Th-then how about Signal? You can use it to send messages to your companions in remote places!"

"Doesn't the other person need to have the Signal scroll, too, to receive it?"

"Mm, yes."

"In that case, you might as well just use smoke signals."

Arisa, a magic enthusiast, was quick to point out the problem with the Signal spell, and Mia affirmed it. When Jojorie added a pragmatic assessment of her own, Mr. Garohal looked ready to cry.

Nana's Foundation included Signal, so it would at least be useful for receiving emergency messages from Nana.

Getting desperate, Garohal pulled out the next scroll, a Light Magic spell called Condense.

"This one's amazing! It'll dry yer laundry even on cloudy days, and ye can read books in the dark!"

"G-Garohal…"

"…Okay, I thought it was the Light spell when I bought it."

Jojorie looked anxious about Mr. Garohal's increasingly desperate state as he soldiered on with the sales pitch.

I felt bad for him at this point, so I decided to give him a hand. I could probably get a good price on them now anyway.

"Mr. Garohal, I'm a collector of rare scrolls, so I'd like to purchase all the scrolls here."

"R-really? Och…"

At my words, tears welled up in Garohal's eyes.

"You'll give him a discount, of course, won't you?"

"O-of course I will, Jojorie. In fact, I'll sell them to ye for the price I paid for them. No markup at all."

I had been hoping for a bit of a discount, of course, but I hadn't expected him to go all the way down to cost price.

"I know! If ye collect scrolls, I have other rare ones for ye, too. I'll go and fetch them at once."

Judging that he might be able to sell them to me, Mr. Garohal disappeared into the back.

Before long, he returned covered in dust with another armful of scrolls.

"How's this? These are very rare indeed."

True enough, it was nothing I'd ever seen before.

The first was an Earth Magic spell, Polish. It looked useful at first glance, but it seemed like a regular rasp or file would be easier to use and fine-tune.

The second was a Fire Magic scroll, Forge. This was obviously a spell for melting metal into ingots.

It definitely sounded like something dwarves would use, but it turned out that you would have to cast the scroll version ten times or more to even melt copper.

"I-it can be used as Attack Magic!"

"If you used this as an attack, you'd hurt yourself, too. There are plenty of other spells that are more MP cost-efficient, like Fire Shot."

To make matters worse, its range was so short that it would even burn the person who used the defective scroll.

Basically, you'd be better off just using a regular furnace.

Besides, there would be little point in attempting blacksmithing on the go, so there was virtually no demand for a product like this.

The third scroll was called Magic Mold.

This spell caused a transparent cube to materialize in midair, where it could be shaped to the user's liking and then reversed to create a mold.

"This one actually does sound useful."

"Yes, couldn't you sell it to people for making prototypes and such?"

"Well…"

Again, although this one seemed useful for blacksmiths, there was a major drawback.

"Intermediate."

"Oh, that's right! This is an intermediate spell, isn't it?"

Mia mumbled a word, and Arisa promptly agreed.

In other words, it would consume much more MP than a lesser spell.

"Plus, they told me clay was easier to use…"

Still, it could be used to make molds out of clay prototypes, but there were more problems, as Mr. Garohal confessed.

Its durability was terribly low; if molten metal was poured into it, the mold would break from the heat damage before the metal hardened.

"Y-you can use it with wax, at least…"

With nothing left to say to Garohal's half-hearted defense, Jojorie simply patted his shoulder comfortingly.

The last scroll was a Practical Magic spell, Cube.

"Why do you have such a bizarre scroll…?" Unable to think of any uses for the spell, Arisa knit her brow.

This was a spell in the vein of Shield and Floating Board that could produce transparent cubes in the air in a size of the user's choice.

It seemed to be mainly used for blocking charging enemies or making temporary desks and chairs.

It didn't last long, and it would disappear as soon as the user moved away from it. Instead of being fixed in the air, it would move if enough weight was applied to it.

So I could make invisible stairs in midair and stuff. Would this spell actually be useful?

"The lowest level of Cube is only about this big, you know."

Arisa drew a square approximately four inches around in the air with her finger. And it could support just a pound of weight at that, she explained. Scrolls could produce only the lowest level of a spell, so I could see why this one was another dud.

"...I thought I was buying two Magic Mold scrolls, but one of them turned out to be this."

"Garohal..."

Mr. Garohal muttered self-deprecatingly, and Jojorie watched him with sympathy.

"Well, this sure is a weird collection of scrolls you've got here..."

"Mrrrr."

Arisa and Mia looked unimpressed.

Tama and Pochi were sleeping at Liza's feet. They must've gotten bored.

These were the last of the scrolls, so I decided to start the negotiations.

"Well, they're certainly all very interesting. So, how much would it be for the lot of them?"

"...Huh?"

All the criticism from Jojorie and Arisa must have had Mr. Garohal convinced that he couldn't sell them. When I asked about the price, he looked completely flabbergasted.

True, these were garbage by normal standards, but to me they were much more fascinating than the ones I bought underground.

"You will sell them to me, won't you?"

"Oh, uh... Yes! Yes, o-of course!" Mr. Garohal stammered in disbelief, but he agreed to sell them when I pressed the question. "I'll sell them at cost—no, that would be greedy. A silver coin for each will be fine. Och, what a great day. Jojorie, yer a goddess."

I handed the money to Mr. Garohal, now thoroughly cheered up, and accepted the bunch of scrolls from him.

If I ever learned how to make magic scrolls, I swore to myself that I would sell the best ones to him wholesale.

Anyway, these were the ones I ended up buying:

> **Scroll, Everyday Magic: Bug Wiper**
> **Scroll, Everyday Magic: Anti-Itch**
> **Scroll, Everyday Magic: Deodorant**
> **Scroll, Everyday Magic: Pure Water**
> **Scroll, Practical Magic: Sonar**
> **Scroll, Practical Magic: Fence**

> **Scroll, Practical Magic: Signal**
> **Scroll, Practical Magic: Cube**
> **Scroll, Practical Magic: Magic Mold**
> **Scroll, Earth Magic: Polish**
> **Scroll, Fire Magic: Forge**
> **Scroll, Light Magic: Condense**

Someday, I would use them from the magic menu, and I eagerly anticipated the effects.

◆

The next day, we went to say our farewells to Elder Dohal before leaving Bolehart City.

"Satou, I'll give ye Jojorie to wife so ye may carry on my legacy."

"M-master! I'm the one who should marry her...!"

"G-Grandfather?! And you too, Mr. Zajuul! What are you saying?"

Elder Dohal's sudden declaration sent Jojorie and Zajuul into a panic.

Jojorie was a great girl and all, but unfortunately, she was miles out of my strike zone.

"Lord Dohal, it is most kind of you to offer, but sadly I have a mission to attend to. Besides, I am certain there are many wonderful young men in Bolehart City who would be better than the likes of me. And you can pass on your magnificent crafting skills to your apprentices as well."

I politely declined, and luckily Elder Dohal didn't push the subject further.

I probably had "Persuasion" to thank for that.

Elder Dohal and many of the other dwarves saw us off as we departed from Bolehart City.

I would have to come back to visit sometime, perhaps with a gift of fine liquor from my journey.

I put a hand on the fairy sword at my waist as I watched the smoke from Bolehart City disappear behind the mountains.

On the Banks of the Great River

Satou here. When I think of big rivers, I always think of the Yangtze River. I know there are plenty of others, like the Nile, the Amazon, and the Mississippi, but my mind always goes to the Yangtze. Maybe it's because of the Battle of Red Cliffs from **Romance of the Three Kingdoms?**

"Lulu, bring us down that side street there."

"Yes, master."

At my instructions, the carriage moved off the main road down a narrower path.

"What's up? A shortcut?"

I smiled back at Arisa and said nothing.

Before long, her doubtful expression turned into a smile as well.

"Ooooh! A flower garden? How lovely! It's enormous, too!"

Just as Arisa exclaimed, a field of colorful flowers was in full bloom.

I had found it by searching the map for the blossoms used in the crowns that Nana and Mia had purchased when we first arrived at Bolehart City.

We stopped the horse-drawn carriage by a stream near the flower garden.

"Let's have lunch here today."

"Understood. Everyone, to your lunch stations! Begin the preparations."

"Aye-aye, siiir!"

"Roger, sir!"

After my suggestion, Liza was quick to give everyone directions.

Tama and Pochi took care of the horses, Mia and Arisa went foraging, and Liza and Lulu helped make lunch.

Nana usually helped with lunch as well, but today she went with Arisa and Mia as their guard.

I taught Liza and Lulu how to use the meat grinder we'd just bought in Bolehart City as I prepared the ingredients for lunch.

After a while, Tama and Pochi finished their duties and came along to watch us cook.

"So roooound?"

"Very unusual meat, sir."

Tama and Pochi tilted their heads as they looked at what I'd made with the new meat grinder.

Tama was particularly intent on following the ball of meat with her eyes as I tossed it back and forth between my hands.

She was fidgeting as if she might reach out and grab it at any moment, but in all likelihood the fear of wasting food restrained her.

I arranged the palm-size patties on a hot plate sizzling with oil. Then, once I'd flipped them over once, I covered the pan with a lid I'd purchased in the city.

"It smells very, very good."

"It might be too soft for you, Liza. Should I prepare a rocket wolf steak as well?"

"Certainly not! Master, I swear to you that I will gladly consume anything you cook without leaving a single crumb of meat behind."

Liza's face was intensely serious as she spoke.

...*You really don't need to get that worked up over lunch, Liza.*

"Ooh! Are you making hamburgers?!"

Sniffing her way over to us, Arisa correctly guessed the dish I was preparing.

"Is it a beef and pork mix? Or beef only?"

"It's long-haired cow beef mixed with wild boar. If everyone likes them, we'll explore some other meat variations, too."

As I conversed with Arisa, I made some standard side dishes, like French fries and glazed carrots.

The carrots in this world were round and a little sweeter than usual. There were many different varieties of potatoes, so I'd picked out a kind that was well suited to frying.

"Done."

"Loading capacity exceeded, I complain."

Nana plopped her haul down in front of the carriage: a heavy-looking bag and a bundle of green bamboo. The bag contained a mountain of bamboo shoots.

"These look delicious."

"Mm. Yummy."

"They take a pretty long time to prepare, so we'll have them for lunch tomorrow, all right?"

"Too bad."

Maybe I should try to make a spell to shorten the cooking time.

According to the AR, the bundle was of the **edible bamboo** variety.

I knocked on the green shaft; it felt as hard as metal. Its exterior was many times harder than ordinary green bamboo, then. I could probably even make armor out of it, but that would be a bit silly.

It had to be fit to eat if the name was anything to go by, but I had no idea how to cook it just yet.

I would have to ask around once we reached the next town. Until then, I decided to stash it out of the way in Storage.

Sorting through the herbs, edible grasses, and materials for various potions that Arisa and Mia collected, I set aside what I needed for the day's lunch and put the rest in Storage via the Garage Bag.

"Shall we make tempura with the angelica sprouts?"

"Mm. Excited."

I asked Lulu to prepare the angelica sprouts. She was better at handling wild plants than Liza.

"Master, I utilized a great deal of Body Strengthening during transport, so my magical power supply has been exhausted, I report. Magical power replenishment is required, I request."

"All right. I'll give you a mana recovery potion later."

When I responded, Nana went perfectly silent. Her expression was as blank as ever, but she somehow seemed dissatisfied.

"…Direct magic supply is preferable, I entreat. Is it impossible? I inquire."

She was still expressionless, but something about her tone reminded me of a child asking for a treat.

"I was planning on doing some magic experiments after we eat, but…I'll prioritize you first as a reward for working so hard."

"Yes, master." Nana's voice sounded much more cheerful.

Immediately, she began to remove her clothes, but Arisa and Mia stopped her in perfect sync.

"Nothing gets past Arisa's Impenetrable Barrier!"

"Mm. Perfect."

Looking beyond the two smug girls, I informed Nana that I would supply her with magic after lunch.

"Now, shall we eat?"

After preparing individual plates, I put a stack of freshly cooked steaks in the center of the table.

Then, with the usual Arisa-led chorus of "Thanks for the food!" we began to eat.

"Mmmm?"

"Mmm!"

As soon as they took their first bite, Tama's and Pochi's eyes went round with surprise.

Liza made a similar expression for a moment, then turned serious as she focused all her attention on chewing.

Finally, her throat moved visibly as she swallowed, and she smiled with satisfaction.

By all appearances, even Liza, who normally preferred tougher food, was a fan of the hamburger steaks.

"It's delicious! ...And very soft. Its texture reminds me of the fish balls we had before, but I much prefer this dish."

"Yummy! It's been so long since I've had this. The fries on the side are delicious, too!"

Lulu and Arisa also seemed excited about the hamburgers.

"Mia, I would like to trade a tempura for a carrot, I request."

"Mm, sure."

Mia and Nana were having fun making swaps. Next time, I would have to make extras of the sides as well as the meat for everyone to enjoy.

Satisfied with the positive reception, I took a bite of my own hamburger steak.

As soon as it entered my mouth, the meat seemed to fall apart and melt all on its own.

The taste of the two meats and the rich sauce made a harmonious combination on my tongue, filling my taste buds with happiness.

It was so delicious that if this were a cartoon, angels would probably be flying around me.

Next, I tasted the side dishes: the sweet, crunchy carrots; the French fries and broccoli; and some freshly cooked rice to cleanse the palate.

Then, in accordance with my youthful instincts, I stretched my chopsticks toward another piece of meat.

Before I knew it, everyone's plates were empty.

The beastfolk girls were starting in on the mountain of regular steaks, but for some reason, their eyes were fixed on me.

"Did you want me to make more hamburgers?"

The answer to my tactful question probably goes without saying. I'd just add that the dwarven meat grinder passed its first performance test with flying colors.

After the meal, I got to— I mean, I had to supply Nana with magic by touching her smooth back.

The strangely sexy noises she made in the process caught me off guard as always, but with children present, I kept myself under control in every sense.

Then, in order to work off that repressed energy, as well as the food, I practiced with the fairy sword for a while.

I swung the sword up, paused, and imbued it with magic before swinging it down. When it was lowered, I reabsorbed the magical power and raised the lightened blade back up.

I increased the speed of this exercise slowly but surely to get myself comfortable with the changes in weight and magic. It was the key to mastering the fairy sword.

After about thirty minutes of nonstop practice, I was finally satisfied enough to take a rest.

Once I stopped, I was greeted with the sound of applause for some reason.

Everyone had sat down to watch from a safe distance while I was focused on my training.

"You really are a cheater. Do you even realize what you were doing?" Arisa demanded.

"Er, practicing with my sword?"

Was my self-taught swordsmanship really goofy-looking or something?

"Nope, you have no idea."

Trotting over to my side, Arisa pulled my head down to her level and discreetly whispered, "Most people can't put magic into a sword any-where near that quickly. And usually they have to release the magic they put into it afterward. No one ever reabsorbs it like that."

Wait, really?

I didn't have a problem doing it with Liza's magic spear, so I figured it was normal…

"Maybe they just can't do it because they've never tried or something?"

"I seriously doubt that. If anyone could do that so easily, there'd be no need for magic recovery potions, would there? You could just recover it yourself—storing MP in a Magic Item to reabsorb it after you use spells, that sort of thing."

Releasing me, Arisa struck a "you're hopeless" pose.

Well, that's good to know. I thanked her for the information. It didn't seem to be enough, so I gave her a quick hug, too.

"Wah! Hey, not so suddenly!"

Just like last time, she gave a weird little exclamation and wriggled in protest.

As usual, even though she was always getting into my personal space, she got flustered when someone else showed her affection. I have to admit, it was fun to catch her by surprise once in a while.

At any rate, I decided to test how effectively I could reabsorb magical power from the sword, then test it further by leaving the magic-imbued sword in Storage overnight to see if it had leaked away at all in the morning.

If my guess was right, this might be a good way to store extra MP, even if I usually had plenty to spare.

Before we departed, I registered in my magic menu all the scrolls I'd bought in Bolehart City.

It was always fun to compare the scroll version of a spell to the magic menu, but I hadn't used them from the scrolls yet. I just tested them out arbitrarily.

Testing out the scrolls earned me the skills "Light Magic," "Ice Magic," and "Ice Resistance," so I maxed those out with skill points and activated them.

I decided I'd test out the magic menu versions off in the mountains somewhere after sunset.

The rest of the day passed without much event, aside from an attack from a group of gray wolves on the road that allowed us a chance to restock our wolf meat supply. Overall, it was a very peaceful journey.

That day, after dinner and my daily magic chant practice, I stole away in the dead of night and took off into the sky with my hang glider. Because I had the Wind Magic spell Blow, I was able to depart from anywhere.

There was a wasteland in the recesses of the mountains more than ten miles away from the road. Fire didn't seem likely to spread there, so I chose that as my site. There were a few shrubs and bushes but not enough to be much cause for concern.

Without further ado, it was time to begin the magic experiments.

My first test subject of choice was Forge.

According to the book on Smithing Magic, Forge was classified as an intermediate Fire Magic spell.

I remembered turning the walls of a labyrinth into lava with the lesser spell Fire Shot, so I decided to use a large meteorite from Storage as a workbench.

This was one of the meteorites that had fallen from the sky when I used Meteor Shower, which should make it fairly heat-resistant by my reckoning.

I slashed at the meteorite with a Holy Sword.

There was a slight resistance as I did so, but I still managed to cut off a piece without a problem, and I put the rest away in Storage.

I placed a copper coin, an iron dagger, and mithril ore on the completed workbench, then selected Forge from the magic menu.

As the spell was used for smelting, it was possible to adjust the intensity of the fire. The amount of magic consumed seemed to change depending on the strength of the flame.

As I slowly raised the temperature, the smell of molten metal began to rise.

Whenever the smell got to be too much, I used the Deodorant spell.

It's getting toasty.

My body in this world was pretty resistant to changes in climate, but standing so close to the flames of the Forge spell was still making me sweat.

The copper coin melted within about ten seconds, and after thirty seconds the dagger liquefied as well.

It took about three minutes for the mithril, but finally that melted, too. The temperature of the flame was shown in an AR display, so I made a note of each metal's melting point.

At this high temperature, my skin felt prickly, like it was burning under the midsummer sun. This might be fatal for a normal person, so I would have to be mindful of my surroundings when I used this spell.

Next, I wanted to test its maximum firepower.

Though it felt a little wasteful, I decided to use a mithril dagger for the test.

I set the spell to full power and activated it.

Within an instant…

Blinding, white-hot flames immediately filled my vision.

Without waiting for my "Sense Danger" skill to kick in, I immediately deactivated Forge and used Blow to send the heat up into the sky.

The "Light Intensity Adjustment" skill must have been working, as my vision returned to its original state right away.

The top of the workbench was charred black, and the mithril dagger I'd put there for the experiment had all but evaporated, leaving behind only a bit of residue. Oddly enough, the workbench itself showed no signs of melting.

When I checked my body, I discovered several minor burns.

That was to be expected; I'd been standing only a few feet away from flames hot enough to sublimate metal.

If anything, it was probably unnatural that I had nothing but a few little burns to show for it.

The hand I'd used to cover my face took the most damage, but even as I watched, it healed itself up like a film clip playing in reverse. This was probably my "Self-Healing" skill at work.

Honestly, my healing abilities are so fast that it's a little disturbing, if I do say so myself.

But I guess I should probably be grateful for that.

So my body was healed thanks to my skills, but my clothes were still scorched.

The parts of my outfit that had been facing the flames were burned into tatters, and even the extremely heat-resistant hydra leather coat had a few holes.

I didn't want to worry everyone, so I decided to change into a similar outfit.

Despite being intended for noncombat usage, the blistering heat of this Forge spell definitely gave it potential as Attack Magic.

Because of its short range, it was a little bit like a suicide bomb, but I decided to keep it in the back of my mind as a very last resort.

That said, I would probably never need to use it like that. Demons could generally only be defeated with Holy Weapons.

I continued my experiments with the other spells.

Curtain, Magic Mold, Polish, Freeze Water, and Pure Water all had potential for some interesting uses. It was going to be difficult to get the hang of Magic Mold, though.

Personally, I didn't need them, but spells like Bug Wiper and Anti-Itch seemed like they'd be good for the kids when they went out foraging.

In my case, mosquitoes and other bugs couldn't pierce my skin, so bug bites were never a problem for me.

Wall, Rock Smasher, and Hard Clay were all really useful for construction. I could literally build a castle overnight. I even tried it out in the wasteland and managed to create one in just under three minutes. Easy as making instant noodles.

On the other hand, I couldn't think of a single use for Condense. Fence didn't seem totally unhelpful, but Shelter or Shield would probably be more convenient in most cases. And Sonar was redundant with my radar.

As for the last spell, Cube...

"This is fun."

The spell could make transparent cubes in the air ranging from four inches to forty feet in size; the amount of weight they could support depended on their own weight.

"I wonder how high I could go?"

As I mumbled to myself, I walked up the transparent staircase I'd made using Cube.

The effect time was ten minutes at most, so an ordinary user would probably run out of magic and fall. In my case, though, it took only a second to recover enough MP for a cube that could support my weight, so I could keep making them indefinitely.

While I was floating in the air, a monster attacked me after I invaded its territory, so I decided to practice some aerial combat.

The level-20 monster looked like a rhinoceros beetle the size of a small truck. According to the AR display, it was called a **soldier beetle**.

Since my goal was to practice fighting up here, I made footholds in the air with Cube and jumped around on them to avoid the soldier beetle's attacks and magic.

I have to say, I felt like a badass video game character.

With the help of my "Spatial Mobility" and "Midair Maneuvers" skills, I was able to figure out the smallest size of cubes I could make to match my mobility. It was very helpful in my ongoing quest for optimal movement.

By the time the soldier beetle's strength ran out, I was able to fight in the air just about as well as I could on the ground.

At this rate, I would even be able to fight dragons or demons in midair.

> **Skill Acquired: "Skyrunning"**
> **Title Acquired: Sky Strider**
> **Title Acquired: Wingless Flier**
> **Title Acquired: Master of the Sky**

As I gained the ability to fight freely in the air, I also gained a skill and a bunch of titles.

The skill name was especially intriguing, so I put the max number of points into it right away and activated it.

"Skyrunning" turned out to produce a similar effect to leaping around with cubes as footholds and had a lower magical cost.

It was highly responsive and allowed me to move without having to think about the size and position of each cube, too.

Even at its top speed, the "Skyrunning" skill took only a little more MP than the amount I recovered automatically, so if I could contrive a good method of flying, I could cruise about as far as I wanted.

I was the only one who would be able to withstand the high winds and low atmospheric pressure, though, so I would probably have to be mindful of my speed and altitude if I was carrying someone else.

◆

It was early morning, a few days after my magical experiment session.

We'd made it through the mountainous region and were getting very close to the main road that went along the river.

"Master, I can see where this road meets the highway now," Lulu remarked from the coachman stand, and I came out to have a look.

There was a lighthouse-esque watchtower set up near the point where the roads met, along with a collection of duchy soldiers. A forest behind the tower obscured my view of the river.

Liza and Nana, who'd gone ahead on horseback to scout out the area, came back toward us. Mia was riding along with Nana.

"Master, please have a look over there. There's something on the other side of the forest."

I looked in the direction where Liza was pointing, but all I could see through the trees were the sails of a large ship. Wait, *that* was probably what she was talking about.

"Those are the sails of a ship. It must be traveling along the big river on the other side of the forest."

Tama and Pochi poked their heads out, apparently having heard my comment.

"Shiiip?"

"Where is it, sir?"

Tama used me to prop herself up and tried to see over the forest.

Pochi, too, grabbed on to Lulu's shoulders and stood on tiptoe, but she still couldn't see it.

"Come here, please. You could hurt yourselves like that."

"Captuuured?"

"We've been caught, sir."

I pulled Tama and Pochi into my lap, holding them firmly so they wouldn't fall.

Tama seemed to enjoy it, but Pochi pouted up at me.

"I wanna see the ship, sir."

"Just sit tight. You'll be able to see it soon." I patted Pochi's head reassuringly.

Arisa came out from inside the carriage as well. "Will we really?"

She draped her arms over Lulu's shoulders from behind in a show of sisterly affection as she looked ahead.

Finally, the river came into view on our right.

"See?"

"Big shiiip?"

"I see the ship, sir!"

No sooner did I point it out than Tama and Pochi exclaimed with delight.

There was a large sailing ship traveling in the same direction as us, albeit faster, as it was heading downstream.

Still sitting in my lap, Tama and Pochi waved frantically at the ship.

Perched on my left knee, Pochi craned around to see the ship on the right.

"Hiii!"

"They waved back, sir."

Pochi continued to wave excitedly.

"Oh? They must have good eyes. I wonder if they're beastfolk, too?"

"Biiirds?"

"They're Mr. Birdheads, sir."

Arisa was correct: The people on the ship were likely some kind of birdfolk.

Pochi and Tama continued to wave until the ship disappeared behind the forest.

Along the way, I decided to reinspect my information about the Ougoch Duchy.

The territory included a huge river, nearly five hundred miles long.

The river started up north in the city of Daregan, where Miss Sara, Miss Karina, and the others were headed. It passed through the old capital, then three more cities, and eventually emptied into the ocean.

As its enormous river would indicate, the Ougoch Duchy was very large.

The Muno Barony was around the size of Hokkaido, albeit with an irregular shape, but the duchy we were in now was far larger—around the same area as Honshu, the main island in Japan. This territory wasn't as long and skinny, though, so it was probably about half the length.

Despite its size, there were only seven cities altogether. The capital had a population of 210,000 people, far larger than any city I'd seen so far. I suppose that was why it was the capital.

The fluvial transportation was probably what supported the locals. There were countless villages along the river, many of which were populated only by demi-humans.

However, 80 percent of the total population was still humanfolk, so it was no different from other territories in its human majority.

As far as I could tell with my map search, there were no demons, reincarnations, or anyone with unique skills.

There were quite a lot of humans and monsters over level 30, so it would be a pain to mark all of them on the map. Instead, I flagged only the ones who seemed likely to encounter us on our itinerary.

There were also several members of the Wings of Freedom, the demon lord–worshipping organization: more than three hundred in total.

They mostly seemed to stay in cities and large towns, so I decided to flag only members in the nearest ones for now.

◆

Once we finished our lunch break by the water, we were nearing the bridge where a stream joined the river when some very troublesome visitors arrived.

The monsters, a group of dog-size creatures called large needle bees, came flying away from the stream as if fleeing from something.

"Pochi, Tama, be careful not to let them surround you."

"Aye!"

"Yes, sir!"

The large needle bees rushed at the beastfolk girls.

"Whoopsiiie?"

"Take this, sir!"

Tama dodged around the needle attacks with ease, and Pochi took the opportunity to attack one of the bees.

When Tama herded three of them into a single-file column, they were easily impaled by Liza's magic spear like dumplings on a skewer.

"Oh crap!"

"Sorry."

A careless ranged attack spell from Mia had inadvertently attracted a swarm.

"Hiyah! Ha!"

Arisa's Psychic Magic and Lulu's Magic Gun sniped the bees one by one, but there was still a huge swarm bearing down on Mia.

"I will protect Mia, I declare."

Nana stepped in front of Mia and used her Foundation technique Shield, but the bees simply navigated around her and kept heading for Mia.

Liza was rushing over, but she was too far away to get there in time.

"Satou."

"Master, heeelp!"

"M-master..."

I wanted to intercept them with magic, but the rearguard girls were between us—I couldn't be sure of my aim.

Instead, I dashed in front of Mia and the others before destroying the swarm with magic.

As I rushed over, I thought I felt something weird and slippery for just a moment, but it must have been my imagination.

While I was puzzling that out, the beastfolk girls finished off the last few needle bees.

"Phew!"

"Good work."

I gave Arisa a drink of cold fruit-flavored water—and distributed more to the other girls, too, of course.

"Thank you. Really, when none of the forwards have the 'Taunt' skill, it's all too easy for one of us rearguarders to end up becoming the main damage dealer."

"There's a 'Taunt' skill?"

Arisa nodded.

The skill Arisa was referring to was a staple of party-based multi-player games like MMOs. It allowed a heavily armored tank character, like a shield user, to draw the attention of monsters.

The difficulty of keeping the enemies' target on one person varied depending on the game, but mastery of this was the mark of a skilled tank player.

"Arisa, please provide additional information on 'Taunt,' I request."

Nana came over to ask about the skill, so Arisa explained it to her.

"Master, we have collected the monster cores."

"Wiiings?"

"Needles, sir."

The beastfolk girls, energetic even after battle, came over to present me with the spoils they'd collected from the monster corpses.

"A second wave of bees will be here soon, so take a break while you can."

I told the girls what I'd learned on the map, so they joined the others in resting up.

Ten minutes later, the second wave arrived.

Just for kicks, I decided to join Nana in attempting to gain the "Taunt" skill.

"Arisa, please offer a demonstration, I request."

"Okeydoke… Hey, you big, stupid bees! Go get eaten by a honey bear, will ya?"

Arisa gave her best shot at angering the bees, but unfortunately they didn't seem to notice.

Flying down unsteadily, the bees practically crash-landed on the bridge and lowered their wings. They seemed more exhausted than anything. In fact, they didn't seem to care about us at all, never mind Arisa's taunts.

"All right, now you try."

"Understood… Hello, you big, stupid bees! Are those wings just for show, I deride!"

Nana followed Arisa's instructions, but again, there was no effect.

Now it was my turn.

"Come at me!"

As soon as I gave a simple shout, the thirty-plus large needle bees that had been lolling around on the bridge immediately charged toward me.

> **Skill Acquired: "Taunt"**

A swarm that big could tear my clothes, so I used "Short Stun" to wipe them out before they got too close.

"Nooo, my experience poiiints!"

"Isspurrieeence?"

"Exporians, sir?"

Tama and Pochi imitated Arisa, who had thrown herself on the ground dramatically.

I patted Arisa on the shoulder reassuringly.

"Don't worry, Arisa. Here come the monsters that chased the bees here."

Gliding toward us from upstream was a thirty-foot-long monster called a **hard newt**. It was level 25 and had a strong acid attack, so I had no intention of letting it hurt Arisa and the others.

"Come at me!"

As a total of nine of them came into view, I used the "Taunt" skill I'd just acquired.

"Everyone, make sure you get in one hit on each of the newts! Don't go anywhere near them, just attack from a distance!"

With those orders, I stood up to the oncoming newts.

Thanks to this powerful grinding technique, the girls jumped up from two to four levels. Mia, at the bottom, reached level 11, while the beastfolk girls were the highest at 16.

Each one learned a few new skills, the most notable being Liza's "Spellblade" and Nana's "Taunt."

The ones who had gained the most levels were starting to get sick from it, so we decided to set up camp for the night right where we were.

Because it would still be a while until evening, we spent our free time on activities of our choosing.

Lulu, Mia, and Nana were all down for the count with level-up sickness and sleeping in the converted bed of the carriage seats.

Liza practiced her new "Spellblade" skill, and Tama and Pochi went foraging in the riverbed.

Arisa was reading one of the spell books we'd picked up in Bolehart City.

As for me, I decided to do some crafting for the first time in a while.

I had occasionally thrown together little things like spare masks and new colored wigs to amuse myself on the journey, but it had been a while since I'd devoted time to making more involved projects like weapons and magic tools.

Well, now that I have some handy new spells and all, I might as well play around with casting.

First, I made four walls to keep fire damage to a minimum. I went with a height of about ten feet to be safe.

I was just messing around, so I melted things like silver coins and brass candlesticks for material instead of wasting something more valuable like the iron ingots and steel bars I bought in Bolehart City.

After about an hour, I'd produced all kinds of silver cups, silver vials, and countless brass accessories.

This included custom pieces for the girls: chick-shaped earrings for Nana, a cat and dog badge for Tama and Pochi respectively, and floral cuff links for the other kids. I applied silver plating to each of them with alchemy.

And now with some extra time to kill, I started making Holy Weapons.

"Now, what should I use for materials...?"

I tapped my chin as I thought.

When I made Holy Arrows before, I used obsidian arrowheads and Mountain-Tree branches, but this time I had no obsidian. Instead, I decided to utilize the rest of the meteorite I'd fashioned my workbench from.

I used a Holy Sword to process the meteorite scraps.

As my go-to Holy Sword Excalibur was in use for magic-storing experiments at the moment, I decided to go with Durandal this time. I did have two other Holy Swords, but I picked Durandal because of the legends back on Earth that said it could be restored if broken by putting it back in its scabbard.

Incidentally, though they rarely saw any action, I also had two Magic Swords and one Holy Spear in Storage.

My understanding was that Magic Swords could be used without a special title, but not only were they flashy, they were extremely heavy, so I was reluctant to have my kids use them.

Besides, against monsters less than level 30, a weapon made with mithril alloy was already overkill.

Anyway, I made arrowheads and spear tips from the meteorite scraps, as well as a tool for carving magic circuits. The remaining fragments went back into Storage as gravel.

Once I'd finished carving circuit grooves into the arrowheads and spear tips, I turned my attention to producing more blue.

I had used up the stock I made before, during our stay in Muno City, and we were due for a new batch. This time, I would have plenty of extra.

I'd made this stuff once before, so the process was fairly simple by now.

I poured the completed blue into my newly made silver vials and stored it away. I made five altogether.

After that, I used a measuring rod to pour the liquid into the magic patterns on the arrowheads and spear tips.

In the end, I'd made ten Holy Arrows and three Holy Spear tips.

Since it'd be impossible to use a bow while wielding a Holy Sword, I made up for that shortcoming by preparing a one-handed Holy Short Spear.

"Master, Lulu is awake."

Arisa called to me from outside, so I removed the walls and went over to meet everyone.

The accessories were very well received.

◆

Dinner that evening was pretty intense. Guess everyone was hungry after the day's battles.

Leaving Liza and the others to clean up after the meal, I went into a grove of trees to fulfill a dream I'd had for a while.

"This area ought to do it."

I had chosen a section of the bank with a good view of the river.

First, I made practical use of the Earth Magic spells Wall and Pit to create a bathtub about ten feet around.

Once I used the Hard Clay spell to make sure it wouldn't muddy the water, I added the pebbles Tama and Pochi had brought from the riverbed at my behest.

This should be big enough for everyone to use.

The ladies' tub was finished, so I made a private one-man bathtub a little ways away.

It would probably be fine if we all bathed together, but I didn't want a bashful adolescent like Lulu to feel ill at ease, so I figured it would be for the best to have the girls bathe separately.

Next, I waded into the river under cover of darkness and put a bunch of water into Storage. Then, I filled the tubs and used the spell Pure Water to clean it. The impurities went into Storage to dispose of later.

Finally, I used the Fire Magic spell Forge at its lowest possible setting to heat the water to near boiling, and with that, the outdoor bath was complete.

I added a few finishing touches by solidifying the ground around it with Hard Clay and building a little washing area.

I also put aside a few barrels and buckets of water for temperature control.

Muno Castle had only a sauna room, so it had been a long time since I'd had a proper bath. Hopefully, everyone would enjoy it.

When I returned to the others and told them that I'd made a bathhouse of sorts, their reactions were mixed. Lulu and Nana didn't know what I meant, so I gave a brief explanation.

"Ah, bathing with a boy! Finally I'll be rewarded for all the hardships I've been through!"

"No, the baths are separated by gender."

"Wh-whaaaaat?! God, don't be such a Goody Two-shoes! This is so obviously a chance for a fan-service-y hot-springs episode!"

Just as I expected, Arisa got all worked up over something absurd. It wasn't really a hot springs anyway.

"Master, I volunteer to wash your back, I declare."

"No."

"She's right—you can't."

Also as expected, Mia and Lulu were quick to shut down Nana's offer.

"We last had a bath quite a while ago. We shall be happy to wash your back again if you wish, master."

"Tama, toooo!"

"Pochi, too, sir."

The beastfolk girls, remembering the bath in the Seiryuu City castle guesthouse, seemed very excited.

A few of our number had a strong reaction to Liza's use of the word *again*, but I chose to ignore them.

I had already made a tool for cleaning my own back anyway, so I would be fine.

For some reason, this information seemed to disappoint the girls. Liza and Lulu offered to let me use the bath first, but I told them that I had prepared a separate one for myself, so they meekly went off for their soak. Naturally, Arisa tried to follow me, but Lulu led her away.

"Ah, that's the stuff."

As I slipped into the men's bath, I looked up at the sky.

The stars were starting to come out. It was too bad that the river wasn't quite still enough to reflect the stars, but the moonlight dancing on the surface was still quite beautiful.

I turned off the utilitarian menu display and enjoyed the view.

"I haven't bathed outside like this since we snuck off that one time in college."

As I leaned back against the wall of the tub and started relaxing, I heard a sudden *plunk* and felt weight against my body. I could tell that someone had entered my bath, but with the radar off, I didn't know who.

I raised my head to find Mia with her long hair loose.

"Mia, this is the men's bath."

"Mn."

Mia, clearly uninterested in my gentle scolding, plopped herself down in front of me with her back to me. I couldn't help remembering when I helped bathe a younger relative while babysitting.

A recovery team seemed to be on the way to collect her, so I decided to let her do what she liked for now.

"Are there baths like this in the elf village?"

"Shared."

Meaning there were public baths, then.

Mia rested her small head on my chest and joined me in stargazing.

Then the recovery team arrived, or maybe I should call them the second attack squad.

"Us, toooo?"

"We're coming in, sir."

Tama and Pochi hopped into the bath from my left and right.

No matter how small the beastfolk girls might be, that bath was definitely over capacity now. It was starting to feel less like a tub and more like a can of sardines.

Tama and Pochi wanted to copy Mia, so I held them up with a hand each so they wouldn't sink.

"Hey, you two! Don't try and get the jump on me!"

Arisa arrived next, clad in a thin bathrobe.

The wet robe was definitely clinging to her body, but I had zero interest in a little girl's figure.

At any rate, the two older girls behind her soon drew my gaze away.

There was no way to comment on Nana's figure without being indecent, but I'd admit I did feel a certain sense of almost fatherly pride in noticing Lulu's proportions were growing.

"Master, I think you ought to come join us in the large bath instead."

Arisa's proposal was met with unanimous agreement from the girls, so I ended up being dragged over there.

I guess bigger is better for baths after all.

"Damn, it's too dark! I guess I ought to learn Light Magic next…"

Arisa kept muttering to herself in between short dives under the water.

I had a hunch as to what her goal might be. Unfortunately for her, I was wearing brand-new swim trunks, so she wouldn't see anyway. *I know that runs counter to the idea of natural bathing, but just think of it as an emergency measure.*

"C-collarbone…"

Lulu, who was submerged up to her shoulders next to Arisa, was mumbling something while staring at me with her cheeks flushed pink. *Okay, you're making me a little uncomfortable.*

I leaned back on the wall again, resuming my previous pose.

The steam wasn't doing its job very well, so I couldn't really keep looking forward.

I was getting a little hot, so I took my arms out of the water and rested them on the side of the tub, only to immediately have them used as pillows. Tama and Pochi were on my right arm and Mia on my left. Oddly, Lulu was inching closer as if waiting for her turn.

"Master, I have made a discovery! Confirmation required, I request."

Nana's voice came to me from somewhere behind Lulu. When I glanced over nonchalantly…

"They float in the water, I report! They are also light and rather cute."

Nana, who had opened the front of her bathrobe, was looking at her floating breasts. Though her expression was blank as usual, she seemed terribly entertained.

If this were a manga, the protagonist's nose would have started gushing blood. What a sight for sore eyes.

"Miss Nana, you mustn't!"

"Lewd."

Lulu quickly moved in front of Nana, blocking my view. Unfortunately, her wet bathrobe was sticking closely to her body, so now I could clearly see the outline of her bottom.

After a moment, Mia blocked my view of that, too, by standing in the way with her arms spread. She wasn't wearing a robe, so I could see all kinds of things that I really didn't need to. If she were an older woman, I'd be so happy I could cry.

The rest of our bathing time passed in a similar fashion—relaxing, if occasionally boisterous.

The next morning, I found Liza looking sorrowfully at the cold bath, so I warmed it back up for a morning dip. She always was fond of them.

Tolma

Satou here. For some reason, maybe because of a movie I saw long ago, the phrase mountain hunt *always makes me picture men with torches hiking into the mountains in the dark. If you ask me, going into the mountains at night is way too dangerous.*

When we reached a fork in the road about half a day's journey away from Gururian City, we were reunited with a knight who was an old friend of ours.

Because of my radar, I was already well prepared to meet him.

"S-Sir Pendragon… Please, could you lend me a horse?"

I handed the knight a flask of water, and he drained it at an alarming rate.

It was the temple knight Heath from back in Muno City.

"Thieves have captured the oracle priestess. I need to tell the viceroy right away!"

What?! Is Miss Sara in danger?

The phrase *oracle priestess* made me search my map in a hurry, but Miss Sara seemed to be safe in Gururian City. He must be talking about a different person.

"Go ahead and use this horse, then."

I gave him the reins to Nana's usual mount, the fastest steed we had.

He seemed a bit surprised as he accepted them. He must not have expected it to be so easy.

His tattered overcoat was covered in dirt, leaves, and sticks from rushing through the mountains.

"I owe you."

Though he looked fatigued, the knight struck his fist to his chest in salute, straddled the horse, and took off at a gallop toward Gururian City.

"Hey, master. What shall we do with these thieves?"

I turned back to Arisa, who had finished things up while I was talking to the knight.

Behind her, a group of around thirty thieves was tied up, disarmed, and even knocked out with Arisa's Psychic Magic.

This band of robbers had been chasing the temple knight.

Three of them were lying dead at the side of the road, but that was the work of the knight, not us.

When my radar had alerted me to the chase, our group waited at the intersection, armed to the teeth, and rounded up the thieves as soon as they arrived.

Our enemies were surprisingly well equipped; most had bronze armor and swords, and four of them even had Fire Rods and Thunder Rods, which were magic tools reserved for military use. I was a bit concerned about where they had gotten all this.

"The knight will probably come back with reinforcements, so let's just leave the trouble of transportation up to them."

I was more than happy to leave the cleanup of the bandits to the proper authorities.

With that, I opened my map to investigate.

We had to rescue the oracle priestess from the thieves' hideout, after all.

There were ten of them at the base: seven women and three men. The abductees consisted of four men and three women.

One of the captured women was the same temple knight who had been guarding Miss Sara. She had probably been tasked with guarding the oracle priestess along with Sir Heath.

I thought about going by myself, but there were more people to be rescued than I'd initially bargained for.

So I elected to take a few people with me. Arisa's Psychic Magic made her a vital addition, so I would bring her, Liza, and maybe one other.

"I'm going to the thieves' hideout to save the abductees. Arisa, Liza, and Tama, you'll come with me."

The indicated trio nodded, but Nana, Pochi, and Mia seemed disgruntled.

"Master, permission to accompany?"

"Pochi is unwanted, sir?"

"Mrrrr. Going."

Nana was expressionless as usual, Pochi was teary-eyed, and Mia's cheeks were puffed out in anger.

"I need you three to stay here. Protect Lulu and the carriage."

"Master, instructions to defend the base have been registered, I report." Nana nodded immediately, but Pochi and Mia weren't so easily swayed.

I patted each of them on the head and repeated my explanation.

While I did so, Nana swiftly lined up next to the other two, so I patted her as well.

"I'll be *terribly* scared on my own... Aren't there aaany strong swordsmen or brave magic users to protect me?"

Catching my drift, Lulu cleared her throat and loudly tried to draw the pair's attention.

"Pochi will protect you, ma'am!" Pochi was drawn in right away.

At that, the horses flared their nostrils and whinnied.

"I'll protect you, too, Rye and Effie, sirs. And you, New and Bie. Zard too, of course, sirs."

Pochi hurried to reassure each of the horses by name.

The horses whinnied again, as if to say, *Yeah, you better.*

As that conversation played out, I continued trying to persuade the last holdout.

"Please, Mia."

"...Mm. Fine."

When I squatted down to talk to her eye to eye, she reluctantly agreed, giving me a quick hug.

Arisa yelped, "Ah!" with jealousy, but I pretended not to hear it.

Once I sectioned off the felled thieves with three layers of barriers using Shelter, it was time to head to the thieves' mountain hideout.

We ran along a narrow trail to get there. Since Arisa was utterly lacking in physical strength, of course, I carried her on my shoulders.

After a while, the entrance to the cave came into view behind the trees. A broken barrier post or something similar stood in front of the entrance, maybe preventing monsters from approaching.

There were two men standing guard in front of the cave. As we arrived, they were right in the middle of welcoming back more of their number.

"How'd it go?"

"Just two stupid little girls and a bunch of crappy loot."

A thief carrying a couple of large sacks responded grumpily to the watchman's question. My bet was that the sacks contained hostages.

"The coachman abandoned the brats and ran off t' the mountains, so some o' ours chased 'im down like a bunch o' hot-blooded morons."

"Hope they don't ferget the boss told 'em to bring 'im back alive."

"Yeah, right. What's it matter anyway? Even if they did bring 'im back, the boss'd end up torturin' 'im to death anyway."

Hmm, so their boss is some kind of sadistic freak?

Leaving Liza and the others in the bushes, I crept toward the thieves.

"No kiddin'. Ever since she got that weird vase, the boss's been even madder than usual."

"Y'mean the one from those purple robes with all the weapons an' Fire Rods an' stuff?"

"Yeah. I bet that thing's cursed…"

While the thieves had their guards down, I stepped between them, knocking out four of them before they could react. One tried to sound an alarm horn, but Arisa's Psychic Magic spell Mind Blow put a stop to that.

The last two thieves threw down their sacks and reached for their swords, but I quickly kicked the swords away and caught the sacks before they hit the ground.

Signaling for the others to join me, I had them tie up the unconscious thieves.

"Are you all right?"

"Huh? We're…saved?"

The first sack turned out to contain a middle school–aged girl, who looked around and mumbled in confusion.

"Siiiiiis!"

Sobbing, a little girl about Arisa's age burst out of the other sack and latched onto the first, who was evidently her sister.

"Arisa, take care of these two, please. Liza and Tama, keep watch here for other returning thieves. I'm going to scout out the cave."

With that, I headed into the hideout. The three thieves on their way back were all less than level 7, so Liza and Tama should be able to handle them without a problem.

With the help of my cave map, I made a beeline to the abductees.

They were gathered in a large room all the way in the back of the hideout, along with the boss and her right-hand woman.

The number of prisoners had decreased since we left, too; it appeared the bandits had killed three of the men. We had to hurry.

Of the remaining six thieves, four women were gathered at a pool of water, and the other two were coming toward the entrance.

I knocked out the pair as they rounded the corner, then made my way toward the room in the back.

"Hmph... Kill her."

A woman's voice echoed from the hall where the boss had the hostages.

Peering inside from the entryway, I saw Lady Knight chained to the wall.

Her armor had been removed from the waist up, and her shirt was torn open, exposing one of her breasts.

If the bottom half of her armor was still intact, she was probably safe for now. I looked around at the rest of the room to assess the situation.

A middle-aged man with unkempt hair was sitting next to her, trying to show her something with a slimy expression of pleasure.

Beside him was a female thief with heavy makeup and a skimpy outfit, giving Lady Knight a once-over and snickering cruelly.

The other abductees were trapped in a cage a short distance away, staring lifelessly at the floor.

In one corner of the room was a pile of mangled bodies.

There didn't seem to be any traps, so I chose to finish this quickly.

"C'mon, it's no fun if you give up so quickly. I wanna see you fight."

"St-stop... Get that thing away from me!"

The disgusting man held a puppy-size wasp with its wings torn off.

According to the AR display, it was called a **corpse bee**, a horrific monster that laid eggs in animal corpses, where its young would turn the corpse into food with decay-inducing poison. Truly the stuff of nightmares.

"Let's see what happens if this thing stings you..."

I had no desire to watch something like that happen to a woman, so I took a pebble out of Storage and threw it at the corpse bee, destroying it.

"Who dares…?!"

Covered in the green fluids of the corpse bee, the thief whirled around in rage.

Without bothering to answer his question, I quickly dispatched him.

A few pebbles to the knees sent two more bandits tumbling to the ground. They shouted obscenities at me from the floor, so I kicked them in the stomachs to shut them up. That should keep them unconscious for a good half hour.

Lady Knight was still blinking in surprise, trying to process what had just happened, when I walked up to her.

"Y-you're…from Muno Barony…"

I covered her chest with a nearby cloth, then destroyed the restraints on her wrists with a knife.

She'd been splattered with dead corpse bee, too, so I handed her a towel and a flask of water.

"Thank you, Sir Pendragon. But how did you find this place?"

"We dragged it out of some robbers who were chasing a young temple knight."

As Lady Knight searched around for her stolen equipment, I turned to the people trapped in the large iron cage.

"I'm here to rescue you. I'll have you out of there soon, so hang on just a little longer, please."

I smiled gently at the abductees as they gave a weak chorus of gratitude, then checked on the map to see where the key was kept.

Ah, it was on a desk up against the wall.

"A young temple knight? Is Heath with you, then?"

"No, I had him go on ahead to Gururian City to send for reinforcements."

I answered Lady Knight's questions as I approached the untidy desk.

The first thing I noticed was a vase in the center of the desk. It had a suspicious design composed mainly of eyeballs and mouths.

According to the AR display, this lidded vessel was called a **malice urn**.

It must be related to that "chaos jar" thing that the demon I defeated in Muno City said was needed for resurrection. It had probably been gathering resentment and other negative emotions in all sorts of places.

This had to be the vase the thieves had been grumbling about, the one that had driven their boss insane.

Opening the lid would probably curse you right away, so I quickly impounded it in Storage.

Once I got to the old capital, I could probably have the holy woman of Tenion Temple purify it.

I found the key shortly thereafter, so I freed the captives from their cage.

"You're safe now."

"Th-thank you."

I offered a hand to a woman in her mid-twenties who was carrying a baby.

The last surviving man's face was swollen, and one of his arms seemed to be broken.

"What terrible injuries."

"The bandits beat him up when he tried to protect us…"

"I had to protect my wife and daughter, didn't I?" The man grimaced through the pain, trying to summon a smile.

I was surprised that he hadn't been killed, until I saw his bloodline in the AR display. According to his profile, he was a high-ranking noble of the old capital. They'd probably kept him alive to demand ransom.

He was severely wounded, so I gave him a lesser magic potion to heal his broken bones. It was a high-quality product that I hadn't gotten a chance to use in a while.

"Is this a potion? Thank you…!"

As if he had just received a glass of water, the man gratefully guzzled down the potion.

"Well, I'll be damned! It's healed already! This is good stuff."

The efficacy of the potion took the man by surprise.

"I'm Tolma. This is my wife, Hayuna, and my daughter, Mayuna. If you go to the old capital, pay Viscount Siemmen a visit. I swear on the Siemmen name that you'll find a warm welcome!"

"The viscount…?"

If I remembered correctly, the viscount Siemmen who Mr. Tolma spoke of ran a scroll workshop in the old capital.

If Mr. Tolma was his younger brother, this connection might be an unexpected stroke of luck.

And his daughter, Mayuna, was the "oracle priestess."

I smiled at her, and she gave a curious-sounding gurgle. She had to be an exceptionally brave baby not to cry in a place like this.

Mr. Tolma had introduced himself, so I did the same.

"A noble of the Muno Barony? Why, I didn't know my second cousin had taken on a vassal. Is he well, then?"

So he and Baron Muno were closely related. The baron did say that he came from the old capital, so it made sense.

As Mr. Tolma and I carried on this bland conversation, Miss Hayuna suddenly gave a bloodcurdling scream.

The cause turned out to be Lady Knight, who'd taken her revenge.

Blood dripped from her sword as the heads of the thieves rolled away.

I generally didn't think well of killing someone who couldn't resist, but her retaliation was probably natural, considering how close she'd come to joining the pile of bodies in the hall.

There was no law against killing bandits in the Shiga Kingdom, but I still didn't entirely approve.

"What?" She glared at me. "Are you going to tell me that was unchivalrous?"

"I won't tell you not to kill thieves, but please at least refrain from slaughtering people in front of others."

"Fine. I'll be more careful next time."

Returning her sword to her scabbard, she went to put her armor back on in a corner of the room.

Honestly, that's so gross. I don't want to see that.

I sent the rescued captives to meet up with Liza outside, captured the other female thieves, collected some spoils, and secured a means of transportation before rendezvousing with everyone else.

The transport in question included a covered wagon, a beast of burden called a "dullalkosaur" that seemed to be a cross between a hippopotamus and a dinosaur, a velociraptor-esque riding animal called a "runosaur," and some horses.

"Master, this runosaur is an excellent steed. Its movements are quite agile."

"And it turns sooo quickly, meow."

Liza and Tama were impressed with the runosaur. Oddly, Tama appended a meow to her sentence, which was probably Arisa's doing.

Unable to see around the runosaur's neck while seated, Tama was standing on the saddle to operate the reins. The creature was quite docile, despite its carnivorous appearance.

Before we boarded the dullalkosaur-drawn carriage, I handed Mr. Tolma a mithril dagger and luggage bag I'd found in the hideout.

"Oh-ho! It's my dagger with the family crest on it!"

"So it does belong to you, then."

Because the AR display confirmed it as such, I returned it to him.

"I truly appreciate all you've done. This will surely help me save face when I return to my brother. Thank you, Sir Pendragon, thank you!"

"You can just call me Satou."

"Very well, Sir Satou. I'll be sure to repay you in the old capital!" Mr. Tolma paused for a moment and then continued a little awkwardly. "Unlike my dear brother, I have relatively little funds to give, but…I am still a man of good renown in high society. I'm sure I can be of some use to you."

I didn't really want to make my debut in high society anyway, so I asked Mr. Tolma to tell me about the old capital on the road.

Better yet, during the journey, he promised me a tour of the scroll workshop.

"Well, if you're a scroll collector, how do these strike you? These two have already been used, but this Remote Arrow scroll is still brand-new."

"Are you sure it's all right if I take it?"

"Of course, by all means! It's not nearly as valuable as the dagger you returned, but if it pleases you, I'm happy to give it."

I gratefully accepted the scroll that Mr. Tolma produced from his luggage.

When I registered Remote Arrow to the magic menu later and tested it out, it was fairly similar in function to Magic Arrow, but its homing ability seemed pretty handy.

True to its name, the dullalkosaur was about as fast as a donkey, so we made it back to Lulu and the others before the temple knight Heath returned with reinforcements.

◆

Sir Heath brought thirty of the viceroy's knights and yeomen.

Twenty-four of them set off into the mountains to hunt down the remaining criminals.

"Well, I'll leave the rest to you."

"Yes, sir! We shall guard the thieves with our lives!"

The honest-looking older yeoman took on the task with a dependable smile.

He led five other knights and yeomen in transporting the prisoners. Supposedly, they would rope the thieves—quite literally—into pulling the carriage over areas where the slow dullakosaur couldn't.

Back on Earth, they'd probably be sued for abuse of prisoners, but in this world the prisoners didn't have any rights. They meekly accepted their lot—and if they refused, they'd be beheaded on the spot, so I guess I couldn't blame them.

Anyway, I cleared my mind of thoughts about comeuppance and headed back to my own carriage.

Tama and Pochi were riding the runosaur, while Liza, Nana, and Mia were on horseback.

Pochi, Tama, and Mia kept peeking inside the carriage, seemingly fascinated by the baby.

The temple knights, having celebrated their safe reunion, were on standby on their horses as well.

"Master! Look what Liza gave us, sir."

Noticing me, Pochi grinned proudly from atop the runosaur.

It seemed Liza preferred to keep her favorite horse.

"Master, Arisa and the others are inside the carriage."

Lulu gave a report from the coachman's stand, so I nodded and got in as well.

"Let's head out, Lulu."

"Yes, master."

Lulu's technique as a coachman had been improving lately; when we started moving, we didn't accelerate more than necessary.

"I've never ridden in such a fine carriage..."

"Mm-hmm. It's so fluffy!"

"Nice, isn't it? We finally got these comfy seats not long ago."

Across from Arisa and me, the villager sisters we'd rescued were getting excited.

"Heavens, what a comfortable ride! It's just as good as our carriage at home."

"I'm honored to hear you say that."

Mr. Tolma, who was sitting in one of the spare seats in the back, was examining the interior with great interest.

"Wasn't this awfully expensive?"

"Tolma, don't be rude."

Seated at his side, Miss Hayuna scolded her husband for his rather indelicate question.

Little Mayuna, who'd been quiet up until now, began wailing.

The AR indicated that she was hungry. Miss Hayuna was starting to open her shirt, so I quickly turned my gaze away.

With the crying baby in the background, we continued along the highway next to the great river.

I was tempted to keep us moving until we arrived in Gururian City, but at the temple knight pair's recommendation, we stopped in a village along the way for the night.

They told me the road was dangerous after dark thanks to monsters from the river.

I didn't see anything of the sort on my map, so it was probably just superstition.

"Hey, sorry to just show up with so many people out of nowhere."

"N-no, it's no trouble in the slightest."

The village headman responded to Mr. Tolma's friendly remark with a slight screech.

I couldn't blame him for that reaction, given that the likes of a high-ranking noble from the old capital and some temple knights had suddenly shown up on his doorstep.

On the map, many of the village girls were hiding in a barn far away from the village headman's home.

Maybe they thought we might be here to look for women. I didn't know whether to be insulted or just apologetic for frightening them.

At any rate, I would have to give them some money and goods as thanks for hosting us before we left tomorrow.

"I'm terribly sorry to put you up in such an unbecoming place..."

"Is this a meeting hall?"

"Yes, I'm afraid it's the only room spacious enough to accommodate a party this large."

The anxious village headman had guided us to a one-story house across from his home.

The enormous room was more than a hundred and fifty square feet. A group of elderly women were already at work preparing a banquet.

Just as Pochi's and Tama's stomachs started announcing themselves, the finished dinner finally arrived.

Each person received a dish containing a soup of beans, dried sardines, and mushrooms, along with a plate holding a savory mushroom and herb pancake and a small grilled fish.

"Wow, what a feast! Isn't it amazing, big sis?"

"I-it's like a banquet..."

I had assumed this was a standard meal for the farming village, but their comments suggested it was exceptional to ordinary villagers like the sisters we'd rescued.

It was just the right size for the likes of Lulu, Mia, and me, but it might not be enough for the beastfolk girls.

In fact, Tama and Pochi were already looking around for more.

"Um, Mister Satou..."

"What is it?"

The elder sister tugged on my sleeve nervously.

"We don't have enough money to pay for all this food."

"Don't worry about that. It's my treat, all right? Just relax and eat."

"O-oh, okay..."

I encouraged the worried young girl to go back to her seat.

Mr. Tolma and the temple knights didn't seem to have any problem with the presence of commoners or demi-humans.

"Heavens, what a humble-looking meal..."

"It's not so bad to eat like the poor once in a while. As long as it's edible, what's the problem?"

"Tolma! Don't insult the good people who made this for us!" Miss Hayuna hastened to scold her husband for his rude remarks.

The village headman and the old women who had prepared the meal stiffened, so I quickly covered for him.

"Please pardon my fellow traveler. We'd like to thank you for your kindness from the bottom of our hearts."

"O-oh, there's no need for that, sir..."

Maybe it was my imagination, but I was starting to suspect that the village headman thought I was the noble from the old capital.

Tolma and his wife were wearing normal traveling clothes, so my finely tailored robe probably helped me pass for an aristocrat.

In fact, I was the only one with an extra plate. I'd have to share it with whoever wanted some later.

"Well? Let's eat!"

Despite Mr. Tolma's comments about the food, he was the first to rub his hands together greedily and dig in.

He was as fast as a schoolboy who'd missed lunch, but the nobleman's manner of eating was still impeccable.

Hayuna and the village girls followed suit and started eating. They were pretty speedy, too.

""""Thanks for the food!"""""

My kids all chorused along with Arisa, then started on their meals.

It was a bit plainer than our usual fare, but none of the girls complained. Mia and Tama even traded fish and vegetables.

For the most part, the meal proceeded as normal, but Pochi and Tama were acting a bit strange.

I was glad to see them eating more slowly—there was less food than usual—but when they'd finished about half their meals, their eyes started shifting between their plates and Miss Hayuna and her baby.

Then, they got out of their chairs and carried their plates over to her.

What's going on?

"We'll shaaare?"

"You can have half, ma'am."

The pair held their dishes out to Miss Hayuna.

For some reason, they looked quite serious, even a little pained.

"C'mon now. There might not be much food, but we're still not gonna eat scraps from some demi-human slaves!"

Mr. Tolma's insult wasn't particularly loud, but it was poorly timed so that it echoed through the otherwise silent room.

On hearing that, Tama's and Pochi's ears flattened.

"Tolma! How many times must I tell you to think about who you're speaking to before you run your mouth?!"

Miss Hayuna rose from her chair and raged at her husband for his misstep. The next thing I knew, her hand was shooting out.

After getting a firm smack on the head, Mr. Tolma looked up at Miss Hayuna miserably.

I wanted to give him a piece of my mind myself, but Miss Hayuna had already scolded him thoroughly. I elected not to try to follow her act.

Given the enormous wealth gap between the rich and the poor in this kingdom, it might have seemed like a natural reaction for Tolma, but to my mind that was no excuse for lashing out at the well-intentioned girls.

From now on, I'm just going to call him Jackass, at least mentally.

Oh, but forget about Jackass. I had to take care of Tama and Pochi.

"What's the matter?"

"Babies have to eat a lot, or they'll diiie?"

"Babies cry when they can't have nipples, sir."

I didn't quite follow their meaning, but maybe this was why they were acting so strangely.

Come to think of it, what if they thought the baby was starving because she cried the whole way here?

"Master, when we were with our previous owner, there was a leopard-woman who had a child. She was unable to produce breast milk, perhaps because we had so little to eat, and the baby was on the verge of starving to death. So we demi-human slaves all shared half our food with the mother and child. I imagine that's what they're referring to now."

"I see. Well, Tama and Pochi, that was very kind of you. But don't worry—the baby is just fine. So you can eat the rest yourselves, all right?"

Liza's explanation made the girls' reasoning clear. Their former master had indeed seemed cruel enough to do such a thing.

Miss Hayuna patted the girls' heads. "Thank you for worrying about us." Meanwhile, her jackass husband scratched his head and complained about the lack of beer.

The villagers appeared to hear Jackass's demands, but none of them moved to respond.

Once Miss Hayuna and I had spoken to them, Tama and Pochi nodded meekly and returned to their seats.

Then, after the meal...

"I am so, so sorry about my husband."

"Ouch! I take it back, Hayuna, just please stop yanking on my ear!"

"I think not. I won't forgive you until you apologize to these children."

Still smiling away, Miss Hayuna dragged her husband over to apologize.

"Sir Satou, I'm sorry for rejecting your slaves' kindness."

"Shouldn't you be apologizing to someone else?"

"No, this is considered proper between nobles! Besides, it's like I said... Lots of demi-human slaves are unclean, y'know. What if you share food with them and get some strange illness? I can't have my wife and daughter sick!"

So he was worried about the baby's weak immune system? That did make sense, I suppose.

"Please don't argue any longer. Sir Tolma, I accept your apology. Let us put this matter to rest."

"Really? Well, I appreciate it."

We would be traveling with this jackass to Gururian City.

I was absolutely going to use this connection to see the scroll workshop, but I'd have to be careful to keep him from interacting with my kids in the future.

I want to raise them right, after all!

Trouble in Gururian City

Satou here. I like both Western and traditional Japanese sweets, but my favorites are Japanese ones that incorporate Western flavors. I think it's important to carry on traditions while also continuing to evolve.

"When we get to Gururian City, you gotta eat Gururian cakes! But it won't be easy, 'cause they're one copper apiece."

"What kind of pastry is it?"

"Lemme see… It's, like, made out of white grains with sweet black grains on the outside, kinda."

While I was talking to the commoner sisters about the city's famous cakes, Lulu reported from the coachman's stand that the walls of Gururian City had come into view. Meanwhile, the sisters continued chattering.

"You've never even eaten one!"

The elder sister turned to me and explained the origin of her younger sister's story.

"A merchant who came to the village was going on about them, so now she thinks she's had one herself."

"Hmph! When I get a job that pays, it's the first thing I'm gonna eat!"

"It'll be years before you can get paid, dummy."

The sisters were going to Gururian City to apprentice at a mercantile.

Until they came of age, children were provided with food, clothing, and shelter in place of actual wages. Given the lack of initial investment, maybe this kind of servitude made for more economic labor than slaves.

Finally, we arrived at the entrance to Gururian City.

There was a line to enter, but the temple knight led us around to the front of it.

At the gate, some young nobles were giving an address to the merchants waiting to get inside.

"Merchants visiting Gururian City! We are seeking a Magic Sword. If any of you can provide us with one, we'll guarantee you an exclusive deal with the government in the future!"

The young men addressing the crowd were mostly in their twenties and dressed in fashionable knight-style clothing.

Naturally, no one answered them. They were probably affiliated with the similar young noble I saw back in Bolehart City.

"Hey, big sis, he says he'll make us government merchants if we give him a Magic Sword! Isn't that amazing?"

"It certainly is. But we don't have anything like a Magic Sword, so it doesn't matter."

"…You girls won't last a minute if you let every sleazebag on the street fool you like that, you know!" Concerned by the sisters' remarks, Arisa clearly couldn't resist sticking her nose in. "You know what that actually means, right? He's saying, 'We don't have money, but we still want a Magic Sword. Please give us one for free. Then, if we manage to have a successful career in the future, we'll give you special treatment. Don't complain if that never happens, though.' They're all full of hot air."

"Wow, really? I had no idea."

"Gosh, Arisa, you're smart for someone so little!"

As I listened idly to their conversation, I opened the window and looked outside.

The young noblemen were staring greedily at Liza's magic spear, but they weren't quite stupid enough to approach a cart with an escort of temple knights, so they were keeping their distance.

Once we entered the gate, we had to let the sisters off.

As commoners, they needed to go through certain procedures to enter the city.

Fortunately, the gatekeeper seemed to be a friend of Sir Heath, so he promised to finish their paperwork quickly and even offered to guide them to the mercantile. What a kind gatekeeper.

"Thanks, Mister Satou!"

"Really, thank you so much. You rescued us from those thieves, then you took such good care of us…"

"You don't need to worry about that."

"I do! Listen, we're gonna be working at a hardware store called the Green Shop, so please come see us if you need anything, okay? We can't give you a discount or nothin', but we'll make sure you get all the best stuff!"

I imagined the girls would be doing only menial chores at the shop, but I thanked them nonetheless for their kind offer.

After parting ways with the village girls, we continued through the city. There were a lot of people about, making me wonder if there was a festival going on or something.

Even the main street had no separation between roads and walkways, so progress in the carriage was slow. I sent Temple Knight Heath on ahead as a messenger to the Tenion Temple.

In the meantime, I decided to check the map once more. There were no demons, chaos jars, malice urns, or anything of the sort, but I did find twenty or so demon lord–worshipping Wings of Freedom.

I decided to write down on paper the names and whereabouts of the members and mail it off to the city guards in the dead of night.

"Masterrr?" Tama, who was riding the runosaur along with Pochi, called to me from outside the window. "Sword fiiights?"

"Master, humans are fighting over there, sir."

Interested, I came out to the coachman stand to look where they were pointing.

There was a great deal of people gathered in a large park nearby, making for quite a lively mood.

"Over there, master."

"I wonder what it is? An exhibition fight, maybe?"

I looked curiously toward where Lulu was pointing, and Arisa stuck her head out as well.

It was dangerous to drive while distracted, so I had Lulu stop the carriage for a moment.

"Maybe it has to do with the martial arts tournament Miss Jojorie mentioned?"

Right—there was a big tournament being held in the old capital soon.

"It's probably a preliminary battle to decide who gets to enter. Want to go check it out?"

Jackass had gotten out of the carriage to stretch and made a suggestion.

Wait, when did you get out?

"Lord Tolma, we must first go to the Tenion Temple…"

"Oh, don't be such a stick in the mud. Let's pick up some grub at the food stalls first!"

Ignoring the temple knight's reminder, Jackass cheerily slipped into the crowd.

"I'm sorry. Tolma is always like this."

Miss Hayuna tried to apologize to the temple knight, but her expression remained stoic as ever.

"…Sir Pendragon. I'm terribly sorry, but would you mind lending me one of your talented servants to retrieve Lord Tolma?"

"Sure, that's fine."

Since her main duty was to protect baby Mayuna, the "oracle priestess," she couldn't leave.

I sent Liza and Nana to collect Jackass.

Tama and Pochi, still riding the runosaur, sniffed the air.

"Sweet smeeell?"

"It's a different smell from the honey pastries and the licorice, sir!"

After a moment, the scent reached the rest of us as well. It smelled like traditional Japanese sweets, specifically red-bean paste.

"Oh man, that smells great! Is that…? Is that red-bean paste?"

Arisa was getting especially fired up for whatever reason and whipped her head around searchingly.

"You there, young master! Would you like a Gururian cake?"

A girl with a food tray suspended from her neck emerged from the crowd and approached the coachman's stand where I was sitting.

She reminded me of a Showa-era salesgirl selling bento boxes at a train station, or something along those lines.

Alas, she wasn't wearing a Japanese-style outfit to match—just ordinary commoner's clothes with a short apron tied around her waist.

"Sure. Could I buy eleven, please?"

"Yes, of course! That will be eleven large coppers."

I didn't feel like haggling, so I handed her two silvers and one large copper.

That was pretty expensive for a pastry, though. Each one cost the same as a night's stay at the Gatefront Inn back in Seiryuu City.

I handed out the leaf-wrapped Gururian cakes to everyone.

I thought the temple knight might decline, but she gladly accepted it. It seemed girls who disliked sweets were rare even in a parallel world.

"Mrrrr. Black things."

Mia was eyeing her cake rather distrustfully.

"It's a sweet pastry made with grains and bean paste," I informed her, and she cautiously took a bite.

"...Yum."

With this brief statement of approval, Mia cupped the Gururian cake in her hands and began eating it reverently.

"I think it could stand to have a bit more sugar."

Critical though Arisa was, she devoured hers in an instant.

I'm guessing that if they used more sugar, which is always expensive, the pastries would cost even more.

"Hmm. So it's that, is it?"

"Yeah, it must be."

Arisa and I both recognized the pastry as *ohagi*, a traditional Japanese sweet.

Instead of mochi, there was a clump of glutinous rice that hadn't been pounded smooth.

The red-bean *anko* was lumpy, giving it the feel of a very traditional *ohagi*.

"So the name of this city..."

"Yeah, it must be a pun."

I couldn't tell this to anyone else—they would have to understand Japanese to get the joke—but there was no mistaking it. *Ohagi* was made by packing sweetened white rice together, then rolling it (*gururi*) in red-bean paste (*an*). That had to be where the name "Gururian" came from.

Whoever named this city was definitely a Japanese punster.

After we finished the *ohagi*, there was still no sign of Liza, Nana, or Jackass.

"I'm going to look for them. I'll bring Tama and Pochi as escorts, so the rest of you wait here, please."

With that, I headed into the crowd, holding Tama's and Pochi's hands.

Usually, this would end in even more kids getting lost, but I didn't need to worry about that as long as I had my radar.

"Anyone who wants a badge of participation for the preliminary battle, line up here! You don't need to go to the town hall. We'll sell you one right here at this branch office!"

A big bald man was holding up a bronze badge-like object and shouting.

Oh, so these were the badges you needed to bet to enter the match.

"The winner is the Wolf of Walt Village, Ton!"

And this round had just ended.

The young man named Ton received a badge from the winner. His friends crowded around him, handing him drinks and a towel to wipe his sweat.

"Wow, Ton! Three more and you can enter the prelims!"

"Psh, this is nothin'!"

Ton had seven badges crammed onto his shirt.

So you needed to win nine street matches to qualify for the preliminary round of the tournament.

"I'm not gonna stop at the prelims."

"Yeah, I bet you'll get four wins in the prelims and move on to the second round no problem, Ton!"

"Ha-ha, damn! If you get that far, you might get to be a knight."

No wonder people were so excited about making a splash in these matches, with a carrot like that in front of their faces.

This would increase the number of people who could fight off monsters in the territory, too, so it sounded like a good event overall.

The participants mostly ranged from levels 5 to 7, with very few of them more than level 10.

"There're still four more qualifying spots for Gururian City, so you've got this in the bag."

"I wouldn't let yer guard down. Last year, the three remaining spots all went in a day!"

"Yeah, I got no time for breaks. Who's going to be my next challenger? I'll take anybody on!"

A middle-aged man responded to Ton's hotheaded declaration, and another match began.

I was fairly interested in the match myself, but when I spotted Liza and Nana on the other side of the crowd, we went to meet up with them.

"Oh nooo?"

"Liza is being bullied, sir!"

As we got closer, we saw five good-looking young men surrounding Liza and Nana.

"Master, help is required, I request!"

Noticing me, Nana rushed up and grabbed my hand to drag me over.

I stood in front of the youths with Nana still attached to my hand.

"Who the hell are you?"

"I'm these young women's guardian."

These children were all from noble families living in Gururian City. All five of them had a blank space in the **affiliation** section of their profile.

None of them seemed to have a rank or title, and frankly, they probably didn't have jobs, either.

"Do you have some business with my children?"

Normally I would be more polite, but I remembered the advice Viscount Nina had given me during her political purge of Muno Barony: kowtowing to power-hungry young nobles would only go to their heads, so it was better to act haughty with them.

"I—I ordered that demi-human to hand over her magic spear, but she won't do as she's told!"

"A weapon like that would clearly be best suited in the hands of Horan here, the spear master..."

"If you're her master, you'd better order her to donate her spear to Lord Horan!"

So basically, these childish nobles were saying, *I want your weapon; give it to me.* How could someone in their mid-twenties be so unabashedly stupid?

By the way, the so-called "spear master" Horan did have the "Spear" skill, but he was only level 4. Liza could probably knock him out while whistling a tune.

As I was wondering how best to deal with these idiots, I got backup from an unexpected place.

"Hey, guys."

"What do you want? Back off, plebian."

The man who pushed his way through the group was none other than Tolma the jackass, still in his traveling clothes.

"Sorry, but we have to go see Lady Sara at the Tenion Temple, then say hi to our friend Lord Worgoch. If you have nothing else to do here, would you mind getting on your way?"

"Sara... Isn't that the duke's daughter who's staying in the Tenion Temple?"

"And Lord Worgoch is a viceroy, isn't he?"

Tolma's words set the young nobles quaking in their boots.

"Listen, commoner! It's poor manners to act friendly with those above your station! I'll make you pay for that right here and now!"

Horan, the ringleader of the cowering group, flew into a rage and drew his sword.

"My, you're short-tempered. Here, have a look at this."

Jackass reached into his coat and produced the dagger with the Siemmen family crest on it, showing it to the foolish young nobles.

"H-hey...!"

"Th-the biggest noble family in the old capital..."

Horan and the others all knew the name and crest of the Siemmen family; they drew back with exclamations of surprise. It was like when an undercover cop flashes their badge.

Smiling faintly, Jackass took a single step forward.

""""We're so sorry!""""

Immediately, the young nobles apologized in unison, then scrambled away toward the main street with their tails between their legs.

I certainly hadn't expected this guy to come to our rescue.

Guess I should probably go back to calling him Mr. Tolma in my head...

"That was a great help, Lord Tolma."

"Oh, not at all. Actually, I was hoping you could do a little favor for me anyway..."

Tolma pointed sheepishly at several food cart owners, who seemed to be waiting on him.

...So you didn't bring any money, huh?

All right, I'll drop the "Mr." From now on, he's just Tolma.

Once I'd paid for Tolma's food, we went and bought a few things to bring back for the others at his recommended stalls of choice. There were a lot of food cart staples, like chicken skewers and melons chilled in well water.

While we walked around, I asked Tolma why the nobles were so interested in Liza's magic spear.

"I see. So a magic spear would exempt them from the first preliminary round for the martial arts tournament?"

"That's right. Not just spears, either—Magic Swords and mithril blades and such work just as well."

"But even if they did get the exemption, wouldn't they just be sorely defeated in the second preliminary round if they don't have the strength to back it up?"

Did they want to join the tournament in the old capital that badly?

"That's not it. See, if you've gotten through the first round of qualifiers, you can enlist in the duke's royal guard."

"They would go to all that trouble to get into the royal guard?"

"You may not know this, Sir Satou, but the royal guard is something of a dream job to young nobles without titles of their own."

I see. So this was an underhanded way of getting a job offer from a place that would normally be out of their league.

Now I understood a little.

But whether I would actually go along with that was another question entirely.

I just hoped they would keep their little endeavor far away from me from now on.

◆

Once everyone had eaten the food we brought back from the stalls, we resumed our journey to Tenion Temple.

"People of Gururian City! Wake up from your false religion!"

I heard a suspicious-sounding call from outside the carriage window, so I moved next to Lulu and took a look.

The speaker was a man in a purple robe standing on top of a barrel at the side of the road.

He was part of that Wings of Freedom group of fanatics we'd encountered in Muno City.

"The gods do not want people to be happy! It is their will that permits us to go on cowering before the threat of monsters yet labels any movements toward freedom as 'taboo'! Good people! Now is the time to take back the freedom of humanfolk!"

The purple-robed man's speech was so insane that I wouldn't have been surprised to find him frothing at the mouth, but the people passing by gave him no reaction.

Only one person stood up to challenge his speech: Lady Knight, who was accompanying us.

As a knight whose job it was to defend the temple, she probably couldn't just let his heresy slide.

"Stand down, you demon-lord follower!"

"Tch! Damned watchdog of a foolish god!"

The minute he recognized Lady Knight, the purple-robed man jumped from the barrel and took off down an alley like a rabbit.

"Stop right there! You cur!"

His sudden dash must have triggered an instinctive reaction for Lady Knight, who took off after him on horseback.

Won't your boss be angry that you abandoned your duty of guarding baby Mayuna?

With that trivial thought passing through my mind, I searched the city map again for the Wings of Freedom.

For some reason, most of them were moving like they were being pursued. Most likely, they'd attempted to give speeches until the authorities or temple officials gave chase.

...Hmm?

Suddenly, a red spot appeared on the map.

Right on the street we were traveling on...

"Run away! There's a monster in the streets!"

A shout from the crowd caused a panic to break out on the main avenue.

Scores of people began fleeing from where the monster had appeared.

"Arisa!"

"Okeydoke!"

With a single deep breath, Arisa invoked her Psychic Magic spell Repellent Field.

After the Psychic Magic landed, the people fleeing all around us started to avoid our carriage, as if they'd seen something truly disgusting.

We'd used the same spell to deal with the people fleeing from the goblins in Muno City.

Once I saw that it was working, I checked the details of the red light on my radar.

It wasn't just a monster... It was a demon.

"Everyone but Lulu, prepare for battle. Lulu, please park the carriage on the side of the road."

Of course, the only "battle preparations" that really needed to be done were Arisa and Mia collecting their staffs and Tama and Pochi their short swords from the Garage Bag.

While they set about doing that, I pulled up the map.

The creature that had appeared was a lesser demon called a **short-horned demon**.

He was level 30, with only the race-specific abilities Transform and Flame Hand and the skills "Super Strength" and "Hard Body"; he had no magic-type skills at all. He was probably meant to be some kind of advance guard.

By all appearances, he was already engaged in battle, surrounded by knights and warriors from levels 13 to 33.

There were at least three people around the same level as the demon, so they should be all right without me... *No, wait.*

"It takes a full squadron to stand a chance at defeating even a lesser hell demon, and you still risk losing half."

The temple knight Sir Keon's words echoed in my mind.

I didn't know how large a squadron of knights was, but it was probably more than seven.

Besides...near the demon, my radar showed the blue dots that indicated acquaintances of mine. Two of them.

I couldn't just look the other way.

"Lulu, you wait here. Take care of the horses and the carriage. You too, Mia and Arisa—"

"Coming."

"I'm coming, too, of course!"

Mia and Arisa didn't even let me finish telling them to stay before they refused.

"All right. Just hang back and cover me. Nana, keep Lulu safe. Liza, follow me and direct Tama and Pochi."

"Master, here."

Arisa handed me the fairy sword and its belt.

"Thank you, Arisa. Let's go!"

With that, I rushed through the thinning crowd.

As the others followed, I told them that it was a demon up ahead, not a monster, and explained his level, skills, and things to watch out for in the battle.

I planned to leave the fighting to the knights and provide them support from behind, while the others transported or healed the wounded.

The beastfolk girls had higher defense than the knights of the same level, so as long as I covered them well, they should be able to stand up to even a lesser demon.

Still, I had no idea why a demon had materialized in the middle of the city all of a sudden like this.

At the very least, I was certain there'd been no demons here when we entered the city.

In fact, there hadn't been any in the entire duchy. He didn't seem able to teleport, either, so someone had either summoned him or sent him here.

Eventually, there were no more fleeing crowds at all, just abandoned carts and carriages littered around the street.

When we turned the corner at the intersection of the main road, we saw the knights and warriors fighting the demon.

The demon himself was quite different from the one in Muno City. He resembled a huge red gorilla with six arms and short horns.

The remains of demolished carriages lay scattered around the battle-field, as well as several large holes in the buildings facing the street.

A few warriors were slumped on the ground around the demon, unable to fight any longer.

Miraculously, there seemed to be no casualties as of yet. But if this went on much longer, people would surely die.

Judging by the situation, the injured were too close to the rampaging demon to be rescued.

The demon's powerful arms struck a few people fighting at the fore-front, and they were propelled into the air, as high as if they'd bounced off a trampoline, toward us.

If they hit the ground like that, even the heavily armored knights might lose their lives.

"Mia! Use Balloon!"

With the fairy sword, I slashed open a barrel of liquor lying nearby on the ground and flung it toward the area where the knights were about to land.

"...■ ■ ■ ■ ■ *Balloon Kyuubouchou!*"

Mia's magic produced an explosive torrent of steam that canceled out the falling knights' downward acceleration.

That should keep them alive, at the very least. Hopefully they can just walk it off.

One of the fighters was on a slightly different trajectory and also happened to be a beautiful woman. Quickly, I darted over to catch her.

"...Wh-what?"

The woman, clad in a dress, had squeezed her eyes shut in preparation for the impact and now blinked a few times.

"Please try not to put yourself in harm's way, Lady Karina."

"Sa... Er, Sir *Pendragon!*"

Realizing who had caught her, Miss Karina flew into a panic.

I got why she was stammering, but what was up with this ritual of alternately entwining and releasing her fingers over her chest? Was this her way of acting bashful?

On top of that, she kept mumbling increasingly absurd comments in my arms, from "Heavens, to think you would hold me like this twice!" to "You're surprisingly strong, aren't you?" to, finally, "Perhaps we'll go to the royal capital for our honeymoon..."

Clearly, her inability to handle any physical contact with the opposite sex hadn't changed since our last encounter.

"I forbid you to princess-carry anyooone!"

"Mm, forbidden."

Once they'd caught up behind me, Arisa and Mia immediately lodged their complaints.

Meanwhile, Tama and Pochi were giving recovery potions to the knights who had just fallen.

"Thank you for your assistance, Sir Pendragon," said Raka, the sentient necklace blinking blue at Miss Karina's chest. I responded by politely asking him to help his master stop throwing herself into danger.

Even with Raka's protection, Miss Karina had still lost about 20 percent of her health, so I asked Mia to heal her.

As I put Miss Karina down, she grabbed onto my sleeve, but she appeared to have as little idea of why as I did.

Mia narrowed her eyes, but she began casting the spell to heal Miss Karina nonetheless.

"Master, the front lines are about to give way."

"We'll heeelp!"

"You can come, too, Karina, ma'am!"

Tama and Pochi each patted one of Karina's breasts in greeting, then stood on either side of Liza.

Why do they get to do that...?

"All right! I'll take the lead. Liza, you and the others help the wounded first."

I could hardly imitate Pochi and Tama's greeting, so I simply gave a light wave before dashing into battle.

On the front lines, two more people had collapsed, leaving only the level-33 imperial knight Sir Ipasa and a level-29 warrior with a large shield.

Both of them were bloodied and slowing down.

The demon fired three shots of Flame Hand, which rocketed like bullets into the warrior's shield.

The stone paving broke beneath the warrior's feet, sending up enough dirt to cover his ankles.

Before the dirt hit the ground, the demon spun around and hit the warrior with his tail, knocking him away.

The warrior rolled over two times, then three, finally crashing through the wall of a nearby house and landing somewhere inside.

Contrary to his heavy-looking appearance, the demon was very light on his feet.

Sir Ipasa's sword slashed at the demon but was blocked by his tail, and the demon prepared to shoot a Flame Hand at the defenseless imperial knight.

Just as he released the shot, I used the Pit spell right beneath his feet to throw off his balance.

The spell rocketed off course, grazing Sir Ipasa's armor and sending him tumbling across the ground a few feet.

As the knight attempted to rise, I saw a trail of burn marks across his chest plate. It looked painful but probably still a lot better than a direct hit would have been.

Sir Ipasa attempted to stand up but finally toppled to the ground, gushing blood.

The demon slowly approached the pair to finish them off.

Both of them had less than 10 percent of their health left.

And their position wasn't looking good.

I had no choice.

I didn't want to draw attention to myself, but I could at least shield the fallen fighters until they recovered.

"Liza, fight from a distance! Make evasion your top priority!"

"Understood!"

After giving Liza her orders, I double-checked the information displayed in the AR next to the demon.

This guy was tough. He still had almost 90 percent of his health left.

"Over here! You ugly gorilla!" I shouted, using the "Taunt" skill on my voice.

The demon immediately charged at me, leaping over the heads of Liza and the others with ease as they tried to attack.

As he dropped toward me from the sky, he pulled back his arm.

Then, in the next instant—

He came down at me like a cannonball.

I dodged him at point-blank range by twisting my body to the side.

The Fire Hand flew past me, hot air brushing by my cheek.

"Sir Pe— Satou!"

"Master!"

"Satou!"

I thought I heard Miss Karina, Arisa, and Mia shout from behind me.

The demon's burning hand plunged deep into the ground in a spray of rock and earth.

Looking up, I saw the demon's eyes distorted with hatred.

I guess he hadn't been expecting me to dodge.

The limb shriveled up and vanished into the earth.

Meanwhile, three of the demon's arms on his other side came flying at me with the same force as the previous attack.

It looked potentially painful, so I avoided it with a light jump.

Drawing my fairy sword, I infused it with just enough magic to strengthen it without invoking "Spellblade."

Moments later, the demon's short tail stretched out from behind and lashed at me like a whip. It was the same surprise attack that had knocked out the warrior not long ago.

I narrowly avoided giving in to the instinct to slice off the tail. Instead, I hopped back to avoid it and its cloud of dust, waited for the right moment, and nailed the demon directly in the face.

With an incomprehensible gurgling shriek, the demon stopped moving for a moment.

It was a perfect opening, so I decided to give a light slash to the demon's ankle with the fairy sword.

It took a lot of effort not to carelessly lop his leg off in the process.

"Ooh! It cut through the demon's super-tough pelt!"

"Even the knights couldn't get anywhere with it! That's crazy!"

"What a beautiful blade..."

"It's gotta be a dwarven mithril sword!"

"He must be some famous swordsman, then. Who is he?"

What's with all the comments from the peanut gallery?

Springing lightly aside to avoid another tail attack, I searched my surroundings.

In a nearby alleyway, five or so well-dressed children were peeking around the corner. I had an audience. I'd drawn the demon away from the previous battlefield, and people who'd been hiding in the nearby buildings worked together to carry away the injured, including Sir Ipasa and the warrior.

By now, hopefully they were getting recovery potions in the safety of the buildings.

Suddenly, a clear ringing echoed through the street, and the demon's movements slowed mid–Fire Hand.

The AR display next to him showed the words **Power reduced by 30 percent**.

Turning to the source of the sound, I saw Arisa ringing the demon-sealing bell, which was emitting a pale-blue light. Miss Karina had probably handed it off to her.

"Aim for his legs."

"Aye-aye, siiir!"

"Roger, sir!"

Tama and Pochi jumped in under Liza's instructions.

The beastfolk girls darted around, jabbing at the backs of the demon's knees.

Irritated, the demon tried to drive them away by swinging his tail around, but by that time all three of them were already out of his range.

So they were going with the same "attack once, then retreat" strategy we'd employed in monster battles in the Seiryuu City labyrinth.

"Over here! I'm your opponent!"

I used "Taunt" again to draw the demon's attention.

Just then, two Flame Shots struck the demon's body and exploded. Arisa and Mia were using the Fire Rods we'd confiscated from the thieves.

"Magic won't work…"

"His fur must be resistant to flame."

"Maybe if you hit inside his mouth?"

According to the peanut gallery, the Fire Rods wouldn't have any effect here.

"I shall assist you! Sir Pendragon!"

Miss Karina, rushing in like a whirlwind as usual, sent a flying kick square into the side of the demon's face.

I wish she hadn't shouted my name. Is she deliberately trying to advertise my identity?

She was glancing this way as if hoping I would call out her name, too, but I stoutly refused.

I couldn't spoil her like that.

Realizing that the Fire Rod wasn't working, Mia instead used the Water Magic spell Irritation Mist, burning the demon's lungs.

I shot her an accusing glare when my lungs started stinging, too, but she carefully avoided my eyes.

While I was distracted, the demon came at me with a Fire Hand.

"You mustn't look away during a battle, you know." Miss Karina diverted the incoming attack with a kick and looked at me with a triumphant grin.

"Lady Karina! Do not let your guard down!"

Raka's advice came too late, as a Fire Hand from the demon's opposite side promptly flung her across the battlefield.

Maybe next time you shouldn't look away, either.

Luckily, Raka's powerful defense protected Miss Karina, so she would be fine.

Even after receiving such a fierce blow, she was almost entirely unharmed. It would probably just leave her head spinning for a moment.

The defense of the multilayered "scales" that Raka produced around her was far stronger than the comparable Practical Magic spell Shield, so much so that I wished I could equip my own kids with such a durable automatic self-defense mechanism.

That little incident aside, our battle continued steadily. It was tedious, but I just had to deal. I couldn't become distracted and let one of my kids get hurt.

WHOOOOOSH!

Fed up with his inability to hit me, the demon swung his arm around and around in the air above his head.

"Get back!"

The beastfolk girls jumped away on my command, and seconds later the earth exploded into clouds of dust under the demon's attack.

""""Waaah! My eyes, my eeeyes!""""

The kids in the alley shrieked and covered their faces. So the dust got into their eyes, did it?

No one could see me in the debris, and I took this opportunity to circle around behind my foe and incapacitate his other leg with a slash.

While I was at it, I got in a few jabs at his shoulder joints.

I didn't manage to hold back as much as I intended, though, and the demon's health was cut down by about 70 percent.

I hurriedly shook the blood off the sword and wiped it clean before the dust cleared.

"Look, look!"

"We're winning now!"

"There's blood all over his legs and back!"

"It must've been the Scalefolk lady with the magic spear!"

"Did those little kids do the legs, then?"

The noisy onlookers had already recovered, but luckily they seemed to have fallen for my trick.

As blood dripped from his wounds, the demon chased after me, fists raised, whipping his tail at me.

Then, a blue light shimmered from the roof of a nearby building.

"Karinaaa Kiiiiiiick!!"

Calling out a silly-sounding attack name, Miss Karina rained flying kicks down on the demon's head.

The demon was starting to dodge when I kicked his jaw upward, trapping him between me and Karina's barrage of attacks.

I felt an unpleasant crunch under the sole of my foot as the demon's skull cracked open.

His health gauge was draining with incredible speed now.

"Liza! Now!"

"Understood!"

Liza's magic spear drew a red arc of light in the air as it drove into the demon's neck. "Ha!" She twisted it in deeper.

For just a moment, the tip of the spear glowed red.

Liza herself didn't seem to have noticed, but she'd used "Spellblade" just now.

His health drained to zero, the demon crumbled into black dust. The wind swept the chaff away, erasing the traces of his existence.

Stooping, Liza picked something up from the ground where the dust had been.

"Master, I've collected a core and what appears to be a horn."

"A horn?"

The objects Liza handed me were a small core about the size of my thumb and a tiny red horn.

The core was normal enough, but when I looked closer at the other object, the AR display showed the name **short horn**. The detailed description read, **Transforms an intelligent creature into a demon**.

So that was why a demon had suddenly appeared in the city.

I searched for other similar items on the map, but I couldn't find any.

However, I couldn't search inside other people's Item Boxes, Garage Bags, and so on. I couldn't say for sure that they didn't exist.

Well, I could think about that later.

After putting the thing away in Storage, I set out to rescue the wounded.

First, I headed back to where Sir Ipasa and the others had been fighting—specifically, the area where three or so carriages had smashed together.

The blue spot on my radar was close now.

I jumped onto a simple temple carriage and entered the open door.

"…Lady Sara."

I called out to her, but her eyelids remained closed, trembling in pain.

Her HP was down by about 40 percent, and her status conditions read **Unconscious** and **Internal Injuries**, so I produced a magic potion to pour into her mouth.

However, the potion simply trickled back out of her lips, making it difficult to get her to swallow it.

Though I felt bad about it, I had no choice but to convey the potion to her mouth-to-mouth. This time, I felt the magic potion pass through her soft lips and flow down her throat.

Miss Sara's eyes opened weakly.

I drew my face away from hers, waiting for her to wake up completely.

"...Sir Pendragon?"

"Are you awake now?"

"Y-yes..."

I lifted Miss Sara in my arms and carried her out of the carriage.

I wasn't sure when exactly Miss Sara regained consciousness. She had her head down and kept pressing her fingers to her lips, so I couldn't read her expression.

But I did what I did only as an emergency treatment method, so it didn't count, all right?

◆

Just because we rescued Miss Sara didn't mean the chaos was over.

Once we had brought her and the other wounded parties to the temple, we parted ways with Tolma and his family there. We were then summoned to the viceroy's castle, where I received his thanks, a medal, a hundred gold coins, and an invitation to stay for a banquet.

Only Miss Karina and I were able to enjoy the superbly delicious dinner, so I decided to do my best to reproduce the dishes for the rest of the group later.

Once the banquet was over, we moved to the salon for some friendly conversation.

Courtly ladies who were indulging in some romantic gossip surrounded Miss Karina.

"Lady Karina, is Sir Pendragon your fiancé?"

"...N-no, he is not."

Miss Karina answered the viceroy's wife after a suspicious pause.

She acted haughty but was actually quite shy, so she was having a hard time interacting with all these new faces.

I would've liked to throw her a lifeline, but I myself was being besieged by men with questions about the defense of Muno City and the battle with the demon earlier that day.

"If you can defeat a demon, surely a swordsman like yourself could even aspire to victory at the martial arts tournament!"

"Thank you, but as I said before, all we did was deal the finishing

blow after the knights and warriors had already brought the demon near death. And without the help of my comrades and the protection of magic, I am certain I would have fallen in battle myself."

One of the nobles was insisting that I should enter the tournament, so I repeated my explanation while politely declining.

I would really rather watch a tournament than fight in it.

Oh, and speaking of knights...

I found out why the imperial knight Sir Ipasa was defending Miss Sara from the lesser demon that afternoon instead of the temple knight Sir Keon.

As it turned out, the temple knights were away on a mission to take down the Wings of Freedom.

That must have been why it looked like someone was chasing around the cult members earlier.

Incidentally, the female knight who'd abandoned her post defending baby Mayuna in favor of pursuing the cultist had received a sound scolding from a higher-up at the temple.

"You're saying that even if you go to the old capital, you won't be participating in the martial arts tournament?"

The viceroy seemed bewildered to hear that I wouldn't be participating. Did I really look like that much of a fighter?

"That's right. I'm not terribly well suited to competition, I'm afraid..."

"You know, if I formally recommend you, you can bypass the preliminaries and participate in the final selection."

"I think such an honor would be better bestowed upon your own worthy warriors, Your Excellency."

"Hmm. I see... What a humble young man you are."

After I repeatedly declined, the viceroy finally accepted my decision.

"Incidentally, Sir Pendragon, I've been told that your sword was able to cut through the demon's hide. Is it the work of a master sword smith, perchance?"

"Yes, Elder Dohal of the Bolehart dominion did me the great honor of forging it." I gave an honest answer to the old noble's question.

"Wh-what did you say?!"

"You got that crusty Elder Dohal to make a sword for you? I'm impressed, Sir Satou!"

"That old fellow refuses to make a sword for anyone who doesn't suit his fancy, even a high-ranking noble..."

"P-perhaps it was Viscount Lottel's recommendation?"

The nobles raised a chorus of surprise. The only person who seemed relaxed was Tolma, who'd managed an invitation to the dinner. He was dressed like a proper noble now, apparently having borrowed clothes from the viceroy's home.

Still, Elder Dohal's reputation carried impressive clout.

The viceroy and company were all dying to see the sword, so we had it brought to the salon. I had given it into their custody when I came to the castle.

"It can't be—a seal?!"

Accepting the fairy sword from the steward, the viceroy gave an exclamation of shock when his eyes landed on the hilt.

The rest of the clamoring nobles had a similar reaction.

"That's the seal that they say is only affixed to true masterpieces, even among Elder Dohal's works!"

"I've never seen it in person before."

"The craftsmanship on this hilt is incredible, too."

"Heavens, the sheath alone has value as a beautiful work of art. I would love to have such an elegant piece for my own sword, to be sure. What workshop produced this?"

The sword was causing a fuss before it even left the sheath.

I had actually just fashioned this in a hurry upon being invited to the viceroy's dinner party, since I didn't want to show up with a plain black sheath, so I didn't really have a good answer to that question.

Instead, I decided to just say that I got it from Elder Dohal as well.

Drawing the sword, I placed it on a stand that the steward produced to show it to the viceroy.

"Its inscription is 'the Fairy Sword.'"

"What a beautifully patterned blade."

"This green and silver edge is difficult to produce even with the finest mithril."

"Truly, only Elder Dohal could have fashioned such a sword."

It certainly was a beautiful weapon, but I hadn't expected it to captivate these discerning nobles so completely.

I'd have to be careful not to show it off to any strangers.

"If you'll pardon me, I'm going to get a bit of air."

I excused myself from the salon for a short time. The viceroy had been regaling us with tales of his youthful mischief while we enjoyed his prize liquor, but when the topic turned to Gururian City's private politics, I thought it best to take my leave. An outsider probably shouldn't be hearing this anyway.

I opened the balcony door and went out onto the veranda. Though we were on the second floor, the courtyard was level with the terrace.

I closed the glass door behind me. According to what I'd heard earlier, it was made in a workshop in the old capital. Glasswork was relatively common in the Ougoch Duchy.

"Sir Pendragon?"

A clear voice called my name, and I turned to see Miss Sara, her hair glimmering silver in the moonlight.

She looked almost like...

"...A fairy."

"Oh my, Sir Pendragon..."

The second half of my thought escaped from my lips against my better judgment. My "Fabrication" skill must have betrayed me because of all the alcohol.

"Good evening, Lady Sara. Please forget my comment; it was a slip of the tongue."

"Hee-hee. I certainly will not."

Perhaps because there was no one else around, Miss Sara's usual restraint had given way to a more relaxed manner typical of girls her age.

Because my long name seemed a bit difficult for her to pronounce, I told her she could simply call me Satou.

"Well, Mr. Satou, shall we take a stroll around the garden?"

"Yes, it would be my pleasure."

Miss Sara gave a mischievous smile.

The courtyard contained a small water feature resembling a creek, lined with evening primroses blossoming with a faint glow under the moonlight. They seemed to be emitting the light themselves, so they must have been different from any primroses I'd seen in Japan.

From beneath the flowers, I heard what sounded like the call of crickets.

"Oh, fireflies...!"

Following her gaze, I saw two fireflies twirling among the primroses in a dance.

"It's quite beautiful."

A mysterious young beauty in a fantastical garden. It was a scene perfect enough to paint. If I could, I'd insert Lulu into the painting as well.

Miss Sara and I walked along the waterway amid the sounds of the bubbling brook and the chirping insects.

I could feel the calm returning to my heart and mind.

What a therapeutic atmosphere.

"Satou...can I ask you something?" Still gazing straight ahead, Miss Sara murmured to me quietly. "Do you think...you can change fate?"

Well, that's a pretty heavy topic.

Sure, I was all about that stuff when I was still going through puberty, but not so much now that I'm older.

A vaguely positive answer was probably my best bet here.

"Of course." Miss Sara reacted with surprise at my prompt, clear response, so I decided to elaborate a little. "There's no such thing as a destiny that can't be changed."

I mean, I don't think anyone can change things like the Big Crunch or whatever, but that's probably not what she's asking about.

"You...really think so?" Miss Sara faltered, as if she was struggling with some inner conflict.

I had no doubt that a girl like Sara, who was both a duke's daughter and an oracle priestess, had all kinds of troubles weighing on her.

"Yes, I do. So if someone tries to force some silly fate on you, just let me know and I'll put a stop to it with my own two hands if I have to."

I answered as lightly as possible, trying to lift her spirits and help her forget her worries.

Her fingers entwined behind her back, Miss Sara turned to me with a little giggle.

"Even if a demon lord is about to kill me?"

"Yes, of course I'd save you from a demon lord. Why, I'd knock him out before he knew what hit him." I responded in kind to Miss Sara's lighthearted prod, finally eliciting a genuine chuckle from her.

She laughed so hard that tears came to her eyes, so I gave her a handkerchief. "...I'm glad you're here, Satou." Miss Sara wiped the tears from her eyes and crinkled them up in a smile. "Thank you."

Her faint smile looked about to disappear at any moment, and I had a sudden urge to embrace her. Still, I managed to resist the impulse.

A strange silence fell over us for a moment.

What was I thinking? This girl was practically half my age. Maybe if she were five years older it'd be a different story, but...

...well, I guess technically, in this body I *was* her age.

"Oh? If it isn't Sir Satou and Sara. Having a little rendezvous?"

A voice from the darkness made Miss Sara flinch. From behind a particularly tall shrub, Tolma emerged onto the path.

"T-Tolma! Satou and I would never do something so unseemly!"

"Oh really? Because you appear to be calling him by his first name..."

At times like this, Tolma's constant inability to read a situation actually came in handy.

"Oh, you!" Miss Sara pouted crossly at Tolma's teasing.

"Lord Tolma, no need to tease her any further, please."

"You're awfully mature for your age, Sir Satou. I can't get a rise out of you, huh?"

Well, yeah, because I'm actually almost thirty on the inside.

"I was simply thanking Satou for his help today."

"So far away from prying eyes?"

"Tolma!"

"Sorry, I'll stop, I'll stop."

I thought it was a fair enough question, but Miss Sara put the brakes on Tolma's remarks by furrowing her lovely eyebrows.

"I wouldn't want any of us to catch a cold from being outside too late. We should go back to the salon soon."

"...I suppose so."

"Oh? You're going back? I was just about to leave so you could continue your little date."

With that, the nobleman jokingly fled toward the path back to the salon as if to avoid Miss Sara's last exclamation of "Tolmaaa!" The two of us followed after him.

As we walked, Tolma struck up a new conversation.

"Still, it's a miracle that there wasn't a single casualty in that little demon brawl today."

"Yes, thanks to God's protection and the help of Satou and his friends. The injured can be healed with magic, but there's nothing we can do for the dead..."

Though Tolma's tone was casual, Miss Sara responded in a manner befitting a person of the temple.

I appreciated her giving credit to my group as well, but one of the things she said grabbed my attention even more.

"Is there no magic that can resurrect the dead?"

"...No, none."

Caught off guard by my question, Miss Sara took a moment before responding.

Man, I can't believe a fantasy world like this has no Resurrection Magic! What a damn shame!

"Aren't you forgetting something, Sara? When that young noble was murdered, the holy woman—"

"Tolma!"

Miss Sara's expression darkened at Tolma's latest slip-up, and her admonition came in a completely different tone.

"Sorry, sorry, I forgot we aren't supposed to talk about that. Sir Satou, please forget what you just heard, all right?"

"Certainly. I didn't hear a thing."

I readily accepted Tolma's request.

My guess was that either the existence of some resurrection item was being kept a secret, or perhaps the requirements for using it were so strict that it could be used only under specific conditions.

If some half-baked rumors about resurrection went around, it would surely cause an uproar from people wanting to use it.

"Were you out for a walk, Lady Sara?"

The viceroy greeted the three of us when we returned to the salon.

It was a good thing Tolma showed up. If Miss Sara and I had returned together, it would have undoubtedly sown the seeds for some unwelcome gossip.

For some reason, Miss Karina seemed to be eyeing me rather sharply. Perhaps she was angry that I left without bailing her out.

"I went to the garden to look for you myself, but we must have missed each other," said the viceroy's wife.

"Did you need something from me?" Miss Sara tilted her head.

"Yes, in fact, a courier came from the Tenion Temple just a short while ago..." The viceroy's wife's tone was gentle.

Thanking her, Miss Sara started toward the room where the courier was waiting.

For some reason, Tolma went after her, so I ended up following along as well. I was curious about the nature of the courier.

"...An urgent summons from the Tenion Temple in the old capital?"

"Yes, but it was conveyed with signal lights from the great river, so I'm afraid I don't know the particulars."

"I understand. I shall borrow an express ship from the viceroy and return home at once, then."

As I listened to Sara's exchange with the priest, I opened the map to check the situation around the old capital and the Tenion Temple, but I didn't see any signs of a major disturbance.

It was probably an internal problem in the temple, then.

Sailing at night was banned even in emergencies, so it was decided that the viceroy would prepare an express ship so that Miss Sara could leave for the old capital first thing in the morning.

"Take care on your journey home, Lady Sara."

"Thank you, Satou. Let us meet again in the old capital."

I saw Miss Sara off that morning at the docks for the exclusive use of nobles.

Arisa and Mia were watching from behind as if they'd caught me with a mistress, but I didn't feel a single shred of guilt about saying my farewells to a friend.

The bells of Gururian City rang to announce that a vessel was passing through on urgent business.

The sound echoed off the water as if the great river were calling out in response.

Someone waved a flag from the control tower of the docks, and the express ship waiting on the open river suddenly took off in a spray of water.

"Faaaast?"

"So speedy, sir!"

Watching at my side, Tama and Pochi waved frantically in surprise.

As I understood it, express ships were equipped with a high-speed propeller that operated on magic, so they could move over the water at speeds up to sixty miles per hour.

I caught only a brief glimpse, but it seemed to be related to the hydrofoil.

Express ships had a very small capacity for passengers, I'd heard, so the only person accompanying Lady Sara was the temple knight Sir Keon. Tolma and his family, as well as the other temple knights, would be taking a larger ship provided by the viceroy to the old capital.

I planned to request passage on the same ship as a reward for defeating the demon.

Journey on the Great River

Satou here. My parents always thought of travel by boat as a luxurious cruise, but as a member of the lower middle class, I tend to think of taking a ferry to a remote island. Either way, I believe the image of a boat leaving a wake through the waves is classic.

Two days after Miss Sara departed, we embarked on the viceroy's ship with Tolma and his family, Miss Karina's party, and the temple knight guards.

The ship was bigger than I'd pictured, with enough room to load several carriages onto the deck.

Ours was the only carriage this time, so we had some of the harbor workers load it up the day before. Most of them were twenty-foot-tall golems or little giants, and watching them use the harbor's loading crane to move our carriage onto the ship left us impressed.

The steam whistle sounded, signaling our departure.

Actually, since it's a tool that operates on magic instead of steam, maybe I should call it a magic flute?

"Weigh anchor!"

The sailors moved quickly at the captain's command.

The captain was a human, but more than half the sailors were beastfolk. Flying-type demi-humans, like birdfolk and batfolk, were in charge of lookout duties on the main mast.

I leaned against the deck railing, waving to the people who had come to see us off.

"Lord Satoou, Lady Mia, come play again somedaaay! Oh, and you too, Arisa."

The loudest voice belonged to the viceroy's daughter.

She was one of the children who'd been in the peanut gallery during the demon battle. I had assumed that they were all boys, so I was quite surprised when I first found out.

She had begged for magic lessons upon learning that Mia was an elf, and Mia had delivered, with interpretation and supplementary explanations by Arisa and yours truly.

She had evidently gotten a little attached to me in the process, not that I let that go anywhere. She was only around middle school age.

Despite being acknowledged as an afterthought, Arisa was waving back quite cheerfully.

That was Arisa for you, though. Being a reincarnation and all, she was really very adult—

"Mwa-ha-ha! Like I was going to let a new character raise any flags. Disappear from our story forever!"

A "new character"...? Was that how Arisa saw the viceroy's daughter? She was particularly wicked today.

As the ship turned, I bopped Arisa lightly on the head. Then we both walked to the bow, where Pochi and Tama were gleefully watching the water.

"Are there members of that cult in the old capital, too?"

"Yeah. It's a bigger group than I realized at first."

As we spoke, I dutifully supported Arisa by the waist as she stretched her arms out wide at the prow.

"Will you be cleaning them out again, then?"

"As much as I can. Some of them are high-ranking nobles this time, though, so it might not be as easy as before."

The Wings of Freedom members in Gururian City had been rounded up and imprisoned after I gave their names and whereabouts to the authorities.

A few had escaped, but I captured them in the dead of night under a black hood and brought them to prison with the rest.

"Are you going to tell the duke about that horn?"

The horn Arisa was referring to was the "short horn" that could turn humans into demons.

"Probably. I just want to meet him and get a feel for him first."

"Yeah, good idea."

Sure, the idea of lesser demons suddenly appearing in cities was scary, but so was the idea of an insurgence bred by paranoia and fear.

"I never expected terrorists to exist in a fantasy world."

"No kidding." I agreed wholeheartedly with Arisa's complaint.

"Um, Sir Viscount, this is rather dangerous, so if you wouldn't mind..."

Where we were standing was supposed to be off-limits, but we had managed to get permission at Arisa's insistent request.

The guide who was in charge of meeting our needs looked distressed, though, so I returned to the deck with a satisfied-looking Arisa in tow.

"That's one more thing I can check off the bucket list from my old life!"

It seemed she had wanted to reenact a scene from a famous American movie.

It did seem familiar, and the movie had achieved enough acclaim for me to recognize the title, but I had been too busy with work to see anything but the trailer.

"Now then, allow me to show you to your rooms."

The tour guide led us down the stairs to the guest rooms at the rear of the ship.

The sizable ship had three floors altogether, including the deck; the second floor had guest rooms and the captain's cabin; and the third floor had rooms for livestock, cargo, and the sailors' quarters.

The old capital was almost two hundred miles downriver, but with the viceroy's special vessel, we would get there in a scant two days.

On a normal ship, it would take three or four days with all the stops in the four other cities and towns on the way to the old capital.

I'd been concerned about seasickness, but the only victims were one of Miss Karina's maids (who was down within the first half hour of the trip) and Tolma (who went down after an hour).

There were many others who had never been on a ship before, but nobody else got seasick.

The tour guide gave seasickness medication to Tolma and the maid, so they would recover soon enough.

After we put our luggage in the room, I gave everyone some free time.

"I love this breeze."

"Yes, it smells very nice. Like the river and the flora."

I leaned back on the sofa that the tour guide had set up for us on the deck and took a sip from a goblet of fruit-flavored water. Instead of a fancy sofa you might see in a noble's house, this one was simple and moisture-resistant.

Liza was sitting nearby on a round mat made of woven grass, squinting into the gentle wind that rippled through her vermilion hair.

Even on the ship, she still had her beloved magic spear close by her side.

Obviously, wearing armor would've been a bit much, though, so today she had put on a simple dress that matched the other kids' clothing. Each of them had a unique pattern; Liza's was designed after red flames.

The other kids were off exploring the ship.

I hadn't expected Lulu to join them, but I could understand why her curiosity got the better of her when she'd never been on a ship this size before.

While I reflected on this, Miss Karina came back from touring the craft.

"I've nothing to do at all."

"Lady Karina, why don't you join the girls in exploring the ship?"

"…Am I not welcome here, Sir Pendragon?"

Miss Karina looked down at me with a pout that was almost entirely obscured by her enormous chest. I exchanged glances with Liza, who stood to prepare a spare sofa for her.

Well, the only "preparation" involved was just removing the waterproof sheet draped over it.

"Of course you are. Would you like to have a seat?"

"…Yes, thank you."

Miss Karina sat down gracefully on the sofa Liza had readied for her.

Making a mental note of how the law of inertia affected her giant breasts, I addressed Miss Karina.

"Would you like some fruit water? It's quite energizing."

"It's…energizing?"

"Certainly. It's like nothing you've ever had before."

"Energizing… Like nothing I've ever…"

Mumbling something incomprehensible, Miss Karina glanced a few times between my mouth and the goblet I was holding out to her.

"N-no, thank you, I'm…I'm not terribly thirsty at present."

Flushing bright red, she emphatically shook her head and both her hands no. The dance of her magical boobs was captivating.

I don't know what she thought I meant, but I suppose a young woman of her age had quite a powerful imagination.

After a few minutes, she seemed to calm down a little, but she remained scarlet-faced and avoided my eyes.

Just then, Tama and Pochi returned from their exploration.

"We're baaack."

"Sir!"

"Welcome back."

I caught them in midair as they leaped at me, placing them on either side of the sofa.

They looked thirsty, so I offered them more fruit water from the side table.

"So fizzyyy?"

"It's bubbling in my mouth, sir!"

The two beastfolk girls jumped to their feet on the sofa, staring at the cups they were clutching in both hands.

Both of them were widening their eyes in surprise. Tama's tail was even puffed up.

"Ooh, this is carbonated, isn't it?! Goodness, it's been so long!"

Arisa stole my goblet, took a sip, and exclaimed loudly.

In this duchy, natural carbonated water existed, so it was sold relatively cheaply in the cities along the great river.

"Unfair."

Mia yanked the goblet from Arisa's hands and put it to her lips.

She didn't seem surprised by the carbonated fruit water, so maybe it was common in the elf village.

"No need to squabble, girls. There are plenty more cups right there on the table."

"You just don't get it, do you...?"

"Mm. Dense."

That was rude. All I did was point out the obvious.

Lulu smiled affectionately at the scene as she poured the drink into a new goblet.

"Lulu, make sure you only fill it halfway."

"R-right... W-waah!"

Lulu panicked as the carbonated liquid started to bubble up.

Quickly, I scooped away the goblet and slurped up the foam before it could overflow.

"There, it should be fine now."

"Thank you very much, master. Stay still for a moment, please."

Lulu wiped away the foam on my upper lip with a handkerchief.

"Well done, my dear sister. Allow me to dispose of this handkerchief for—"

"No, thank you, Arisa. I'll wash it myself."

Arisa, who had somehow reappeared next to Lulu, tried to tug the handkerchief out of her sister's hands.

While Lulu seemed occupied with their little game, I poured some fruit water for Nana in her place.

"Thank you, master, I report."

"Be carefuuul?"

"It's very fizzy, ma'am."

Tama and Pochi gave a serious warning to Nana as she lifted the carbonated beverage to her lips.

"Your advice has been registered. I will be careful, I report."

After nodding to Tama and Pochi, Nana took a sip...

"Master!"

...and jerked toward me with a doll-like movement.

"Master, this fruit water is alive, I report."

"It's just carbonic acid. It fizzes because of a chemical reaction."

Nana seemed alarmed despite her ever-present blank expression, so I tried to reassure her.

For a moment, I'd considered making up a story to tease her a little, but I decided against it; she'd probably believe me.

"Sa— Sir Pendragon, could you perhaps spare a glass for me as well?"

Miss Karina, who'd been peeking at us surreptitiously for a while, finally gave in to her curiosity.

"Sure, I'll pour you one."

"Let me take care of that, master."

Having triumphed in her battle with Arisa, Lulu returned to her work with a lively smile.

Tama and Pochi, already tired of the novelty of carbonation, clambered onto the sofa to sit next to me.

It was meant to be a two-seater, so it was pretty cramped.

"Togetherrr?"

"Sir!"

Once Tama and Pochi were settled on the sofa, Liza handed them the rest of their drinks.

"I call the lap!"

Arisa raised her hands demandingly, so I picked her up and placed her on my lap as requested.

"Mrrrr."

Mia grumbled crossly, but there was no space left.

Instead, she tottered around behind the sofa and sat on the back behind my head, messing around with my hair.

"Mia, please stop touching my hair."

"...Mm."

Mia did leave my hair alone, but then she started prodding at my ears with her fingers instead.

I would prefer only adult women to do that, thanks.

"It's disgraceful to be acting so improper this early in the day!"

Miss Karina, apparently miffed by the perfectly innocent snuggling going on, narrowed her eyes, snatched the goblet Lulu offered her, and knocked it back in one gulp.

Uh-oh.

I think everyone else present had the same thought in that moment.

With a loud sputter, an orange spray arced through the sky.

Miss Karina, having encountered carbonation for the first time in her life, performed a dramatic spit take, dropping the goblet from her hand.

The drink sprayed all over poor innocent Lulu, while the goblet bounced off Miss Karina's ample breasts to nearby Nana's, then to the ground.

Oh boy.

I put Arisa on the floor and stood up, handing out towels from the Garage Bag to the three victims.

Nana's and Lulu's white dresses were soaked through, providing a glimpse of their modern-style underwear beneath. I forced myself to avert my eyes.

Arisa designed and I tailored the underwear, by the way. The three-dimensional sewing was pretty difficult.

Miss Karina's clothes were transparent, too, but the chest wraps of this world didn't hold any sex appeal for me.

Speaking of which, I would've thought Raka would be able to fend off a goblet— Oh, wait. If Raka's defense had activated, the fruit water would've bounced off it and caused even more damage, so it was probably a deliberate decision.

"Miss Nana! You mustn't undress to dry yourself off in public."

"But, Lulu! This fruit water must be removed at once for sanitation's sake, I insist."

"No."

Lulu and Mia scolded Nana as she tried to take off her clothes.

"Nana, go back to the room to change. That's an order. You can dry yourself off there."

"…Master, your order has been registered, I report."

The sticky soda probably felt pretty gross.

For whatever reason, there was a short pause before Nana's reply.

"Lady Karina, you may change clothes in our room as well, if you'd like."

"O-of course."

"Lady Karina, please clean me off as well, if you could."

Miss Karina was still frozen in place when Raka spoke.

The unladylike incident must have distressed her, as she had made no effort to cover her chest with the towel.

Her eyes followed Nana and Lulu to the room. She must have been feeling guilty.

Taking another towel out of the Garage Bag, I draped it over Karina's shoulders, hiding her chest.

"Lulu and Nana aren't angry. And it's difficult to look at you without being rude in this state, so please, go ahead and change clothes."

At my second prompting, Miss Karina turned red, clutched the towel to her chest, and hurried to the stairs to follow the others.

In the entrance, I caught her apology to Nana and Lulu thanks to my "Keen Hearing" skill.

While the crew cleaned the area around the sofa, we stood at the railing on the side of the ship and watched the river go by.

"Look, look! Mermaids, mermaids!"

Did you have to say it twice?

I followed where Arisa was pointing, and sure enough, there they were.

The AR display called them **finfolk**—water-dwelling demi-humans.

There were gillfolk soldiers on the ship, but I hadn't realized there were other kinds of fish people, too.

The finfolk were gathering mollusks, prawns, and so on and carrying them to people on a small fishing boat.

Somehow, they seemed less like beautiful female divers and more like trained cormorants.

I was content just to watch the little boat, but when the guide noticed, she flagged them down.

The conversation quickly turned to the buying and selling of marine products, so Liza and I headed over to the lift at the front of the ship.

Liza, the guide, and I were loaded into a gondola on the lift, which was lowered to the water's surface so that we could see into the small boat.

There were mollusks the size of plates, prawns the size of spiny lobsters, and even octopuses that were more than six feet long.

I didn't think octopuses could live in fresh water, but I guess there was no point in assuming this world would operate on the same logic as mine.

"Th-this bizarre creature is edible?"

"Yeah, it's called an octopus. I know it looks strange, but it's actually very tasty."

Liza looked alarmed, so I explained.

She didn't seem to be aware that she was clinging to my arm in her shock, but I decided it wasn't worth pointing out to her.

"Sir Hereditary Knight, how much shall we buy?"

I figured a prawn for each person, a few mollusks, and three or so octopuses should be enough.

When I gave my order, the tour guide reacted with surprise.

According to her, most nobles or people from other territories tended to avoid octopus.

The price of all the products came to two large copper coins, which was far less than the price my "Estimation" skill suggested.

"Octopuuus?"

"Let go, sir."

Tama and Pochi caught an octopus as it tried to escape the bucket, only for them to get tangled in its tentacles.

Fed up with the suckers, Pochi was gnawing ferociously on one of its appendages.

It might taste good and all, but I wish she would stop biting raw food.

Tama finally freed herself, then went to join Pochi, scratching at the offending tentacle with her nails.

Quit playing around and rescue Pochi, would you? It was cute how mad she was, though, so I couldn't blame Tama for not being more helpful.

All right, I guess I should help them out…

"Satou."

Hearing Mia call out miserably behind me, I turned to find that she, too, had fallen prey to an octopus.

If an older woman were in this helpless situation, it might bring to mind some unsavory associations, but with Mia it had no such effect.

I wished Arisa would rescue her instead of cracking jokes about sexy elves.

With help from Lulu, who had just returned from changing clothes, I extracted Mia. Meanwhile, Nana and Liza helped Pochi escape.

"Sticky."

Mia looked very unhappy indeed.

At my request, the tour guide went to fetch some water.

Behind me, I heard Pochi exclaim, "Help, sir!"

When I turned, I saw that she was covered in black ink from the octopus. Liza and Tama had managed to dodge it.

"Master, permission to use Magic Arrow, I request."

The octopus they'd removed from Pochi was now entwined around Nana's upper body.

Unlike with Mia, this was way too sexual.

Liza and I pulled the creature off her, but like a skunk defending itself, the octopus managed to shoot off one last ink attack, soaking the shirt that Nana had just changed into.

"Master…"

Though Nana was expressionless, she looked miserable as she stared in my direction.

I got the feeling that she was going to develop an aversion to water.

Because the ship was in motion, we couldn't use water in our rooms in case it sloshed over the sides of the container.

Instead, we had to set up a partitioning screen on the deck for the three octopus victims to bathe behind.

I stealthily put up an Air Curtain spell around them so that the screen wouldn't get blown over.

This was to prevent them from getting colds as much as it was to prevent anyone from seeing them, including myself.

The knights and sailors were kind enough to turn their backs to the whole affair as they worked. What a gentlemanly lot.

"Dry."

"Please dry Pochi, too, sir."

Mia and Pochi came around the screen to ask me to dry them off, but I instructed them to do it themselves and hustled them back behind the screen.

It wasn't my fault that I happened to catch a glimpse of Nana in the process. So there was no reason for me to feel guilty.

"You're smirking, you know."

"Oh, hush."

At Arisa's words, I covered my mouth under the pretense of stretching and yawning.

Well, since I got to see something good today and all, I might as well try my hand at cooking some octopus myself.

The guide asked the captain whether I had permission to cook on the ship.

I was told that it was no problem as long as I didn't start a fire, so I agreed to use a magic heating tool designed for cooking.

"Piiink?"

"Rolled up, sir."

Tama and Pochi were gazing curiously at the boiled octopus.

I sliced it into thin pieces, added herbs, and divided them into small bowls to be pickled.

"Master, the rice is ready."

"Thanks, could you bring it here?"

I used the rice Lulu brought me to make octopus pilaf. For Mia, I used carrots and broccoli instead of meat to make a vegetable pilaf.

Meanwhile, I had Liza prepare the mollusks and prawns, then line them up on wire mesh.

When I finished the pilaf, I put the wire mesh over the high-powered magic heating tool to start grilling.

When I sliced them up and scooped some soy sauce over the mollusks, a tempting aroma filled the air.

"Ooh, smells amazing!"

"Can't waaait?"

"My stomach is shriveling up, sir!"

Arisa, Tama, and Pochi sniffed around excitedly near the wire mesh. While we were waiting, I sliced the uncooked octopus and tasted it. I'd been concerned that it would taste muddy, but it seemed like it would actually make good sashimi.

"Lemme taste it, too!"

"Me toooo?"

"Pochi too, sir."

I handed a slice to each of the sharp-eyed children.

"Ah, fresh octopus is always a treat."

"Chewyyy?"

"It doesn't taste like much, sir."

Arisa seemed to like it, but Tama and Pochi weren't as thrilled.

"Master, you'll get sick if you eat it raw like that."

"Forgive my insolence, but I do agree with Lulu, master."

Lulu and Liza looked concerned.

"Don't worry. Something this fresh should be fine."

Sashimi, the classic Japanese method of serving sliced raw fish, might not be very popular here due to health and freshness issues.

But I had used my oft-neglected "Analyze" skill to check whether it was safe, so it should be fine to consume.

The crew looked a bit envious, so I gave the guide a gratuity and requested that she make sure they got a good lunch.

By the time I was done preparing the food, the youngsters returned with Miss Hayuna, as I'd instructed them.

She was carrying baby Mayuna, but Tolma was nowhere to be seen.

The temple knights weren't here, either. The second they saw that I was cooking octopus, they'd excused themselves on the pretext that they had other food.

Instead, they were standing upwind on the rear deck to avoid the smell, surveying the ship's surroundings.

…*Well, their loss.*

"Young Master Pendragon, thank you for inviting us. Tolma said that he had no appetite, so I left him in the room."

Miss Hayuna was using very formal words with me, perhaps because she was originally a commoner. Tolma's family wouldn't allow him to marry a commoner, I'd learned, so the two of them had eloped.

Later, when they learned that the couple's child Mayuna had the oracle gift, Tolma's family approved the marriage and welcomed them back to the old capital.

"All right, it's ready. Take your seats, please, everyone."

The only "seats" were circular floor mats, but oh well.

Miss Karina's maids took care of the serving, and we all chorused "Thanks for the food" and began to eat.

"Yummy! I can't stop!"

"Tasty, sir!"

Arisa eagerly snatched up some octopus sashimi with her chopsticks and threw it into her mouth along with the pilaf.

Pochi imitated her, too, filling her cheeks like a chipmunk.

Their faces lit up like the sun as they chewed their huge mouthfuls of food.

In the face of such joy, I couldn't bring myself to tell them to slow down.

"The unique crunchiness, the sweet, strong flavor of the prawn that wells up from within the bitterness... Quite wonderful."

"Yummy yummyyy?"

Liza and Tama were chomping wildly on grilled prawns without peeling away the shell.

They seemed to like it that way, so I didn't bother correcting them about how to eat it.

Miss Karina, intrigued by how much they were enjoying the whole prawns, tried to imitate them and received a prompt scolding from her maid, Pina.

"Yum."

Mia looked a little forlorn as she chewed on her vegetable pilaf.

I grilled some vegetables on the wire mesh, whipped up a quick sesame miso sauce, and served them to her.

"Satou."

Breaking into a pleased smile, Mia gave me a little hug. I was just glad to have cheered her up.

"Mia, please share one of your stars, I entreat."

"Mm, here."

The "stars" Nana referred to were carrot slices that had been cut into star shapes.

My attempt at having a little fun while I sliced the veggies must have struck a chord with Nana.

Maybe I could try making more shapes out of the vegetables next time we made stew.

"Master, you seem to be enjoying yourself."

"Yeah, I am."

Lulu passed a particularly plump mollusk onto my plate, and I responded with a smile.

How could I not, eating delicious food with cute girls and pretty young women under a blue sky?

I hope I can spend times like these with Zena and Miss Sara, too, someday.

Miss Karina's maids took care of the cleanup, so the rest of us stretched out on some soft furs the tour guide had spread on the deck for us to enjoy an afternoon nap.

Miss Hayuna joined us with Mayuna in her arms, as did Miss Karina.

I learned this was the fur of a monster called an eight-legged leopard. With a quick glance at my map, I discovered that they lived in the southeastern part of the duchy, so I would have to go hunt some when I had the chance.

As I entertained such idle thoughts, I gradually drifted off.

◆

...I had a dream.

A dream of a hot summer day from my childhood.

Below me, amid the incessant cries of cicadas, a young boy sprinted up a long flight of stone steps.

It was me. I was tugging the leash of my grandfather's pet dog as I skipped every other step.

If memory served, the backpack hanging off my shoulder contained the latest portable game console of the time.

This dream seemed to be from a bird's-eye view, so I turned my gaze farther up the stairs.

On the grounds of a Shinto shrine, my childhood friend with chestnut hair was quietly kicking a rock around for fun.

As soon as my childhood self arrived at the shrine grounds, my point of view merged with his.

*   *   *

As *I* entered the grounds, a little girl with *blond* hair turned around excitedly to face me.

"My, my! I've been waiting for you, Satou!"

"Man, call me Ichirou when we're not playing games, will ya?"

Satou was my grandfather's dog's name. It was a weird name for a dog, but he inherited it from the person who gave the dog to my grandfather. My family has always had a tendency to be arbitrary about that kind of thing.

"Hmph, I was speaking to the dog, not you."

"Really? Then I guess we'll skip the games for today and play with the dog outside."

As soon as I made this teasing remark, the girl dropped her haughty attitude and started flailing in a panic. As usual, she was sticking with her weird, old-fashioned way of speaking.

"W-wait, just a moment! If not us, then who will save the Trojans from the Achaean Empire?"

"Yeah, yeah. Let's go play in the shade, then."

We sat side by side on the shady porch of the shrine. His leash removed, Satou the dog dashed around the grounds in defiance of the summer heat.

I pulled out two handhelds from my backpack and gave one to the girl.

She liked the one that made a clicking sound when the joystick moved.

As she always did, she fiddled with it even before turning on the power, relishing the sound it made. Once I'd connected the two consoles with a link cable, I turned them on.

"Oh-ho, it begins!"

The game was a space-battle simulation themed around the Trojan War. Despite being for children, it included mechanics like supplies and enemy detection.

"Hmm, attacking me from outside my enemy detection field, eh? You dog. This is why I call you Satou."

I grinned wryly at her irrational complaint.

"Fine. Starting next map, you can have one 'Map Search' as a handicap."

"Huzzah! Then you ought to throw in a 'Comet Shot,' too."

"What? No way! That can turn around a whole battle in one go."

"Indeed! C'mon, just one. Please? Have mercy—only one."

Shaking her *red* hair, she pleaded with me until I finally gave in. As they say, there's no winning against a crying child or a count, after all. Although I'm not sure why a count, specifically.

"Bwa-ha-ha! Take this!"

She looked downright gleeful as she obliterated my main force with a "Comet Shot." She continued cackling as she plundered my now-immobilized main battleship.

"Ah, 'Comet Shot,' you are too kind. Why, I even got a battleship as a souvenir."

However, her smugness turned to shock after she brought the battleship over to her side.

This game was modeled after the Trojan War. So of course it included a "Trojan Horse" strategy.

"Robots are coming out of the battleship! Argh, I just completed that carrier... Nooo, you must not touch that factoryyyy!"

Once my robots destroyed her supplies from the inside, I revealed my real main force and went after her army. It was a close fight, but I somehow managed to pull out a win.

"Alas, so cruel. Have you no mercy for a little girl?"

She pounded the porch with both hands in regret, her beautiful *indigo* hair brushing the floor.

"I mean, it's impolite to fight someone with anything but your full strength, right?"

"Hmph! I despise you, Satou. May only the most flat-chested of lasses fall for you!"

Even as a joke, that's a pretty mean curse.

Everyone in our class was crazy about idols with big boobs, after all.

"Anyway, you sure get upset whenever you lose, huh?" That was what made it fun to play with her, though.

"But of course! You must lash out with all your strength if you lose, or else you will never grow! People mature only by making mistakes!"

With tears in her eyes, the girl brushed her *orange* hair out of her face and struck a pose as she made her declaration.

As she raised her arm, the blue bells on her bracelet reflected the sunlight.

"Huh? Hey, have you always worn that bracelet?"

"Ho-ho, it is my lucky charm today!"

The girl puffed up her little chest, then took off one of the bells and presented it to me.

"I shall give you one, too, Satou. You must treasure it always so it can bring you fortune, understand?"

"Sure, thanks."

I carefully tucked the bell into my breast pocket…

◆

What a nostalgic dream.

I didn't remember when exactly it had happened, but I did remember playing games with my childhood friend on the grounds of a shrine.

What I hadn't remembered until now was that the origin of my go-to game character name, Satou, was actually the name of my grandfather's dog.

I'd have to make sure no one else ever found out about that…

Just like in the flashback I had at the Travel Gate back in Seiryuu County, the girl's hair color was totally inconsistent. Dreams do tend to come with a little randomness.

As I sat up to get a drink of water, my eyes fell on the bell sitting at the sleeping Miss Karina's side.

It was the demon-sealing bell, a gift from the forest giants.

Still half-asleep, I started to connect it to the dream I'd just had, when…

Suddenly, Arisa bounced over to me.

"What's wro—?"

"Master!"

Before I could finish speaking, Arisa latched onto me and wrapped her arms and legs around me tightly.

At first I thought she was just harassing me as usual, but this seemed different.

She anxiously repeated "Master…" into my chest, so I patted her head.

"Arisa…?"

"I-I'm sorry." Arisa pulled away abruptly, apologizing with uncharacteristic sincerity.

"Did you have a bad dream?"

"Yes, it was about…"

She stopped without finishing her sentence.

"...I can't say it."

"Arisa?"

"I can't tell you it was about you being surrounded by muscly macho dudes in a festival of manliness, master!"

Arisa clutched a handkerchief to her face, feigning tears.

Most likely, she'd actually had a dream about the past that she didn't want to relive, so I decided to let her fool me.

"Then why did you just say it?!"

I wrapped an arm around Arisa's head, pretending to put her in a choke hold.

I was being extremely careful, but Arisa still shrieked, "Uncle! Uncle!" and batted my chest dramatically, so I let her go before too long.

All that horseplay ended up waking the others.

"I don't wanna be cooold..."

"I don't wanna be hungry, sir."

"Master! You're safe!"

The beastfolk girls hugged me so hard I could barely breathe.

"Satou."

Mia, still half-asleep, latched onto my head and started rubbing my hair.

"Master."

And Nana did the same thing as Mia.

As I enjoyed the sensation, I looked around and made eye contact with Lulu, who was silently crying.

When I did, a relieved smile appeared on her face, and she wiped away the tears.

I wasn't sure why, but it seemed like everyone had had some kind of bad dream.

For some reason, my eyes fell on the oracle priestess, baby Mayuna, but that probably had nothing to do with it.

If she could influence people's dreams just by sleeping nearby, her mother, Miss Hayuna, would probably be stuck with strange dreams every night, after all.

Because traveling on the river after dark was prohibited, our ship entered the harbor of Zurute City near sunset.

Still, the journey was going quite smoothly. We'd gone a hundred miles downriver today alone, so we should reach the old capital as early as tomorrow.

Along the way, pirates attacked us once and monsters three times, but before my group or the knights could get involved, the ship's gill-folk and birdfolk soldiers disposed of them easily.

◆

"You truly shan't be joining us, Sir Pendragon?"

"I'm afraid I wasn't invited."

Miss Karina entreated me in front of a carriage that had stopped at Zurute City's harbor, but I shook my head.

Fortunately, her evening gown was a modest one.

If it had been a more revealing design that showed off her bust, I might have gotten charmed into nodding despite myself.

The event she was referring to was a dinner party hosted by the viceroy of Zurute City.

Tolma's family, Miss Karina, and the imperial knights had been invited. The temple knights would be going to the viceroy's castle as Mayuna's guards.

While I had been invited to the banquet in Gururian City as thanks for vanquishing the demon, hereditary knights like me were the lowest class of noble and rarely received invitations to an event like a viceroy's dinner party.

Joining Tolma and his family, Miss Karina boarded the carriage sent by the host.

She continued looking back at me as the carriage pulled away, so I waved and smiled cheerfully.

"So we'll explore the shopping district near the harbor, then head to the restaurant Sir Tolma told us about, shall we?"

"Can we get in without a reservation?"

"Not to worry. I had the tour guide book a table for us."

She'd told us we should be fine thanks to our connections, and even if they canceled our reservation, we could always go to some other eatery or food stand.

After all, part of the joy of travel was dealing with the unexpected.

The shopping district of Zurute City had narrow streets, and the shops themselves were only about twenty square feet. Instead of asking patrons to go inside, most of the vendors stood out front to make sales and attract customers. Generally, there were no storefronts at all.

There was no rhyme or reason to the layout; it wasn't unusual to find restaurants next to galleries.

I didn't want to lose anyone in the chaos, so I had everyone hold hands in groups of two or more.

As another precautionary measure, the beastfolk girls and Nana were equipped with cheap bronze weapons instead of their usual equipment.

"Master! It's kombu!"

"Oh, dried kelp, huh?"

"You should make *kobumaki* with it!"

That was a pretty complicated request. But the seaweed would be good for making stock and such, too, so I decided to buy a few bundles.

"How about some dried sea slugs, sonny? They're good for stock, too."

"Then I'll take a bag of that as well, please."

"Thankee."

The bundles of kombu and bags of dried slugs were very cheap at only a copper coin each.

"Master!"

Nana pulled my arm to her chest and urgently steered me to the shop next door.

"I would like to request one of these objects, I entreat!"

Nana was pointing to some small glasswork hair ornaments.

The accessories came in many designs, fashioned after baby chicks, fish, cats, dogs, and so on.

"How about it, young man? They're all one large copper apiece."

"Hmm, that seems a bit high…"

According to my "Estimation" skill, they should be only one regular copper.

The other children came over as well, so I let them each pick one out.

While I waited, I decided to chat with the shopkeeper.

"Is there a glassblowing workshop around here where all this is made?"

"There is indeed. But it's past the inner wall in the nobles' quarters, so you can't buy 'em directly, you know."

The shopkeeper seemed to be on guard, perhaps suspecting I was a foreign merchant or something along those lines.

"Do you have any mirrors?"

"In a place like this? 'Course not. Flat panes for mirrors and windows are only made in the glass workshop in the old capital, so you'll have to stock up there."

Thanking the shopkeeper, I checked on the girls, and they seemed to have made their choices.

To kill time, I picked out a few extra pieces for friends like Miss Karina and Miss Sara.

For a moment, the face of my friend Zena from Seiryuu City came to mind, so I decided to get something for her, too. For that, I chose a blue glass brooch that would match the clothes she'd worn on our date.

Haggling over all of it would've been a pain, so I simply paid up.

Obviously surprised that I'd bought everything without trying to talk down the price, the shopkeeper smiled as he finished up the transaction.

"Young master, if you're buying souvenirs, why not pick up an orc glass goblet?"

He had probably pegged me for an easy mark and pulled out a box from the back of the shop.

"What is orc glass, exactly?"

"It's glass made in the Orc Empire, of course," he answered as he opened the case. "Did you know that this area used to be shared with the orcs until the ancestral king defeated the demon lord?"

"Yeah, so I've heard."

"Well, it's called orc glass because it was a specialty of that empire."

Out of the box came a red glass goblet.

It had silver decorations around the handle, and blue glass in the shape of a flower was welded to the center of the body. The welding was so seamless that it looked as if it had all been one piece from the start.

"...It's quite impressive."

"Isn't it, though? I only have two, so how about six silver coins?"

That was actually slightly cheaper than the market price. Perhaps he hadn't been able to find any buyers around here.

I decided to buy it at the asking price and use it for drinking alcohol and such.

After shopping at a few more stalls, we arrived at the restaurant as planned.

I wasn't sure what sort of introduction the tour guide gave for us, but even the beastfolk girls were welcomed in without a problem. We were given a private room and an excellent feast.

The main dish consisted of giant prawns made into boat-wrap sushi, with carefully crafted sides in small dishes and bowls, as well as a spread of colorful fruits and vegetables for the taking.

As far as I could tell, the tour guide had even informed the place that some of us couldn't eat meat or fish.

If I ever built myself a mansion, I'd like to have a butler or a secretary as talented as her.

"Tummy's fuuull?"

"So happy, sir."

Tama and Pochi murmured contentedly, their stomachs swollen with food. All that eating had made them sleepy, so they were starting to stagger around.

In fact, all of us had eaten a bit too much for dinner, so we took a stroll along the harbor before heading back to the ship.

"The steamed prawns were adorable, I report."

"Yes, the plating was exquisite."

"The food was delicious, and the prawn shells were delightfully crunchy."

Nana, Lulu, and Liza all spoke highly of the meal.

Liza's comment was a little strange, but I decided to do the polite thing and ignore it.

"Full," Mia mumbled as she took my hand.

Arisa, who was holding my other hand, was very quiet.

She'd been very cheerful during dinner, but once we started our walk, she took on a worried expression and seemed to be deep in thought.

"Did you eat too much and give yourself a stomachache?"

"…Yeah, a little."

That almost certainly wasn't the cause, but I didn't want to bring up the dream she'd had during our afternoon nap.

If she wanted to talk about it, she would probably bring it up herself.

We walked in silence for a while, enjoying the night breeze. The stars and the city lights reflected together in the great river, creating a beautiful picture like none I'd ever seen.

When I stopped to gaze quietly at the scenery, Lulu gave an emotional sigh.

"How dreamy."

"Lulu's observation is correct, I affirm."

By all appearances, they were enjoying the view of the river, too.

I had a strange suspicion that they weren't actually looking in that direction, but... There wasn't anything else around to call "dreamy," so it must have been my imagination.

"Should we get going?"

Sensing something was off, I looked down.

In the brief time that we'd stopped walking, Tama and Pochi had fallen asleep at Liza's feet.

Since both their bellies were so full, I had Nana and Liza carry one each, instead of Liza carrying both under her arms like usual.

"Master, there is a ship moving on the river," Liza murmured discreetly into my ear.

Wondering who would be sailing after sunset when travel on the river was prohibited, I opened up the map to check.

Affiliation: Wings of Freedom

"What, these guys again?"

Arisa broke her long silence to react to my muttering. "Is it that group of demon-lord worshippers?"

"Yeah, looks that way."

The city's Wings of Freedom members were going somewhere on that ship.

It'd be one thing if officials were just chasing them away, but I couldn't let it slide if they were off to get up to no good somewhere. If I ignored them and they summoned a demon lord or something, that'd be a huge pain.

I put a marker on the ship itself and the most important-looking members.

Wondering if Miss Sara's emergency summons had anything to do with this development, I opened the map to check her status.

—What?!

"What's wrong, master?"

I was too shocked to answer Arisa about what I'd found.

Condition: Possessed

It was Miss Sara's current status.

A Secret Night

Satou here. There's this line I read in an exorcism novel once: "One must never negotiate with demons. They tempt and seduce humans with their honeyed words." I still think back on that sometimes.

"Master! What's wrong?"

As I stood frozen in shock, Arisa repeated her question.

"Go back to the ship without me. I have a little business to take care of first."

"Wh-what do you mean? Come on...tell me."

Arisa looked pale. Unlike her usually joking expressions, this one was completely serious.

"Lady Sara is in danger in the old capital. I'm going to go and help her."

"The oracle priestess...? You don't think they're trying to resurrect a demon lord, do you?!"

That was probably taking it too far.

We'd destroyed the chaos jar necessary for the ritual, after all, and I'd also confiscated the malice urn I found on the way here. If a demon lord was going to be resurrected, it shouldn't happen for a very long time.

For now, they had probably summoned a minion as a first step toward their ultimate goal.

"No, no. It should only be a lesser demon."

"D-don't go! What if it does turn out to be a demon lord?!"

The other children seemed convinced, but Arisa was unusually worried.

"It'll be fine. I'll come back safely; don't worry. I promised I'd make you some tasty *kobumaki*, remember?"

"D-don't jinx yourself, stupid!"

True enough, it did sound like the kind of line you'd say before going off to your death, but I had no intention of getting myself killed.

Uncharacteristically distressed, Arisa clutched my robe so tightly that I thought her delicate fingers might break if I pulled it away.

"Lady Sara has been possessed. I have to go help her before things get really bad. Let go of my robe, Arisa."

"I can't... Do you remember when I mentioned having a bad dream this afternoon?" Arisa's voice trembled. "I was lying... It was actually about you fighting a giant man with a boar's head. You were wielding a black sword, but the giant used a golden blade to cut you down..."

Arisa's halting confession was a bit too serious to dismiss out of hand as "just a dream."

For one thing, she didn't know about my black Holy Sword. But even if there was a demon lord there, I couldn't just leave Miss Sara to fend for herself. If I just waited for a hero to come from the Saga Empire, it would probably cost Miss Sara her life.

"Don't worry. Even if a demon lord is there, I'll just beat him. So let me go."

"No! Don't go... I'm worried." Arisa shook her head obstinately.

I felt guilty about the tears in her eyes, but I had no time to argue like this.

"If you won't listen to me, I'll have to give you an order, all right?"

"Go ahead and try... My heart won't lose to some stupid order."

I had no choice. I didn't like to use orders, but right now, Miss Sara's life was on the line.

"Then...this is an order. Let go of my robe, Arisa. I order you to go back to the ship and wait."

"I won't! I won't let you go!"

Even after that, Arisa refused to release my robe. Her breathing grew ragged, and drops of sweat formed on her forehead.

She was probably suffering for disobeying her slave contract.

"D-don't go... Sa...tou..."

The pain rendered Arisa unconscious, and she collapsed, still hanging on to my robe.

"A-Arisa!"

Anxiously watching the proceedings, Lulu rushed over and caught her by the shoulder.

I carefully pried the unconscious girl's fingers from my robe and put her hand in her lap as Lulu held her.

I patted Arisa's head. She still looked agonized even in unconsciousness, so I murmured in her ear that I was calling off the order.

I wasn't sure whether it would work, but after a moment, the pained expression left her face.

"Lulu, take care of her, please."

"O-of course."

I gave a gentle kiss to Arisa's cheek, wiping away her tears. "May fortune favor you."

"Master, good luck, I encourage."

"Please don't push yourself too hard, master."

"Satou. Come back safely, okay? You can't get hurt. Promise?"

I nodded at Liza, Nana, Lulu, and finally Mia's uncharacteristically long statement, then disappeared into the night dressed as the silver-masked hero.

Incidentally, Tama and Pochi stayed asleep the whole time.

◆

Before my urgent trip to the old capital, I stopped at the viceroy's mansion to see Miss Karina. I needed to borrow the demon-sealing bell back from her.

When I looked up her location on the map, though, I noticed something strange.

Condition: Paralyzed

Guess there's trouble at the viceroy's place, too.

I came down from the sky onto the balcony of the evening party's venue.

"Now, where should the torment start? Which of you will be the first to offer your despair to the malice urn?"

A man in a purple robe was standing on a table in the center of the room.

He was a member of the Wings of Freedom and a level-31 necromancer. The spirits floating around him had the inherent ability **Paralysis**. Without my AR indicator, they would've just looked like translucent brown objects.

"Well, who better to sacrifice than a maiden? Go, my poltergeists…!"

At the necromancer's instructions, a rope flew out of his bag and wrapped around the fallen Miss Karina, hauling her up.

She must have left Raka behind to participate in the banquet.

"Ngh, Satou..."

"Bwa-ha-ha! Calling the name of your beloved in your final moments? By the time this man arrives, you'll be in such a state that he'll cry out in despair at the sight of you!" The necromancer sneered down nastily at Miss Karina. "Let's start with that chest of yo... Gah!"

I rained Short Stun spells on the man to protect Miss Karina and her magical breasts.

With an utterly unoriginal screech, the man flew backward, crashed through a wall, and disappeared from the room.

I was careful not to kill him, but his condition read **Serious Injury**, and his HP was almost gone.

The spirits and the rope-wielding poltergeist came after me, but I used a Holy Sword from Storage to destroy them in a single blow.

I also collected the malice urn from the table into Storage.

"It seems you lead quite a turbulent life, Daughter of Muno."

Trying to remember how I'd played the hero last time, I gave Miss Karina a potion to heal her paralysis.

"...Th-thank you, S-Sir Hero."

"I apologize for asking this in such a situation, but I must request that you lend me your demon-sealing bell. I'm afraid it is terribly urgent."

Miss Karina hesitated a moment, then undid the top button of her shirt and pulled out the bell from her chest.

The valley from which it came threatened to steal my gaze, but I forcibly resisted, reminding myself of the situation at hand.

"H-here you are..."

"Yes, this is it. Thank you."

Miss Karina looked like she wanted to say something, but I simply promised her, "I'll bring it back to you when it's all over," handed her enough anti-paralysis potions for the other guests, and left the mansion behind.

Later, when the viceroy returned with the troops he'd gone to summon, they collected the near-dead necromancer.

◆

I soared through the night sky above the river on my hang glider, arriving over the old capital in less than a half hour.

According to my map, Miss Sara's current position was in the **Boar Lord's Labyrinth: Ruins**.

When I turned on the map's 3-D display, I found her marker shining far below the capital in a blank zone of the map.

Using that information, I searched for a way underground.

Beneath the old capital was a complicated mazelike sewer. There was even a shelter below the nobles' quarters.

As I continued my survey, I found dozens of the Wings of Freedom moving through the sewers.

That's suspicious.

I put markers on all the members in the old capital, then headed toward the entrance to the sewers.

I kept the markers open in a corner of my vision, where I soon saw the location for some of them change from **Ougoch Duchy** to **Boar Lord's Labyrinth: Ruins**.

So my hunch was right.

As I monitored their movements, the members all collected in the same place and somehow moved into the labyrinth.

Once I'd determined the fastest route to their meeting place, I headed into the tunnels.

As I approached the entrance to the tunnels, I had to use a perfumed handkerchief to cover my nose and mouth and ward off the horrible smell.

The passages of the sewer were filthy, so I used "Skyrunning" to sprint through the air without touching the ground.

As I flew along, I checked my equipment.

I definitely had enough weapons. Aside from the Divine Blade, I had the Holy Sword I usually used, Excalibur, as well as three other Holy Swords and a Holy Spear, plus two magic blades and the Magic Bow that the giants gave me.

Most of them had been stashed away in Storage since I first got them in the Valley of Dragons, but I should be able to use them without a problem.

In addition, I had ten disposable Holy Arrows, plus the three Holy Short Spears I made in the same batch.

With the help of my "Overload" skill, I had already filled these disposable weapons to the brim with magic power.

My armor, on the other hand, was a bit of a problem.

My Meteor Shower had destroyed most of the high-quality armor from the Valley of Dragons, I think, so all I had was a single Holy Shield. The rest was armor I'd made myself.

Still, it was better than nothing. I used my "Quick Change" skill to put on some armor.

On the off chance that there really was a demon lord waiting for me, I didn't want to be the idiot who showed up in a cloth outfit.

Before long, I arrived in the area where the cultists were congregating.

There were a few alarms disguised as spiderwebs along the way, but I used my "Trap Detection" and "Sense Danger" skills to avoid them with ease.

As I continued through the sewers, I stole a purple robe from a lone member and put it on.

The uniform was designed to hide the wearer's face and body shape, as befitting a secret society. It was so loose that I could even wear it over my leather armor.

"The wings dance..."

"In the skies of freedom."

My "Keen Hearing" skill picked up on a conversation from the other side of the tunnel.

This was probably a code members used to identify each other.

I passed through the tunnel quickly, repeating the password to the man standing in front of a suspicious-looking door at the end.

The man stepped aside silently, allowing me through.

On the other side of the door was an enormous room. A scarlet object, perhaps a giant magical device of some kind, was enshrined in the center. Conveniently, the room was dimly lit, so my face was barely visible under the hood.

Several members were gathered around the object, arguing about something.

"What shall we do? Our young nobleman Purple Three has yet to arrive."

"Knowing him, he may just be resting somewhere."

Apparently, one of the executives was running late.

"There is little time left before the ritual. We shall have to go on without him. Do you have enough magic?"

"Indeed."

The male who spoke first seemed to be the leader, while the woman who responded was checking the control panel of the magic device.

The word *ritual* definitely disturbed me a little, but I took comfort in the fact that it hadn't taken place yet.

If they'd just send me along with these guys, I should be able to save Miss Sara.

"...The gate has opened."

"The time is now, comrades! Let us set forth toward the ritual!"

All the members responded to the executive's words by raising one arm toward the sky, so I imitated them just to be safe.

Once we stepped into the circle at the center of the object, we were transported from the room to a vast underground cave.

The circle must be some kind of teleportation device. My radar was now showing the unexplored area where I'd seen Miss Sara's marker.

I used "Search Entire Map" from the magic menu to learn about my new location.

As it turned out, I was in the deepest part of the labyrinth underneath the old capital.

There were no monsters in this maze, and the only people present were the ones in this large cave. It was shaped like an egg laid on its side, and it was almost two miles across in width alone. I was surprised it didn't collapse in on itself.

There were several strange objects lined up in the enormous cavern, the smallest being about six feet across and the largest being upward of sixteen.

I touched one curiously; it seemed to be made of stone, about as hard as marble.

There was a noticeably brighter region in the distance, where the members appeared to be performing some kind of ceremony. I could hear voices chanting something, maybe sutras. It was somewhat different from the usual incantations for casting spells.

"So the ceremony has already begun..."

Wait, what?!

"Hurry! We must make it in time for the Rite of the Second Coming!"

At the executive's words, the members all hurried through the forest of stone objects.

As I followed them to the site of the ritual, I gathered the information I'd need to rescue Miss Sara and escape. In addition to Miss Sara, there were two other girls around her age with the same "Oracle Priestess" skill. Like her, they seemed to be possessed.

There were a total of two hundred Wings of Freedom present. Most of them were below level 5, while three were above level 30, including the cult's leader.

The leader could use Gravity Magic and Space Magic. On top of that, I noticed that the two high-ranking executives around the same level each possessed a short horn, so I'd have to be careful of those.

There were three escape routes to the top floor. The northern route seemed like the best way to lose anyone trailing us.

By the time I finished my information check, the ritual was right before my eyes.

In the shrine where the leader stood was a stone bed, where Miss Sara was lying unconscious.

As for the other two captured maidens, the high-level executives had tied their hands and were holding them over Miss Sara's body. They each held one oracle priestess's wrists in one hand and grasped a frightening ceremonial dagger in the other.

The pair of young women were stone-faced, probably because of their possessed condition.

All three of the captured women were entirely exposed, with mysterious purple patterns painted over their skin.

I absorbed all this information in a flash. However, before I could determine the best timing for my rescue operation, the ritual proceeded.

"We offer these pure maidens in prayer for the second coming of the great lord!"

""""The second coming!"""""

The members echoed the leader's shout.

The executives holding the two oracle priestesses raised their daggers.

Immediately, I shot forward like an arrow. There was more than six hundred feet of distance between us.

A loud *crack* echoed through the cavern, and I heard cultists shrieking behind me.

The recoil from my sudden launch into "Skyrunning" had probably blown a few of them off their feet. As I took my second stride forward, I threw a few pebbles from my pocket.

Startled by the commotion, the cult leaders turned toward me.

Before I took my third step, the pebbles smashed the ceremonial daggers to pieces.

However, this wasn't enough to stop the executives, and the shattered daggers plunged toward the maidens' hearts.

Almost there!

At that moment, I felt a strange sensation around my body, as if I were running through water.

The next thing I knew, I was right on top of the cult executives, kicking the daggers out of their hands.

> Skill Acquired: "Warp"

It seemed potentially useful, but given the urgency of the current situation, I'd have to postpone it for now.

The executives still hadn't let go of the priestesses, so I sent each one flying with a strike to the jaw and yanked the young women away.

"Who dares?!"

That's probably what the man who seemed to be the leader of the cult wanted to say, but before the words could leave his mouth, I fired a barrage of Short Stuns into his stomach to knock him out. No matter what rare skills he might have, it didn't matter if I beat him before he got the chance to use them.

Paying no attention to the leader as he keeled over in a spray of blood, I took a bell out of Storage and directed it toward the possessed maidens.

It was the demon-sealing bell, of course.

A clear sound rang out, and two translucent shapes, one red and one blue, were driven out of the two young women.

For some reason, there was no effect on Miss Sara.

This chilled me to the bone with an awful sense of dread, but I decided to finish off the ones who'd been exorcised first.

Grabbing the blue and red shapes, I flung them far away from the site of the ritual and sent a pair of Fire Shots after them. If they were lesser demons, that should be enough to disable them.

The cult members closed in around us with staffs in hand, so I knocked them out with a shower of Short Stuns.

Unlike their leader, these guys would probably die from a direct hit, so of course I was careful only to graze them.

Behind the mob of cultists who were dropping like flies, two demonic figures appeared—the same two I'd just thrown away.

So they're not lesser demons?

I felt the same intense power from them that I'd sensed from the greater demon I fought in the Seiryuu City labyrinth.

"What A Boorish Fellow, Interrupting Our Ritual, Indeed."

"Truly A Vulgar Human, Yes."

"Indeed" had red skin, elk-like horns, and was thirteen feet long from head to tail, while "Yes" was a little shorter with bluish-bronze skin, water-buffalo horns, and two sets of wings.

The former used Space Magic, while the latter used Gravity Magic. Both were level 63.

The blue-skinned demon howled, and Miss Sara appeared in his crossed arms.

Was that Teleportation Magic?

"Quite so. You must be incredibly foolish to interrupt the rites of my second coming, surely." Miss Sara showed not an ounce of shame as she addressed me, using the kneeling demon as an armrest.

Her eyes flashed open, glimmering purple.

...That's not right.

Miss Sara's eyes were light green.

I rang the demon-sealing bell again, trying to banish the creature that had possessed Miss Sara.

This time, I tried putting magic into it to strengthen its effect like Arisa had done in the fight in Gururian City.

"Hmm. How unpleasant, surely."

...But the result was the same.

The demon possessing Miss Sara was barely perturbed.

"Master, Leave This To Us, Yes."

"Very well. You will defeat the hero, surely."

The blue demon stepped forward, and a rift like a mouth opened up in his shoulder, unleashing a howl.

Without waiting for "Sense Danger" to warn me, I picked up the two priestesses and leaped backward.

The cult leader and two executives lying at my feet were crushed as if by an invisible hammer.

There was no way I could've helped them, and I had to at least save the two kidnapped maidens first.

To aid in my escape, I allotted some skill points to "Warp" and activated it.

"Rather Impressive Reaction Speed, Indeed."

If I ran away, they would probably chase me.

With that in mind, I leaped back to put distance between the demons and myself, then created a series of barriers with the Wall spell.

"Earth Magic Seems Plain For A Human, Indeed."

"But Walls Are No Use If I Can Fly Over Them, Yes."

The winged, blue-skinned demon poked his head over the wall.

As soon as I laid eyes on him, I launched a salvo of Magic Arrows, Short Stuns, and Fire Shots right at his face.

It probably wouldn't be enough to defeat him, but it should at least delay him for a moment.

Without waiting to see the results of my attack, I grabbed the maidens and escaped with "Warp."

I was a bit worried about damaging the delicate young women by warping too quickly, but they seemed to be fine. There was no change in their HP.

"Warp" used some magical means to move the user like the Practical Magic spell Skyrunning, not a physical technique. Each "Warp" used about ten points of MP.

After using the skill over and over, I reached the northern passage in the blink of an eye.

I glanced back at the site of the ritual, but the demons didn't seem to be chasing me. Laying down the unconscious maidens, I used Shelter and Wall to create a barrier to protect them.

This way, they should be safe even if the ceiling caved in.

When I returned to the site of the ritual, it had become a sea of blood.

"...You slaughtered them all? Weren't they your followers?"

"As my devotees, their greatest desire must have been fertilizing my revival, surely," the creature answered with Miss Sara's body.

The red and blue greater demons stood behind her.

"You have no intention of leaving that body, then?"

"Hmph. This girl is important to you, surely?" The demon smirked and casually laid Miss Sara's hand on one of her breasts. "Would you still say that if I were to cut these breasts, surely? Or how about this beautiful face?"

He held the dagger in Miss Sara's other hand to her cheek threateningly.

Unfortunately, since the demon-sealing bell didn't seem to work on him, my only hope to win her back was through a war of words.

I decided to take a shot at betting on his pride.

"Release Sara, and fight me yourself! Or are you afraid to take me on without a hostage…"

If this creature had greater demons as his servants, then he could be only one thing…

"…demon lord?!"

"Bwa-ha-ha, you dare to challenge me? Then you must be a hero, surely!"

Oh, that went surprisingly well.

"I may have lost once to the hero Shiga Yamato and the sky dragons but only when they worked together. I have no time to waste on mediocre heroes. If you wish to fight me, defeat my subordinates. If you win, then I'll return this girl's body to you as a prize before our battle."

I'd gained the demon lord's word, though I had no way of knowing if he would keep that promise.

If it came down to it, maybe I could get the holy woman of Tenion Temple to perform an exorcism.

"Be Careful Of His Magic, Yes."

"Fear Not, I Have The Reflection Defense On My Side, Indeed."

Just to be sure that Miss Sara's possessed body wouldn't get caught in the crossfire of our battle, I used "Skyrunning" to get some distance from the altar.

"You Shall Not Escape, Indeed."

The red demon appeared before my eyes, splitting through the air itself. He was probably using his Space Magic.

I fired a barrage of Remote Arrows and Short Stuns from the magic menu to ward him off. Of course, I chose 120 arrows, the maximum amount.

"I Shall Return These, Indeed."

The spells I'd fired at the red demon all bounced back toward me.

The homing arrows changed course back toward the demon right away, but the Short Stuns continued to fly right at me.

That had to be the "Reflection Defense" thing the demon mentioned earlier. That could be a bit of a pain.

I avoided the shots using "Warp."

Behind me, I heard a rumbling as the Short Stuns struck the odd stone figures and knocked them over.

"How Annoying, Indeed."

The red-skinned demon gave a howl, and a crack appeared in the air before the Remote Arrows, destroying them.

I pulled the Holy Sword Durandal out of Storage.

I normally would've used Excalibur, but it was chockablock with magic as part of an "Overload" experiment, so I was reluctant to start waving it around.

The last thing I wanted was to throw away a Holy Sword like that.

Durandal wasn't quite as powerful as Excalibur, but it was still much stronger than Gjallarhorn, so it shouldn't be a problem.

My "Sense Danger" skill alerted me to something on my left, so I used "Warp" to get away.

The ground where I'd been standing just moments ago suddenly caved in.

"Don't Keep All The Fun For Yourself, Yes."

This must have been the blue-skinned demon's Gravity Magic.

I used "Warp" to teleport around, landed directly in front of the blue demon, and sprang up to slash my Holy Sword—

Suddenly, an enormous pressure weighed down on me.

> **Skill Acquired: "Gravity Magic: Demon"**
> **Skill Acquired: "Gravity Resistance"**

I forced my sword upward against the powerful gravity, but just as the Holy Sword was about to slash the blue demon, I stopped abruptly and jumped back.

"This New Hero Has Sharp Intuition, Yes."

"If Only He Had Cut Me, He Would Have Been Sliced In Two As Well, Indeed."

So both of them had Reflection Defense.

If my "Sense Danger" hadn't sounded an alarm at the last second, I would've been in trouble.

Just then, I felt my body being pulled slightly toward the red-skinned demon. The log told me he'd used a spell called Attract, another technique you'd expect to see a boss use in a game.

> **Skill Acquired: "Space Magic: Demon"**
> **Skill Acquired: "Space Resistance"**

I activated my two new resistance skills.

"For Such A Low Level, Magic Hardly Works On Him, Indeed."

"Har-Har-Har, You Are Making Excuses In Your Old Age, Yes?"

While the two greater demons bickered among themselves, I decided to try my next trick.

I fired more Short Stuns at the two demons. Sure enough, they reflected back at me, so I avoided them with a light backstep.

When I observed the trajectory of the attacks, the reflected shots didn't move in the exact opposite of their original direction.

Once again, I fired a bunch of Short Stuns at the two.

"No Matter How Many Times You Try, It Will Not Work, Indeed."

So this Reflection Defense didn't have limited uses... What a pain.

The red and blue demons' extra mouths each howled incantations.

My "Sense Danger" skill tingling, I dodged to the side.

A deep crack opened in the ground where I'd been, and an invisible gravity hammer struck large craters in the ground, moving toward me.

I dodged with "Skyrunning," then made more walls between the blue demon and myself to buy time.

First, I wanted to defeat the red demon so I wouldn't have to deal with that troublesome Space Magic.

When the attacks stopped for a moment, I made my next move.

I used the Wind Magic spell Blow from the magic menu and scattered salt from Storage into the gale.

The fine grains floated through the air.

"What A Poorly Planned Distraction, Indeed."

But the whirling salt did render the red demon's Reflection Defense visible to my eyes.

Old-fashioned as the method was, the results were excellent.

Instead of a perfect reflector, Reflection Defense seemed to be made up of countless holes that floated around the user at random, some absorbing objects and others ejecting them.

Each hole was smaller than a dust particle, which was why I couldn't see them.

The salt grains were clearly larger, but as soon as one made contact with an absorber, it would immediately be transferred to an ejector. So they weren't physical holes but minuscule teleportation gates.

Just to be sure, I threw a thin nail toward a gap between the absorbers.

As soon as it started to pass between them, it was sucked into the nearest absorber and spat back out by a nearby ejector.

So even a rapier or an arrow wouldn't be able to get through.

Noticing that the blue demon hadn't attacked in a while, I looked around and saw that he was standing off to the side with his arms folded, watching my fight against the red demon with great interest. He seemed unworried.

I pulled out a wad of thread from Storage. It was made from the fibers of Mountain-Tree fruit, with excellent magic conduction.

I poured magic power into the wad, creating Spellblade in all the threads.

"Making A Hedgehog, Hero? If You Think That Thread Will Pass Through The Gaps In My Reflection Defense, Go Ahead And Try, Indeed."

The red-skinned demon chuckled confidently.

Laugh it up while you still can, pal.

I leaped in front of the red demon with "Warp," jabbing him with the ball of Spellbladed thread he'd called a "hedgehog."

"A Suicide Attack, Indeed?"

As soon as the countless bits of thread shot back at me, I used the Shield spell that I'd already invoked to block them.

The Shield broke in an instant, but that was all I needed.

Got you.

I canceled the Spellblade in the threads but left alone the magic power strengthening them. Next, I grabbed a handful of the thread shooting back at me from the ejectors and gave it a sharp tug to the side.

The countless holes filled with the thread went along with it.

The confident sneer vanished from the red demon's face and was replaced by an expression of surprise.

The free absorbers moved to fill the gap—but it was too late for that.

A single moment's opening was all I needed.

By the time the blue light trails of the Holy Sword Durandal melted into the darkness, the red demon had already dissolved into black dust and scattered.

> Skill Acquired: "Light-Speed Attack"
> Title Acquired: Thread Master

"That Was A Surprise, Yes."

The blue-skinned demon used Gravity Magic to destroy the Reflection Defense around his body. He wouldn't be falling for the same trick, I guess.

I activated the skill I'd just acquired.

"I Will Show You My Secret Technique, Yes."

The mouths on both his shoulders began to howl alarmingly. At the same time, I infused my Holy Sword with magic.

Demons' chants are much faster than humans'...

The Holy Sword glowed blue with devastating magic power.

...but they still take time.

I used "Warp" to clear the distance between the blue demon and myself, and before he could finish his chant, I struck with "Light-Speed Attack."

My sword sliced right through with almost no resistance, and the blue-skinned demon turned into black dust and vanished.

...Well, that was anticlimactic.

It was truly impressive how effective Holy Swords were against demons. As long as I could reach them with the blade, there was hardly even a difference between lesser and greater demons.

◆

When I returned to the altar via "Skyrunning," the demon lord in Miss Sara's body was sitting with one knee drawn up on the edge of the stone bed.

As I approached, he stood up and applauded me.

"Wonderfully done, surely. I must apologize for mistaking you for a small-time hero, surely." Standing naked in an imposing stance, the demon lord spoke like a stage actress. "I did not expect a lone hero to defeat my courtiers entirely on his own, surely."

Miss Sara's body glowed with a faint purple light.

Something feels wrong here.

I had to get the demon lord out of her right away.

"I've upheld my end of the bargain, demon lord! Leave Sara's body at once!"

"Very well. It is a ruler's duty to reward those who have completed a trial, surely."

Good. He was cooperating more than I'd expected.

The demon lord cast his arms open, and the purple light covering Miss Sara's body deepened in color.

"Hero. I have judged you to be a worthy opponent, surely," he declared, and an intense violet glow burst forth from Sara's eyes and mouth.

What's going on?

"Black-haired hero, hunting dog of Parion. I know not why you disguise your appearance, but you will entertain me as Yamato did, surely? I will not forgive any disappointment, surely."

At the demon lord's words, I touched my hair and realized that my blond wig was no longer there.

I did have spare wigs and masks, but this was hardly the time to worry about that.

I have to get him out of her body or...

"Certainly! Once you leave that body, I'll gladly take you on!"

"Then *I accept your challenge*, surely."

I heard a crackling sound.

Sara's back tore open.

The head of a boar emerged.

...No...

"Satou...can I ask you something?"

* * *

"I have enough power now that you have sacrificed my courtiers for me, surely."

The boar-headed, purple-skinned demon lord appeared and cast Miss Sara off like old clothes. His childlike form expanded immediately, growing to five times larger than a normal adult.

Violet rings of light rippled across his body, turning his skin to a shining gold.

...Why had I believed a demon lord?

"Do you think...you can change fate?"

My conversation with Sara replayed in the back of my mind.

As soon as the hairless demon lord started to appear, the flame of Sara's life was extinguished.

How could I promise her I'd "save her from a demon lord"?!

A storm of regret raged inside me.

However, it lasted only a moment.

In real time, it was probably less than a second.

My high MND stat quickly restored my mind to its normal state, clearing away the clouds of guilt.

Once I was lucid again, something in my memories sparked a glimmer of hope.

Resurrection Magic.

The phrase suddenly came back to me.

Sara had denied it at first, but Tolma had confirmed that Resurrection Magic existed. And if I remembered right, Sara hadn't contradicted him.

Which meant it was too early to give in to despair.

"The Time Of My Resurrection Has Come. Quiver In Fear, Humans! Today The World Takes Its First Step Toward Utter Destruction, Surely!"

I warped closer to the demon lord during his triumphant speech and shoved him away from Sara's body with a full-power palm strike.

Then, I picked up the still-warm body and collected it into Storage. Including the blood that had spilled onto the ground.

In my Storage system, things didn't deteriorate over time. It might

be possible for the holy woman of Tenion Temple to restore a recently deceased body back to life.

There might very well be risks and specific conditions for the use of Resurrection Magic, as Sara had hinted at back in Gururian Castle.

But there was no point in worrying about that right now.

So…pull it together, Satou.

For now, all I had to think about was pouring my all into destroying this guy.

"Hmm? What Are You Trying To Do, Surely? You Ought To Be Coming After Me, Not Recovering A Corpse, Surely."

Ignoring the demon lord's arrogant goading, I prepared for battle.

Before the fight started, I checked over the demon lord's information.

His name was **Golden Boar Lord**, and he was a level-120 orc demon lord.

In addition to this unprecedentedly high level, he had three unique skills: "Unbeatable Strength," "Mighty Warrior," and "Protean."

I guessed by the names that these skills were strength-enhancing, endurance-enhancing, and some kind of transformation, respectively.

As befitting a demon lord, he had a great deal of other battle abilities, too, including normal physical skills like "Sword" and "Evasion," along with rarer ones like Destruction Magic and Explosion Magic.

The gold covering his skin seemed to be one of his unique skills or support magic; the AR displays next to it read **Physical damage cut by 99 percent** and **Magical damage cut by 90 percent**.

What ridiculously high defense.

In this case, magic attacks would probably be better, except he also had an annoying skill called "Lesser Magic Nullification."

This had to be the advanced version of the "Lesser Magic Resistance" skill belonging to the demon I fought in the battle for Muno City.

"As I Have Just Been Revived, I Am Weaker Than I Once Was, Surely. This Is A Rare Chance At Victory For You, Surely?"

If this was him at his weakest, how strong must he have been normally…?

The black rift of an Item Box opened up next to the demon lord, and he removed a mantle and two sabers.

When the demon lord donned the red mantle, it transformed into an extravagant outfit.

According to the AR, the sabers were classified as **Magic Swords** and boasted impressive stats on par with those of a Holy Sword.

The golden shroud of light around the demon lord spread to bathe his swords.

As it did so, the sabers' attack power increased in my AR display. They'd already been comparable to a Holy Sword, but now they were actually stronger than Durandal.

"Now Then, Come At Me With All Your Body And Soul, Surely."

I was already planning to do just that.

This demon lord would suffer my revenge for Sara and my own personal rage. Besides…

"…I have no intention of holding back."

The demon lord smirked with pleasure at my words.

I drew the black sword from Storage and glared at the demon lord.

I would go all-out from the beginning this time. I had no reason to try to hide my power here.

In fact, in order to destroy the demon lord with my first blow, I decided to strengthen the Holy Sword.

Normally, adding magic to a mere wooden sword would enhance it, never mind a Magic or Holy Sword. Surely that would apply to a Divine Blade, too.

I pushed some of my magic power into the sword.

What the—?!

I added a mere ten points to start, but immediately afterward, all the magic in my body started getting sucked into the Divine Blade at an alarming speed.

Stop, damn it!

I managed to slow the consumption of my magic power, which hadn't been drained this much since I used Meteor Shower, with sheer force of will.

By the time it slowed down, though, it had drained nearly half my MP, and the Divine Blade was continuing to absorb it at a rate of about ten points per second.

"Only An Inexperienced Hero Would Be Thus Hindered By A Sword Unbefitting His Stature."

The words of the demon lord stung.

As my "Sense Danger" skill alerted me to something, I looked to see a jet-black aura around the Divine Blade. There was no information on it in the AR display.

What's going on?

"If You Are Unsure How To Proceed, Allow Me To Demonstrate, Surely."

I used "Warp" to dodge away from the right-hand saber as it swung down at me, then used "Skyrunning" to dodge over the left one sweeping in from that side. Moving forward at the same time, of course!

The demon lord's violet eyes glinted with a light that made me suspicious.

I'll have to finish him off before he can do anything.

I slashed the Divine Blade straight down toward the demon lord's boar-shaped head.

Before the sword reached its target, magical shields like the ones Raka created around Miss Karina sprang up to stop it.

Then, crackling like a thin film of ice, the shields shattered into shards of white light.

It was probably some very powerful defensive magic, but that meant nothing to a Divine Blade.

"Imposs—"

I had no interest in hearing his last words.

Before he could finish speaking, I sliced right through the demon lord's head.

As soon as the sword made contact with it, the demon lord's face began crumbling away. Only a Divine Blade could do that.

Suddenly, "Sense Danger" was screaming on my right!

I used "Skyrunning" to escape high into the air.

Moments later, a saber cut through where I'd just been with a heavy *whoosh*.

It would be one thing if this were just a dying spasm, but that wasn't the case.

I could scarcely believe my eyes as a new head grew from the demon lord's neck.

...Guess a demon lord wouldn't go down that easily.

"To Think That You Would Force Me To Use The Effects Of 'Mighty Warrior'..."

The restored demon lord sprang backward, keeping his distance.

...Strange. Even after the demon lord backed off, my "Sense Danger" skill was still sounding strong.

At first, I'd been sensing danger from the demon lord, but now I was having a stronger reaction to the Divine Blade in my hands.

"What A Terrifying Sword, Surely. It Is Far Stronger Than Yamato's Sword, Claíomh Solais, Surely."

As I steadied the sword in front of me to point it toward the demon lord, something strange caught my eye.

The jet-black aura coiled around the sword was writhing like a living creature, reaching from the blade toward my hands.

...*Not good.*

This was undoubtedly a sign of something very bad.

I quickly put the Divine Blade back in Storage.

Then I took out Durandal, the sword I'd used against the greater demons, and changed my title back to Hero.

It certainly wasn't as strong as the demon lord's sabers, but using the Divine Blade any longer seemed like a worse idea.

When I checked my log for any strange status conditions afflicting me, a chill ran down my spine.

> Skill Acquired: "Instant Death Resistance"
> Skill Acquired: "Helmet Splitter"

So that strange glint in his eyes earlier had been an insta-kill attack.

If I didn't have a high level and the "Evil-Eye Resistance" skill, I might've been done for then and there. I quickly activated "Instant Death Resistance."

"I Shall Take This Seriously As Well, Then, Surely."

A second purple glimmer covered the demon lord's body.

This was the same light I'd seen before. It looked like when Arisa used her unique skills.

Judging by my foe's declaration, he had probably used his other two uniques.

"What Happened To That Black Sword Of Yours, Surely?"

Noticing that I was holding a different sword, he seemed dubious.

"Sorry, but I switched it out. You'll have to make do with this Holy Sword now."

The demon lord's lips curled.

"I See, So It Had A Limited Number Of Uses, Surely."

I actually just couldn't use it anymore because I did something stupid, but I didn't really want to explain that to him.

Instead, I strengthened the Holy Sword Durandal with a little bit of magic power, then protected the surface with Sacredblade, the holy equivalent of Spellblade.

This sort of thing was probably necessary if I was going to face off against the demon lord's "Saber III" or whatever.

Here goes.

First, a diversion.

To test whether they would work, I first fired a barrage of my usual combination of Remote Arrow, Short Stun, and Fire Shot at the demon lord.

But the three types of magic all disappeared just before touching his golden skin. All that reached him were the last traces of the Fire Shots.

Unfortunately, though not surprisingly, it looked like I wouldn't be able to scratch the demon lord with lesser magic spells; he did have "Lesser Magic Nullification," after all.

Using the spells as cover, I warped into the demon lord's blind spot and swept my Holy Sword up at him.

Far before my sword reached the demon lord, the same shields that had blocked the Divine Blade hindered Durandal as well.

They broke easily when the Holy Sword touched them, but...

Slowly but surely...

Yes, ever so slowly, they were whittling away at the momentum of my blade.

After it had broken through nearly a hundred shields and advanced about eighteen inches, the Holy Sword stopped in place.

I tried to use more force to push it through, but of course the demon lord wouldn't simply stand by and watch.

"You Shall Not Reach Me With Such A Weak Attack, Surely!"

With a roar, the demon lord slashed down at me.

I caught the saber with the Holy Sword Durandal.

Immediately, blue and gold sparks lit up the underground cavern, blinding me for a moment.

What a powerful attack. It took all the strength in my legs to bear it.

Unable to withstand the pressure, the floor beneath my feet started to cave in with a loud *crack*.

My "Light Intensity Adjustment" skill quickly restored my vision.

As I lost my balance slightly, the demon lord aimed another swing with the saber in his left hand.

I instantly pulled a Holy Shield out of Storage to block it.

However, since the shield wasn't secured to my arm with a belt, the blow launched it across the cavern.

As the demon lord recovered from his swing, I took that moment to jump back and put some distance between us.

Then, I heard a bass-heavy boom from the demon lord's direction.

"Take This, Surely!"

Jet-black rings began forming around the demon lord.

They attacked me as if they were independent creatures. I used Short Stun and Homing Arrows to try to intercept them, but both spells evaporated when they hit the rings.

An anti-magic attack?

I threw some stones from Storage at the rings, but they fizzled out like water hitting a hot frying pan. So physical attacks wouldn't work, either.

This time, I stowed away my sword and pulled out a bronze spike infused with Sacredblade, then flung it toward one of the rings.

With a loud *crack* like a plate being broken, the jet-black ring shattered. In that case, I should be able to fend them off with a Holy Sword.

My "Sense Danger" skill suddenly reacted to something.

I instantly jumped to the side to avoid some invisible attack.

The stone object behind where I'd been was immediately pulverized.

"How Did You Avoid My Greater Destruction Magic, Surely?!"

So the demon lord could use magic without a chant, just like Arisa and I could.

He is *a demon lord, after all. No wonder he's so strong.*

Even if I counterattacked now, the scale shields would just get in the way. If I wanted my attacks to reach him, I'd have to do something about those first.

On top of that, if I tried to put distance between us, he would just attack with magic.

I had to come up with more ways to deal with his offense.

After the last exchange of blows, with a quick glance, I checked the condition of the Holy Sword, which had lost its Sacredblade protection.

The blade had a few chips. If I kept using it to block, I might even be down a Holy Sword.

Instead, I decided to hang on to my spare Holy Swords and Holy Spear and instead use a magic blade to deal with the sabers.

With that, I took out the Magic Sword Balmung in my free left hand. It wasn't a Holy Sword, but its attack power was on par with Durandal's. And not that it mattered, but they both had gold-patterned hilts.

I infused the Holy Sword with Sacredblade and the Magic Sword with Spellblade. It was impossible to use Sacredblade on a Magic Sword.

"Using Spellblade And Sacredblade At The Same Time, Surely?!"

The surprised demon lord nonetheless bore down on me with his twin sabers.

I fended off the attacks with the two weapons of my own.

I could barely keep up with parrying and evading the demon lord's unpredictable onslaught of attacks from all sides.

> Skill Acquired: "Two-Sword Style"

Judging that the sabers alone wouldn't be enough to defeat me, the demon lord started tossing in more of those invisible bullet attacks.

One shot grazed me. My skill sensed more danger from the sabers, so it was difficult to avoid the invisible shots.

> Skill Acquired: "Destruction Magic: Demon"
> Skill Acquired: "Destruction Resistance"

I promptly activated the resistance skill and "Two-Sword Style."

The invisible bullets could evaporate bits of my clothes just by whizzing by me, so my battle-torn state probably would have thrilled Arisa.

I tried using Shield from my menu, but a single invisible attack destroyed it. I guess lesser magic couldn't block greater magic.

Every time one of the imperceptible shots grazed my body, it left a prickling itch on my skin. If I wasn't careful, I was going to get distracted and take a direct hit pretty soon.

I wanted to block the invisible attacks with the Sacredbladed Holy Sword, but I was too busy using it to fend off the sabers.

Even with the help of my Magic Sword, I was barely able to keep parrying.

"What Sort of Half-Baked Hero Are You, Surely? You Can Command Both Spellblade And Sacredblade, And Your Speed In Evasion And Swordsmanship May Surpass Even Me, Yet Your Attacks Ring Hollow, Surely. And Your Magic Is Nothing But Absurdly Strong Lesser Magic."

Even as he spoke, the demon lord's attacks with the sabers and invisible bullets didn't let up in the slightest.

Thanks to the "Two-Sword Style" skill, it felt like parrying had gotten a little bit easier.

"You Do Not Seem To Be Holding Back. It Is As If You Have Been Given Power But No Training, Surely."

His analysis was painfully accurate.

"Your Resistance Is Bizarrely High As Well, Surely. Instant Death, Petrification, Curse, Paralysis… None Of My Evil Eyes Have Affected You, Surely."

I did see an array of special attacks in my log, from Petrification to Paralysis, but I had resisted all of them.

"It Is As If I Were Fighting A God…"

Well, that's a bit of an overstatement. I'm just a little over-leveled with a bunch of defensive skills.

Between silently responding to the demon lord's words and the itching pain, I lost concentration long enough to bungle a parry.

My Magic Sword Balmung flew across the cavern.

As a desperate measure to avoid his follow-through, I fired off the Forge spell.

I was hoping it would at least cloud his vision for a moment. But the effect turned out to be more powerful than I was expecting.

The shields that had warded off my Holy Sword started burning up like scraps of paper.

"Inferno?! So That's Your Secret Weapon, Surely!"

As the demon lord shouted, I heard an enormous roar.

There was an immense amount of light and pressure directly in front of me. Instead of resisting, I let it throw me backward.

It seemed I'd taken a direct hit from a wide-range magical attack. The strange stone objects in the area had all been blown clean away.

> ## Skill Acquired: "Explosion Magic: Demon"
> ## Skill Acquired: "Explosion Resistance"

I wasn't sure what the difference between "destruction" and "explosion" was exactly, but for now I was just grateful for the resistance.

Frankly, that attack hurt way too much. Where was my "Pain Resistance" when I needed it?

My HP barely even went down, but this pain... If I was in agony from that, I shuddered to think what a direct hit from one of those sabers would feel like.

My "Self-Healing" skill quickly fixed the injury, but my already tattered clothes had pretty much dissolved away.

I didn't really want to fight naked, so I pulled out some clothes that were easy to move in and equipped them in an instant with my "Quick Change" skill. No transformation sequence needed.

While I had the chance, I pulled out the Magic Sword Nothung to stand in for the one that had been knocked out of my hand, Balmung.

Oh, that's right.

To prevent any further blunders due to the itch, I used the Everyday Magic spell Anti-Itch from the magic menu for the first time.

A cooling sensation wrapped around my body, erasing the distracting situation. *Magic really is wonderful.*

As I was appreciating anew the wonders of the supernatural, the demon lord emerged from the cloud of dust.

"Hmph. It Seems That Was A Draw, Surely."

A draw?

It didn't look that way to me.

Half the demon lord's body was covered in burns.

The flames of my Forge spell had broken through his shields somehow. Was he weak to fire? Or maybe it was because Forge was an intermediate magic spell.

"How About This, Surely?!"

The demon lord fired another explosion attack and more of the black rings at the same time.

As soon as I heard the roar of the bomb spell, I fired a Short Stun at the ground for a smoke screen, then used that moment to somersault into the air and skyrun over the demon lord to get behind him.

Below me, I watched the jet-black ring shooting past.

The dust cloud from my Short Stun revealed the path of an invisible bullet attack.

Looked like the demon lord had fired three spells at once, not two. For some reason, I felt like I could see the invisible bullets now even without the dust cloud.

> Skill Acquired: "Magic Vision"

Oh dear. That was a handy-sounding skill, but I had no time to activate it now.

I swooped down to attack the demon lord from far above and behind like a bird of prey.

As I entered attacking range, I activated Forge again, simultaneously slashing down with the Holy Sword and Magic Sword in my hands.

The flames from the Forge spell started burning the shields away.

My swords reached the shields before they had burned away completely, but there were few enough left that the swords didn't lose too much momentum before they reached the demon lord's body.

Tearing through the flames, my swords left blue and red traces in the air as they slashed into the demon lord's skin.

However, ripples of light spread across the surface of the demon lord's golden body, blocking the attack.

As he blocked the attack, though, I felt my swords starting to break through some kind of film.

It was a strong defense, all right, but it probably wouldn't withstand too many attacks. I hacked away with all my might, trying to break through and hit him.

Sneering at my determination, the demon lord swung his arm around like a whip and attacked with a saber.

It didn't seem like it should be physically possible, but I assumed that it was an effect of his unique skill "Protean," and I parried the attack with both my swords.

But it was a trap.

Just as I detected that with my "Sense Danger" skill, countless white spears ripped out of the demon lord's back, straight at me.

I quickly took evasive action, but the lances moved too fast for me to dodge them all completely.

Several white spears pierced through my body.

Ow, ow, owww!

I used my "Poker Face" skill to suppress the shriek threatening to escape my lips.

Overcoming the searing agony with the help of my "Pain Resistance" skill, I broke the spikes over my knee and flung them away. Though I'd mistaken them for white spears at first, they seemed to actually be the transformed ribs of the demon lord.

The pain was intense for only a moment before it washed away like the tide. There was still a dull throb, but I ignored it.

With no intention of letting me alone when the pain briefly immobilized me, the demon lord tossed aside his sabers, snatched me up with both hands, and squeezed.

His grasp was viselike, even though his arms were bent in the wrong direction.

Theoretically, my higher level should have made me stronger, but I couldn't shake him off. His unique skills must have been enhancing his strength several times over.

The demon lord squeezed harder. He had to be trying to crush me with his bare hands.

Ngh, that hurts.

My arms were pinned at my sides, so I couldn't use my swords. I put both of them away in Storage.

Then I called upon my last hope, Forge, at full power. The crimson flames, hot enough to melt even heat-resistant mithril, seared the demon lord's body.

Of course, since I'd fired it at point-blank range, I didn't get off without a scratch, either.

The flames weren't engulfing me directly like they were the demon lord, but they were still strong enough to burn up my second set of clothes in an instant.

My skin turned red, but thanks to my "Fire Resistance" skill, I didn't get any burns.

Of course, it was unbearably hot.

But I was the winner of this game of chicken, as it turned out.

The demon lord's hands slackened.

Just that moment was enough. I forced the fingers apart and freed myself.

I'd lost some feeling in my arms. It would probably take a few seconds before they recovered enough to use a sword normally.

I pulled out one of the disposable Holy Short Spears from Storage, already overloaded with magical power.

Blue light filled the underground cavern.

The excess magical power was converting the Blue in the magic circuit at the center of the Holy Spear to holy light.

The explosive beam carved straight through the demon's defenses, blowing a huge hole through his abdomen and leaving blue tracks of light in its wake.

But it wasn't over yet.

My foe's HP hadn't yet reached zero.

Despite the enormous hole through his stomach and smoking flames enshrouding his body, the demon lord still managed to raise a fist.

Now that's an impressive fighting spirit.

I pulled out the Holy Sword Durandal from Storage, filled it with magic, and activated Sacredblade.

This ends now.

The blazing blue light of the slash was absorbed into the demon lord's heart—and then it gushed out all at once. The holy glow exploded the upper half of the demon lord's body.

I took several strides back and retrieved a recovery item from Storage.

I used an HP recovery potion to restore what little health was missing, then used the magic inside the Holy Sword Excalibur, which I'd been using for an experiment, to fully recover my MP. Finally, I changed clothes and equipped some heavy-duty shoes.

Now I was ready for the next battle.

Yup, it was too soon to let my guard down.

When I had defeated him with the Divine Blade before, he'd still recovered. It would be foolishly optimistic to assume he could revive himself only once.

Golden light welled up from the body of the demon lord. The third round had begun.

When the golden light faded, the demon lord's upper body was fully restored. It was like there was no point in trying to beat him at all.

At least there was one silver lining—his two sabers had flown off to parts unknown when I destroyed his upper body.

I had two more Holy Short Spears like the one I'd just used, but I couldn't afford to waste them when I didn't know how many times the demon lord could be revived.

"I Have Not Had To Use 'Mighty Warrior' Twice Since I Battled Doghead, Surely."

Wait, who's "Doghead"?

It sounded vaguely familiar, but if he was going to start prattling about some guy I didn't know, I wished he'd save it for someone who cared.

As I grumbled in the back of my mind, I activated the "Magic Vision" skill I'd just acquired.

"The Hero Yamato Only Defeated My 'Mighty Warrior' Skill By Working With The Sky Dragons. Tell Me, Nameless Hero, How Do You Plan To Destroy Me Without Their Breath Of Light, Surely?"

Hmm. He called me that because my name field is blank, huh? Maybe I should start calling myself "Nanashi," the Japanese word for "Nameless," instead.

"The sky dragons are on vacation right now."

In the Graveyard folder of my Storage, that is.

So I would have to fight hard to make up for their absence.

The demon lord attacked with Destruction Magic, but I altered its course with a palm strike.

"Impossible!" the demon lord exclaimed, but I ignored him. My hand was tingling painfully. *Better not touch that magic too much.*

Instead, I prepared for battle by magically infusing the swords that were back where they belonged: the Holy Sword Durandal and the Magic Sword Nothung.

"By the way, the full-time hero is also on vacation. He's off with a pretty girl with huge boobs."

I cracked a random joke, trying to keep the demon lord distracted.

If there really were a hero on vacation, I'd like to give him a good smack.

"The Full-Time Hero, You Say? Then What Are You, Surely?"

"I'm just a part-timer. Normally, I'm just a traveler who likes sightseeing."

I gave my body a quick once-over.

Thanks to the recovery potion and my "Self-Healing" skill, the wounds from the rib spears had healed.

They still hurt, but not enough that I couldn't fight. My guess was that I wasn't going to have time to heal anymore for a while.

He used Destruction Magic again, but his aim was easy to read. *If you really want to hit me, try using ranged magic.*

As if the boar had read my thoughts, a ranged area-of-effect spell came flying at me.

I crossed my Magic Sword and Holy Sword to parry the attack, then jumped backward to cancel out its power.

But that wasn't all. The demon lord followed up with a Breath attack, and I kicked off the ground to evade it in midair. At this distance, my swords couldn't reach.

The gray Breath attack kept chasing me, so I used "Skyrunning" to get some distance.

I stowed away both swords and swapped them out for the Magic Bow.

Just as I was passing directly over the demon lord, I aimed the bow at him and fired an arrow.

It was a magically enhanced Holy Arrow, of course.

The blue light shot straight through the Breath attack and pierced through his mouth into his stomach.

I landed behind the demon lord, turned at the hip, and shot three Holy Arrows at him as the golden glow of resurrection began to engulf his body.

But the bolts passed right through the golden glow.

He's invincible while resurrecting? Enough with the game mechanics!!

I was just going to have to keep this up until he ran out of lives.

"To Think You Would Throw Away Even More Holy Weapons—"

I had no motivation to listen to whatever the resurrected boar was trying to say.

Before he finished recovering, I surrounded him with walls and fired three more Holy Arrows while he was unable to dodge, felling him again.

But of course, the golden light appeared and revived him once more.

"Impossible... My Forbidden Technique—"

I continued ignoring him and focused on reducing his remaining lives.

Another three Holy Arrows settled round five. However, those were my last ones.

With no further use for it, I put the Magic Bow in Storage and created more walls around the resurrecting demon lord.

"How Can You Use The Divine Gift Of A Holy Sword So Carel—?"

I flung two Holy Short Spears overloaded with magic at him, cutting off his latest complaint.

This time, I tried destroying his head and heart at the same time, but he still started reviving again.

At this rate, I'd have to mince him and incinerate the pieces or something.

I switched back to the Holy Sword Durandal and invoked Sacredblade on it.

"Where Did You Get So Many Magic Weap—?"

I made them myself.

Answering silently, I burned up the boar's defense with Forge, then used the "Light-Speed Attack" skill with Durandal to slice him in half.

Before the halves could hit the floor, I brought the blade back around to bisect those, too.

As his hand reached toward me in the throes of death, I stabbed through it, only to meet the bone in his arm flying at me like a bolt from a crossbow.

I gave up on attacking further and flipped out of the way like an acrobat.

These attacks were getting more ridiculous by the minute.

Watching the golden light washing over the demon lord yet again, I took out the Magic Sword Nothung and invoked Spellblade.

"What's Wrong, Hero? You Have No Way Of Destroying This Immortal Body, Surely?"

The moment the resurrection finished, the demon lord fired wide-range Explosion Magic at me.

My "Light-Speed Attack" cut deeply but failed to bring him down completely.

The boar reached into the wound and pulled out two ribs. Then he gave a short howl, and black flames wreathed the bones.

"Taste The Wrath Of My Black Flame Bone Swords, Surely. Let Us Begin The Dance Of Death!"

My opponent attacked with a sword in each hand, but the bone swords were brittle compared to the sabers. When our blades met, the black flames scalded my hands a little, but that was all.

"Who In The World Are You, Surely? How Can You Be Unharmed By The Black Flames Of Destruction, Which Burn Even Dragons To Cinders?!"

Because my level's so high, maybe?

No, maybe it was because my "Destruction Resistance" skill was maxed out.

Besides, I was harmed a little. I just recovered really fast.

Still, "Self-Healing" used magic power, and I wanted to avoid injuries as much as possible. I didn't like pain anyway.

"If You Are Not Hurt Now, I Will Attack Until You Are, Surely!"

Since the Black Flame Bone Swords endlessly regenerated every time they were destroyed, the damage to my Holy Sword Durandal and Magic Sword Nothung was reaching worrisome levels.

I used Forge as a distraction to get a bit of distance so I could switch weapons.

This time, I chose the Holy Sword Gallatin. According to the detailed description, it was a sister sword to Excalibur.

In my other hand, I equipped the Holy Spear Longinus. It was difficult to use with one hand, but Gjallarhorn probably wouldn't be a match for the Black Flame Bone Swords.

I strengthened the Holy Sword and Spear with magic, then wrapped them in Sacredblade.

This combination was three times stronger than the last.

This should whittle him down.

"Let's go, demon lord!"

"I Challenge Thee, Nameless Hero!"

When I gave a shout to motivate myself, the demon lord responded with a line straight out of an epic fantasy.

◆

After that, I defeated the demon lord five more times, but he had still more lives to spare.

As he was going through yet another revival sequence, I assessed the situation.

My Holy Sword Gallatin and Holy Spear Longinus were wearing down, so I should probably replace them soon.

Over the course of the past few fights, I'd learned a skill called "Triple Helix Spear Attack," which made for an even more powerful finisher than "Light-Speed Attack."

But even that wasn't enough to destroy the demon lord completely. I was stuck in an endless loop.

Of course, it might be possible to defeat him if I took certain risks.

If this were some desert wasteland, I could probably beat him down easily with Meteor Shower, but we were underneath the old capital.

If I used Meteor Shower here, the city above us would be destroyed. Then I'd be the one flaunting a Great Demon Lord title.

On the other hand, if I didn't mind risking losing the Holy Sword Excalibur forever and making the whole labyrinth cave in, I could probably do it with the overloaded Holy Sword Excalibur.

With the Divine Blade, I risked getting swallowed in that mysterious black aura, but at least then I'd be the only casualty.

If possible, I wanted to avoid using any of these three solutions.

If I had only an intermediate or advanced attack spell stronger than Forge, I could defeat this thing so easily...

And I should've mass-produced more overloaded Holy Arrows.

I had enough Blue to make more Holy Weapons, but there wasn't enough time to do that in the short breaks while the demon lord was reviving.

While I was preoccupied, the golden light covering the demon lord started fading.

Round thirteen was about to start.

"PUUUGUEEEEE!"

The demon lord raised a strange war cry while a suspicious purple glimmer filled his eyes.

I'd noticed the past few times that his pronunciation was breaking down. It appeared he had finally lost the capacity for human speech.

Maybe he was getting close at last.

"BUUUGWOOOOOO!"

Transforming his lower half into that of a snake, the demon lord struck at me with the tail.

I slashed at him with the Holy Sword Gallatin, and his scales came flying at me as if I'd struck a land mine.

I avoided them with "Warp," then fired three "Triple Helix Spear" attacks with the Holy Spear Longinus, but his arms transformed into ten whips and knocked them away.

The creature's chest opened up like a maintenance hatch.

In between the folds of purple flesh, I could see his ribs.

From their shroud of black flame, the bones shot out toward me like living things while I was briefly stationary.

I quickly retreated into the sky, but the ribs were faster than I thought.

Somehow, I managed to stop them with my Holy Sword and Spear.

Below me, I could see the demon lord's mouth opening wide.

The same dark flame was rising from inside…

Immediately, I used Forge at full blast to counter the black flame breath.

There came a roar as blasting heat filled the cave.

The attacks seemed to be amplifying one another as they battled for supremacy.

If that Breath attack rivaled Forge, which was strong enough to evaporate mithril, I definitely wanted to avoid that.

Evaporate?

Something about that word stuck out to me.

When I checked my body, I discovered several minor burns.

An image floated across my mind's eye.

That was when I'd figured out mithril's evaporation point in an experiment, right?

My skin turned red, but I didn't get any burns.

When was that?

Right, that was when I'd first used Forge at full power against the demon lord.

What was the difference?

Why did I get burned one time but not the other?
Of course. The difference had been the presence of metal particles heated with enough energy to evaporate.
Specifically, a magical metal that conducted MP easily.
A flicker of hope crossed my mind.
But at the same time, I knew.
It wouldn't be enough to destroy the demon lord.
This thirteenth round was for all the marbles.
I needed just one more move to defeat the demon lord.

What appeared in my mind was a glittering blue bell.

"You must treasure it always so it can bring you fortune, understand?"

Right, of course.
Beneath me, the demon lord leaped up through the Breath attack with his arms transformed into sabers. But now, he looked about as threatening to me as a bug flying into a zapper.
I put the Holy Sword and Holy Spear in Storage and pulled out something else.
Instead of a bell, it was a silver vial full of cerulean liquid.
I poured the rest of my magic into the Blue, the metal solution that formed the core of Holy Weapons.

"This is it…"

In less than a second, it was overloaded with magic, and bright light beamed through the cracks between my fingers.
I reached toward the demon lord in the midst of his unswerving charge.
Then, as the shining blue beacon left my hand, I aimed at it and activated Forge at full throttle.

"…for yooooou!"

The metallic liquid evaporated under the inferno and turned into a conical shower of luminescent blue over the demon lord.
Within moments, the boar was completely engulfed in the holy

aura. He burned away, without leaving so much as the shadow of a trace.

A rumble echoed through the underground cavern.

The cone of light bored deep into the hard floor of the labyrinth before vanishing completely.

◆

Using "Skyrunning" to reach the bottom of the newly formed pit, I found a broken purple orb that must have been the demon lord's core.

So this didn't burn, huh?

I was concerned for a moment that he'd somehow resurrect from this, but it seemed like it was finally over.

As proof, I now had some visitors...

"Hee-hee, looks like he lost."

"Just like he lost to Yamato..."

"Now he lost to the nameless hero."

From the shards of the core rose three small violet lights like the ones I'd seen after the Undead King Zen passed on during the Cradle incident.

No, their color was a bit darker. It would have been better described as dark purple, bordering on black.

They felt quite similar to the ones I'd seen before, but maybe they were different individuals.

"So much for orcs."

"What should we use next?"

"Those weasels seem rather clever..."

Their words suggested that they thought I couldn't touch them, so they weren't expecting me to attack.

My dark blade slashed three times.

The deep-purple lights vanished, leaving only faint traces behind.

I quickly put the Divine Blade and its black aura away in Storage and changed my title from Godkiller back to Hero.

At first, I thought I saw the black sword absorb the purple remnants, but the sword's status hadn't changed, so I must have imagined it.

My Holy Sword went straight through them last time, so I'd taken a gamble by using the Divine Blade.

After I crushed the three dark-violet lights, the rewards log filled at an absurdly high speed, but I scrolled back up just to be sure.

The words **You defeated the fragments of a god!** had appeared, so I must have really destroyed them.

In retrospect, I guess you could call that making an enemy of a god, but I had acted without really thinking. Still, if this "god" was the type to lend its power to a demon lord, it would be hostile toward me anyway, in all likelihood.

If it was going to retaliate, hopefully it would do it in a time frame befitting a god, like maybe a hundred years from now.

> **Title Acquired: Demon Lord Slayer**
> **Title Acquired: Demon Lord Slayer: Golden Boar Lord**
> **Title Acquired: True Hero**
> **Title Acquired: Savior with No Name**

The Price of a Miracle

Satou here. When the era of home video-game consoles first dawned, there was a time when there were no real save files. Instead, they say you had to write down a long code called a "Spell of Restoration" to pick up where you left off.

Whew, that was exhausting.

Thanks to my heavy use of Forge during the battle, the underground cavern was as hot as a sauna.

I used Freeze Water from the magic menu to cool things down a bit, then chugged a pinch of salt and some sweet fruit juice to rehydrate and replenish my salt and sugar.

Once I'd taken a little break, I drank a stamina recovery potion and a nutritional supplement to fully restore myself physically. As I did so, I checked the clock.

It hadn't been as long as I thought. Only about an hour had passed since I arrived underground.

I opened Storage and checked to make sure that the items I'd lost during battle, like the Holy Shield and the Magic Sword Balmung, had been recovered via the automatic loot collection.

Since my clothes had once again been burned away in the last battle with the demon lord, I put on some cheap ones from Storage.

Before I went to collect the two kidnapped maidens, I ventured into the dust cloud to take care of that teleportation device. The last thing I needed was for a new group of creeps to find it and start some more trouble under the old capital.

"So the base is about six feet around..."

With the help of a Spellbladed fairy sword from Storage and the

"Light-Speed Attack" skill, I sliced through the base of the teleportation device.

Of course, once it was cut off, I put the teleportation device in Storage.

Between this and the Magic Cannon I'd picked up in the castle in Muno Barony, I was beginning to build up a serious collection of junk.

But with the unlimited space of Storage, that shouldn't be a problem.

On the base that had housed the teleporter, I found a cross section of what looked like red wire.

It had probably been started up by external magic powers.

Well, I could worry about all that later.

Now I was covered in dust, so I hopped into the air with "Skyrunning" and washed off with water from the great river. Then, after quickly toweling off, I changed into more proper clothes.

This time I chose some chic, high-class robes that resembled a clergyman's outfit.

I also donned a white mask and a spare purple wig. My silver mask had been incinerated in battle, and I didn't want to wear my dust-covered blond wig.

Once I put on a cloak over everything, I was ready to return aboveground.

I went back to where I'd left the oracle priestesses and removed the walls I'd put up around them.

It turned out they were already awake, huddling against the far side of the shelter and trembling.

"Wh-what are you planning to do with us?"

"Please, just let us go back to the temple."

The maidens looked alarmed when I released the spell and approached them.

...Well, if a suspicious-looking man in a mask approaches you when you've been kidnapped, of course you'll think he's one of the kidnappers.

"If it's money you want, our parents will—"

As the braver one tried to negotiate, I handed them some clothes and blankets to cover themselves up. I had no interest in middle schoolers and could hardly let them stay naked any longer when they were already in such distress.

"Here, put these on. Or did you want to return to the temple naked?"

I disguised my voice just in case they were friends of Sara.

When I had imitated a voice actor during the battle of Muno City, I acquired the "Change Voice" skill, so now I could easily make myself sound like a different person without even thinking about it.

"...Y-you're letting us go home?"

"Of course. There's a battalion fighting the kidnappers right now. Once you've changed clothes, I'll bring you to the surface."

I turned my back to the maidens as I spoke.

There was no battalion, of course, but it would probably be more alarming to tell them that a demon lord slaughtered all the kidnappers.

"We're done changing."

"Good. I'll carry you out, so hang on to my neck, all right?"

"Wh-what...? Cling to some strange gentleman?"

"H-how improper!"

Their reaction was fitting for a pair of pure holy women, but if we tried to walk out of an underground labyrinth like this, it could be days before we made it aboveground.

"Just think of me as a carriage or a golem. If we wander around in a place like this, there's no telling when the kidnappers might find us."

With the help of my "Fabrication" and "Persuasion" skills, I talked the young women into letting me carry them.

"Please forgive me, Goddess Parion."

"My purity has been sullied..."

When they said that, I noticed for the first time that these two were the oracle priestesses of Parion Temple and Garleon Temple.

Once I lifted them up, I ran through the course I'd plotted to escape, using "Skyrunning" and "Warp" to speed the process along.

Thanks to my "Transport" skill, I was able to carry them without too much jostling, but I was so fast that it probably felt a bit like a roller coaster.

Prim priestesses though they might be, they were still adolescent girls, so I had a chorus of high-pitched shrieks next to my ears.

By the time we reached the top floor, they were sleeping, possibly fainted. They had been kidnapped and nearly killed, so I was sure they were just exhausted.

Also, I carefully avoided looking at their status conditions.

"Hmm, the path forward is blocked here..."

As far as I could tell, there had once been a stairway here that led from the top floor to the underground of the old capital, but it had been completely filled with Earth Magic.

My best spells for excavation were Rock Smasher and Polish. Anything else would be highly inefficient, MP-wise.

It would have been ideal if I could use Pit, the spell I'd used to dig down to a mithril streak before, but the nature of the spell restricted its use to ground that was underfoot.

...Underfoot?

I looked down at my feet, then up at the ceiling.

I hopped up with "Skyrunning," then took out my fairy sword to cut through the earth above.

After storing away the heavy stones that fell, I landed on the exposed earth of the ceiling.

Then, with the help of the Earth Magic spell Pit on the "ground" that was "underfoot," I created a passage to the surface.

That was pretty difficult, let me tell you.

"Skyrunning" was based on jumping around on invisible footholds in midair, so while I could stand in the air easily, it wasn't meant for ignoring gravity.

To combat this, I made "footholds" for my hands and "landed" on the ceiling by doing a handstand.

Well, either way, I got us back up to the sewer system of the old capital.

I had eyeballed the distance, though, so I messed up and came out several feet away from the room with the transportation device to the old capital.

I covered the exit with some nearby stones, then threw some dirt over the pile to conceal it.

Thanks to certain skills like "Disguise" and "Destruction of Evidence," the cover-up job was so effective that I suspected I might not recognize it later, so I put a marker over it on the map just in case.

Collecting the oracle priestesses, I headed to the teleportation room.

After a little reconnaissance via the map, I found that the room was unstaffed for some reason. The man who'd been on guard outside the door was gone, too, as was the Wings of Freedom member whose clothes I'd stolen earlier.

That concerned me a little, but my only business here was with the teleporter, which I disconnected and put in Storage like the one in the large cavern.

With that, it should be impossible for anyone to get up to no good in the underground labyrinth.

That was the last item on my to-do list, so I shouldered the unconscious maidens and headed for the exit.

Checking on the map, I found a path that let out right onto the premises of the Tenion Temple, so I used "Skyrunning" to follow that route.

As I mechanically stuck to the course, I checked on Sara's body in Storage.

The item name read **Corpse of Sara. Damage: Maximum. Blood Loss: Great**.

First, I attempted to drag-and-drop the blood Sara had lost back to her body, which successfully combined the two.

The item name changed to **Corpse of Sara. Damage: Maximum**.

In that case... I tried using the same method to combine a healing potion with her, but no such luck.

Maybe there was a title that would allow that sort of thing, like the Hero title being necessary to wield a Holy Sword.

It was just a thought, but there was still a little time before we reached the temple, so I decided to give it a try.

I tested out a few titles: Paramedic, Doctor, and Saint, in that order.

For some reason, it was changing my title to Saint, not Doctor, that allowed me to combine a healing potion with Sara's body.

However, it didn't bring her back to life.

The item name simply changed from **Corpse of Sara. Damage: Maximum** to **Corpse of Sara. Damage: Great**.

After I synthesized several more potions with her body, the item name eventually changed to simply **Corpse of Sara**, so hopefully it hadn't been in vain.

As I flew along the tunnels during this operation, I saw some interesting things—mysterious humanoid creatures with glowing eyes and clad in rags, for instance, as well as countless white crocodiles—but they showed no aggression toward me, so I ignored them.

Once we managed to do some sightseeing in the old capital, it might be nice to come down here and bring them some gifts or something.

◆

"Oh my, what an excellent assassin they've sent tonight. I've never had one get so close without my noticing them before."

I crept into the room of the Tenion Temple's head priestess, but unfortunately, she immediately mistook me for an assassin.

I couldn't blame her for not trusting a purple-haired man in a white mask out of the blue.

"Dear me, are you a kidnapper as well as an assassin?"

Noticing the girls I was carrying on each shoulder, the head priestess seemed bewildered.

She had skills like "Holy Magic," "Analyze Person," and "Sense Danger," so I'd set my title to Hero and changed my level to 89, the same as the ancestral king Yamato had in the legends.

"Nice to meet you, Head Priestess Yu Tenion. I am Nanashi. I mean you no harm."

Her "Analyze Person" skill should solve the misunderstanding before too long, but I decided to introduce myself first to save time. It was only good manners anyway.

I laid the maidens down on the guest sofa. They showed no signs of waking up just yet, so I figured it was better to let them rest.

"These two are priestesses from Parion Temple and Garleon Temple. They were kidnapped by demon-lord worshippers."

"I do seem to remember them. Say, Mr. Nanashi... I don't suppose you could show your face? It's quite difficult to hold a conversation with a mask like that."

"My apologies, head priestess. It is my policy to conceal myself when I carry out good deeds. I hope you will forgive me."

"My, what a bashful hero you are."

Her voice sounded quite young. Looking at her in the moonlight, I couldn't believe she was eighty years old. I would probably have believed her if she said she was in her twenties.

"So, Mr. Nanashi. I don't suppose you've seen Priestess Sara of the Tenion Temple?"

"...I have."

My face was hidden, but my voice became darker than I intended.

Her features stiffened, as if she'd somehow guessed everything from my simple statement.

"...She's passed away, hasn't she?"

I nodded once.

"Mr. Nanashi, will you answer me this one question?"

"If I know the answer, I certainly will."

Her voice trembled a little as she spoke. "Was it a human member of the Wings of Freedom who stole Sara's life? Or perhaps..."

She hesitated for a moment before answering her own question.

"…a demon lord. Sara was sacrificed to a demon lord, wasn't she?"

"That's right."

A stream of tears rolled down her graceful face. "So she was unable to escape her destiny…"

The head priestess wept as she told me the story. According to her, several oracles had predicted that a demon lord would appear before too long.

However, the location of his appearance differed depending on which oracle priestess saw the vision, and there were seven all told, so each of them chose to abide by the vision their respective gods had shown them.

The head priestess had prophesied that it would happen in the old capital.

At the end of the vision, she saw an image that alluded to Sara's death.

Sara knew this, which was probably why she'd acted like she was on borrowed time when I met her in Muno City.

The urgent summons that had called her back to the old capital was because the Wings of Freedom had learned about the prophecy and were targeting her.

The Tenion Temple had made every possible effort to protect her, but earlier that evening, she had suddenly disappeared from her room in the temple.

That was probably the work of the Space Magic–wielding red demon or the leader of the cult.

"Thank you, Mr. Nanashi. It pains me to hear of Sara's loss, but as the head priestess, I must confer with the goddess Tenion about the demon lord's revival, send word to the duke, and sound the alarm bell to warn the city." The head priestess slowly rose from her chair, narrowing her tear-filled eyes. "If the demon lord challenges you, then I am willing to help you with whatever strength I can provide."

"Just a moment. You see, I have already defeated him."

"…Really? But your title…"

Only when the priestess spoke did I realize my blunder. Instead of Hero, I should have set my title to True Hero, which I'd acquired after the battle.

I discreetly made the change before I spoke.

"I swear by my title and my Holy Sword that I speak the truth."

I showed the priestess Durandal, which had done the most heavy lifting today, like an ID card.

"I believe you. True Hero Nanashi, allow me to thank you on behalf of the entire city."

The head priestess gave me an elaborate bow.

I learned later that this gesture was an expression of gratitude of the highest degree, normally reserved only for gods.

At any rate, it was time to get into the main reason for my visit.

"Priestess Yu Tenion, do you have the ability to use Resurrection Magic?"

"Yes, I do," the priestess said. Sara had said the miracle of Resurrection Magic came at a certain price. "However, there are certain stipulations."

I listened tensely.

"Firstly, the subject must have been baptized by the Tenion Temple."

No doubt Sara would meet that condition.

I should get the kids baptized here, too, for safety's sake.

"Secondly, it must be performed within four quarters of their death."

If I remembered correctly, a quarter was a period of around thirty minutes.

In terms of elapsed time, we were already past that point, but her body in Storage was still in the same state as moments after her death, so it should be all right.

...Please let it be all right.

"Finally, there must be enough magic stored in the Treasure of Resurrection."

She removed the object around her neck and showed it to me.

"Unfortunately, it was used twenty years ago to bring the duke's child back to life, so it cannot be used for another ten years."

The priestess's voice was bleak.

What, is that all?

I placed a hand over the Treasure of Resurrection she held out to me and began to push magic into it.

However, I was met with a strange resistance, and the power evaporated.

"That won't do, Mr. Nanashi. You must be gentler, like this, as if offering up a prayer."

Her hands still under mine, the head priestess demonstrated how to pour magic into the object.

This treasure seemed to be more complicated than I thought. In fact, maybe *finicky* would be the right word.

Magic was required to open the path to the treasure's core, but when that power was supplied, it would block the path to the core itself.

And there were more than a hundred pathways with such puzzle-like mechanisms inside the treasure.

No wonder it took thirty years to refill the core with magic.

The head priestess's MP was now decreased by half, yet the Treasure of Resurrection's power gauge hadn't budged an inch.

However, thanks to her demonstration, I figured out the trick.

"Allow me to try for a moment."

I took the treasure into my hands and started to push magic power into it.

I narrowed down the flow of my magic to be fine as a thread—no, as molecular wire—and manipulated it along the treasure's complicated channels, opening the path to the center.

It was a very sensitive task, but I somehow managed to do it.

By that point, it felt as if an hour had passed, but it was only a few seconds.

The next part was the real challenge. I sent a steady stream of magic down the opened path. Even after two thousand MP, it still wasn't completely filled. The process was quite difficult, as the path would start to close every time my focus wavered for even a moment.

There was only one option.

I took out the Holy Sword Excalibur from Storage to use it as a magic source.

The head priestess started back in surprise at the fiery blue light of the sword.

Unfortunately, I couldn't stop and explain it to her. I had to stay focused.

In the end, it took a total of ten thousand MP to fill the Treasure of Resurrection.

This sword's magic storage capacity was really something else. I'd relied on it a lot as an MP tank in the fight against the demon lord, too.

As I learned later, the Treasure of Resurrection was supposed to be replenished only by those whose titles were set to Saint or Holy Woman. *No wonder it was so difficult to supply it...*

"Remarkable, Mr. Nanashi. The Treasure of Resurrection is indicating that it's now usable."

The head priestess wore an expression of genuine surprise.

"So you can use Resurrection Magic now?"

"Well, yes..."

She seemed confused because I hadn't explained who I wanted her to use it on.

"I'm going to summon Sara's body here. For her, it's only been seconds since her death, so the conditions should be satisfied."

"But...Time Magic is the stuff of fairy tales. It doesn't really exist..."

Time Magic doesn't exist? That's too bad. I wanted to go back and meet the ancestral king Yamato and things like that.

Whoops. This isn't the time to get distracted.

"Here, use these potions to make sure you're fully recovered first."

I handed her a health potion and a magic potion from Storage.

It might not be necessary, but I wanted to make sure everything went as smoothly as possible.

I waited for the priestess's status to fully recover before we proceeded.

"All right, I'll summon her now. Are you ready?"

"Yes, whenever you are."

The head priestess held the treasure to her chest and nodded.

I removed Sara's body from Storage.

"Sara...!"

The priestess exclaimed in surprise.

Her body was pristine, without so much as a scratch.

It would be unkind to leave her naked, so I covered her with a clean cloth.

"Please begin the resurrection. Can I help in any way?"

"No, I can handle it from here."

"All right, then. May you have success."

The head priestess began a very long incantation.

Holy Magic chants were always long, but this one was particularly lengthy.

As she chanted, I saw magic power cycling among the priestess, the treasure, and Sara, perhaps as a result of my "Magic Vision" skill.

It manifested in the form of beautiful, sparkling light.

Finally, the spell was completed, and the color began to return to Sara's cheeks.

At last, her information in the AR turned from **Corpse of Sara** to simply **Sara**.

Her status condition read **Weakened**, but this was a temple, after all. Her fellows could probably take it from here.

I left the head priestess's room and the sacred ground of Tenion Temple without a sound.

◆

Well, that was a long night.

It would've been nice to find an establishment where I could recover with some pretty older ladies for a while, but Arisa and the others had to be worried, so I decided to hurry home.

I flew over the great river in the dark of night, stealthily returning to the ship in the harbor at Zurute City.

The ship with the Wings of Freedom members that I'd marked when I left had sunk, but I wasn't particularly concerned about such a trivial matter.

After taking off my hero costume, I changed back into my usual robes.

"...I'm back."

As soon as I walked in the door, everyone jumped up to greet me.

"Master! You've come back!"

"Welcooome!"

"Sir!"

"Master, you have returned safely; I rejoice."

"Satou!"

After the beastfolk girls, Nana and Mia embraced me enthusiastically.

"Arisa, master is back."

Lulu patted Arisa, who was hidden under a blanket in bed.

As soon as she heard her sister, she sent the blanket flying as she leaped to her feet.

"M-masterrrrr!"

Arisa dove at me with her eyes red from crying, so just this once, I caught her gently.

"You're not hurt? You're okay, right? You've got your legs, at least. What about your stomach? Did they get your belly button?"

In her panic, Arisa was acting even stranger than usual.

"I'm fine. I promised I'd come back safely, didn't I?"

"W-well, yes. Yes, you did, but…"

Arisa rolled up my sleeves to check for wounds.

I decided to humor her for today.

"Welcome back, master. Are you certain you aren't hurt at all?"

"I'm all right, really."

"I'll go and fetch you something to drink. Arisa, master must be tired, so don't give him any more grief."

Lulu stopped Arisa from attempting to check under my pants.

According to the map, Lady Karina was staying at the viceroy's mansion.

I had to return the demon-sealing bell to her, but I was completely exhausted, so tomorrow would have to do.

I swilled down the mead that Lulu brought back for me, then fell asleep with the girls piled on top of me.

Finally, I could get a good night's sleep.

◆

As it turned out, the seven places where demon lord resurrections were prophesied were as follows.

There was the old capital, as the head priestess had foretold; the Labyrinth City Celivera; Yowork Kingdom, which had taken over Arisa's homeland; Parion Province; the Gray Ratman Emirate; the Weaselman Empire; and finally, a kingdom that was on another continent.

For this to be the one out of seven to be correct, Sara, this city, and I must all have had terrible luck.

When I told Arisa about it, this was her response:

"The gods must be pretty careless, for the oracle prophesies to be so scattered."

"Yeah, really."

"But y'know, if this were a game, I bet a demon lord would show up in all seven places, don't you think?" Arisa grinned with amusement, clearly not believing her own words.

At any rate, the next demon lord shouldn't show up for another sixty-six years, so I should be able to enjoy a carefree sightseeing tour from now on.

"And then, once you defeat all those, there'd be, like, a great demon lord as the secret last boss!"

"Yeah, I could see that in a game, but the whole world would be destroyed by now if that actually happened."

"Fair enough. Ah! Lulu! If you're making potato chips, can you make two kinds? I want salt and consommé!"

Her attention drawn elsewhere, Arisa skipped away.

...No way that *could happen, right?*

I murmured the thought aloud, and the words floated up past the full moon illuminating the night sky and disappeared.

Afterword

Hello, this is Hiro Ainana.

Thank you for picking up the fifth volume of *Death March to the Parallel World Rhapsody*!

Since I'm low on pages this time, let's quickly cover the highlights of this volume.

After giving Karina so much attention in the previous volume, Volume 5 puts the spotlight on Sara, a priestess of the Tenion Temple. Once you've finished the whole story, I highly recommend that you go back and read it again. I think you'll find that you pick up on hidden meanings of Sara's words and the actions of some of the other characters.

Not only are there lots of brand-new scenes, as always—I also elaborated on some of the more popular sections from the web version, like the dwarf city and the journey down the river.

Now for the usual acknowledgments! Thank you to my editors Mr. H and new Mr. H, shri, and everyone else involved in the publication, distribution, and sale of this book!

And to you, the readers. Thank you very much for reading all the way to the end of the book!

Let's meet again next volume to explore the old capital!

Hiro Ainana

PRESS "SNOOZE" TO BEGIN.
DEATH MARCH TO THE PARALLEL WORLD RHAPSODY
MANGA
LIGHT NOVEL
After a long night, programmer Suzuki nods off and finds himself having a surprisingly vivid dream about the RPG he's working on…only thing is, he can't seem to wake up.
YEN ON
www.yenpress.com
Death March to the Parallel World Rhapsody (novel) © Hiro Ainana, shri 2014 / KADOKAWA CORPORATION
Death March to the Parallel World Rhapsody (manga) © AYAMEGUMU 2015 © HIRO AINANA, shri 2015/KADOKAWA CORPORATION